"TOO MUCH, TOO SOON?" EVELYNE ASKED.

Rhyder shrugged. "More like I'm doing just what you said your ex-husband did—running your life. I'm not giving you a fair break, am I?"

"No."

He flinched. "Please don't hold anything back on my account," he said wryly. "Evelyne, I've done a lot of thinking. I've decided that if you prefer to go back to L.A. and not come to Chicago, I won't try to talk you out of it."

"Is that what you want me to do?"

Rhyder sighed. "It can't be what I want. It has to be your decision."

She looked out at the ocean. "I've never seen Chicago, so it wouldn't be a wasted trip," she said finally, turning to him. "Of course I'd have to find a place to stay."

He barely hid his relief as he embraced her. "I happen to know of a place with a great view, and the price isn't too bad either."

She nodded. "Then I believe I'll give it a try."

SPLENDOR
AT DAWN

Linda Randall Wisdom

A CANDLELIGHT SUPREME

Published by
Dell Publishing Co., Inc.
1 Dag Hammarskjold Plaza
New York, New York 10017

Dell ® TM 681510, Dell Publishing Co., Inc.

Candlelight Supreme is a trademark
of Dell Publishing Co., Inc.

Candlelight Ecstasy Romance®, 1,203,540, is a registered
trademark of Dell Publishing Co., Inc., New York, New York.

ISBN: 0-440-17785-5

Printed in the United States of America

September 1986

10 9 8 7 6 5 4 3 2 1

WFH

*For Patricia and Clayton Matthews,
A couple who certainly know what romance is
all about*

To Our Readers:

We are pleased and excited by your overwhelmingly positive response to our Candlelight Supremes. Unlike all the other series, the Supremes are filled with more passion, adventure, and intrigue, and are obviously the stories you like best.

In months to come we will continue to publish books by many of your favorite authors as well as the very finest work from new authors of romantic fiction. As always, we are striving to present unique, absorbing love stories —the very best love has to offer.

Breathtaking and unforgettable, Supremes follow in the great romantic tradition you've come to expect *only* from Candlelight Romances.

Your suggestions and comments are always welcome. Please let us hear from you.

Sincerely,

The Editors
Candlelight Romances
1 Dag Hammarskjold Plaza
New York, New York 10017

SPLENDOR
AT DAWN

PROLOGUE

The large room was dark save for the flickering color images on the silver screen covering one wall.

"This will be a party to end all parties!" The man on the screen announced in his husky southern drawl, his arms gesturing toward a swimming pool dotted with floating candles. "Another memory for our library and another thank-you to my gorgeous wife for giving me another great year of marriage." He mimed a smacking kiss at the camera.

A woman sat in the middle of the room with stacks of neatly piled videotape cases surrounding her. Her life may have fallen to pieces, but that didn't stop her from making sure everything was in perfect order. So far she had viewed three tapes with each video segment representing a different part of her life; her twenty-fifth birthday party, their tenth wedding anniversary, special vacations, and other, more personal times that were for private viewing.

The longer she watched the tapes, the more tears covered her cheeks and the more misery she brought upon herself as she watched the man on the screen.

Rick, with his hair of sunlight, eyes like the sky, and a smile that sent shafts of burning desire through her veins. No man could make love the way he did and no one could hurt her as badly as he had.

The peal of the doorbell echoed through the huge

house, but she ignored it. She'd had enough visitors. Right now she was too preoccupied watching Rick. She pushed the hair sticking to her cheeks away from her face and wiped the tears away. But that didn't make them stop. The silent tears soon turned to full-fledged sobs.

Cursing loudly she jumped up and grabbed the remaining cassettes, throwing them down and battering them against a chair until they broke open and streams of dark-brown metallic tape streamed over the carpet in their own gesture of mourning as black chunks of plastic flew all over the plush cinnamon carpet.

"Evelyne!" A woman's voice filled with horror echoed around her.

She spun around to face the couple standing in the doorway. "The front door was locked." She may have looked like a lost waif with her dark-brown hair streaming around her shoulders and tearstained face, but no one could match her for composure when necessary.

"We used the extra key," the man standing next to the woman explained. He stepped forward to examine Evelyne carefully. "You haven't been drinking, have you? You know what the doctor said about alcohol."

"Drinking?" She arched an eyebrow. "Come now, Brian, I know very well what he said, and I certainly wouldn't go against that tyrant's orders." She stared at him with defiance before turning to the woman. "Why have you come, Celia?" She wasn't in the mood for company and chose to let her friend know it, even if it meant acting rudely.

"You haven't answered your phone in days and we were worried." Celia looked around the room with its mess of torn tapes draped over the carpet and a

14

group of singers shouting a bawdy ditty on the screen. "We can't get ahold of Rick either. What is going on here?"

During Celia's speech Brian noticed a paper lying on the back of the couch. He sidled over in that direction and scanned the official-looking document long enough to understand the meaning before turning back to Evelyne.

"When did this come?" he asked quietly, holding up the paper.

Evelyne shrugged, her deep-green eyes betraying her bitterness. "Yesterday at three-thirty. No wonder I haven't seen him in the past week. He's had better things to do—such as filing for divorce."

Brian swore fiercely under his breath while Celia looked too upset for words.

"What can you expect?" Evelyne shouted. "I'm not a whole woman any longer, am I? I'm not the proper image for Rick Winters's wife now because people whisper about me and look away if I happen to see them. They're afraid to get too close to me for fear it might be contagious. I'm not perfect anymore. . . ." The last words dropped to a painful whisper. She sank down to the floor, too tired to battle the world any longer.

Brian and Celia would have disagreed without hesitation, but they knew Evelyne wasn't in the proper frame of mind to listen. They saw her kneeling on the carpet looking beautiful in spite of her tears and the pain etched in her too-thin features.

"What will you do?" Celia whispered, unused to seeing her friend so downtrodden. Evelyne had always been a fighter; this woman filled with self-pity was someone new.

Evelyne's lips trembled. "I guess I'll have to find a way to put myself back together, won't I?"

CHAPTER ONE

Rhyder spent the morning by the pool, allowing the tropical sun to sink into bones he considered old and chilled from too many Chicago winters. Two hours later he tossed a towel over bare shoulders still glistening with suntan oil and sauntered back to his hotel room. Passing near the reception desk he paused to study the new arrival.

The woman's mink-brown hair was secured back in an intricate braid that hung almost to her waist. Her trim and nicely rounded backside was encased in a pair of tan leather pants, a rare sight in the tropics even if the month was November, and a rust silk shirt. A fur jacket lay draped over her arm.

The lady either didn't lack money or had a rich old man to take care of her, he decided. She also could practically look at him eye to eye thanks to those high-heeled boots she wore, and that wasn't something he appreciated in a woman. Standing a couple of inches under six feet, Rhyder liked his women petite and dainty, not tall and looking well equipped to take care of themselves.

Rhyder loitered long enough to enjoy the view and listened to her speak to the desk clerk before he moved on to his room for a shower and change of clothes before indulging in a late lunch. That was one thing he liked about a tropical island: he didn't have to stick to a timetable, and as an apprentice beach bum, Rhyder was living it up. During the next hour he carried the image of the dark-haired woman with the cameo face in his mind.

Evelyne filled out the registration card, silently damning the airline's erratic schedule. She hadn't had time to change into something lightweight in Los Angeles, since her flight from New York had crept in two hours late and she'd barely had time to make her connecting flight to Honolulu and on to Kailua. Not wishing to try some strange contortions in the tiny jet's lavatory, she suffered wearing the leather pants that stuck to her skin from waist to ankle. She offered the clerk a brief smile and followed the bellhop to her room.

Ten minutes later Evelyne examined the large room with its two king-size beds, a table and two chairs, and a chest of drawers against the wall with a television on top. She was glad to see a small refrigerator, since she enjoyed a cold drink at all hours. But it was still a far cry from the luxurious suites she and Rick had shared during their vacations. No, she mustn't think about him. As long as she remembered she was on her own now she could remain in one piece.

She stepped out onto the balcony and looked down at the hotel's saltwater pool. It was fashioned after a large tidal pool, with lava rock walls along three sides and an opening allowing the seawater to splash in during high tide.

When Celia had first suggested that Evelyne get away and recommended a resort hotel in Hawaii, Evelyne had balked, thinking of the two weeks she and Rick had spent in Waikiki touring the nightclubs while Rick checked out the bands and singers. He may have been the head of Midnight Records, a company he had built himself, and didn't need to scout for new talent,

18

but he still enjoyed doing it. Due to his unerring sense of what would be the coming thing his choices never failed.

Rick. Her insides twisted in agony. The divorce had been finalized under a blaze of publicity, and Evelyne had left Los Angeles as soon as possible. She had known Rick was a hard-nosed businessman, but the divorce had brought to the surface the glaring truths about his hidden personalities.

She turned away and reentered the room, stripping off her clothing and heading for a much desired shower.

As Evelyne stood under the cool spray, she thought back to the painful last weeks of her marriage before it had deteriorated completely. She remembered Rick's attentive manner while she had convalesced in the hospital. He had rarely strayed from her bedside and had showered her with more flowers than her room could hold. She recalled his solicitous attitude when she was released and how he had made sure she didn't lift a finger for anything once she reached their home. No one could have wished for a more loving husband. Then his rejection had come when she needed him the most, and she had thought she would surely die.

She had returned home from the doctor's office after receiving his stamp of approval and planned for a sensual evening of reacquaintance with her loving husband. She had donned a negligee purchased specially for the occasion, used the perfume Rick said drove him crazy, and chilled a bottle of their favorite champagne. She still couldn't drink alcohol, but there was no reason why he couldn't enjoy it while she sipped a glass of Perrier.

Instead of the beautiful reunion she had expected, Rick had shied away from her touch. When she finally demanded an explanation he told her bluntly he couldn't make love to her for fear something would happen to her during the peak. After all, he knew how passionate a woman she was and he couldn't take a chance of her blacking out on him—or worse. Rick left the house that night and a little over a week later a stone-faced man came to the house and served divorce papers to Evelyne. If it hadn't been for Celia and Brian, her closest friends, she doubted she would have survived the next harrowing months. Rick was a well-known figure in the entertainment field and Evelyne's illness and their divorce was a source of industry gossip for months.

With an abrupt twist of the hand she switched off the shower and stepped out of the tub enclosure, snatching up a large white towel.

"There is nothing wrong with me, Rick!" she had screamed at him that night. "You were there when the doctor said it was a small, abnormal blood vessel that broke in my brain. I certainly don't suffer from any paralysis, do I? Or have slurred speech? Does my face sag along one side? Tell me what's wrong with me!" She had demanded wildly.

He had refused to look at her. "For all we know it could happen again."

"The doctor said it was a fluke!"

"Doctors don't know everything. You don't even remember what happened the week before you became ill. We made love the night before everything happened and you don't remember one damned thing about it!"

The words kept repeating themselves in Evelyne's mind. The news media had had a field day when the divorce had been announced and speculation ran rampant among the tabloids. EVELYNE WINTERS SUFFERS FROM STROKE. POSSIBLE BRAIN DAMAGE. It had even been insinuated that she had suffered a drug over-

20

dose. Her mother had suffered a nervous breakdown during Evelyne's early years, and even that story had been dredged up. As Evelyne had been the only daughter of the movie mogul Victor King, and her mother a former film star, she had known the media from an early age and how it could help and, especially, how it could hurt.

All Evelyne knew was that her headaches had increased until she went to bed early one evening and didn't know anything until she woke up in the hospital three days later.

At first Evelyne refused to acknowledge the doctor's diagnosis. Middle-aged men in high-pressure jobs had strokes, not thirty-two-year-old housewives. But she was reminded she was so much more than a wife who cooked the meals and cleaned a four-bedroom house with a hobby for her free hours. Her life consisted of planning several large parties a month, working on charity committees, and attending rock concerts with her husband. She managed two homes and a staff for each, and her free time was at a minimum. No, her three times a week at the health club couldn't count as relaxation. When it came down to it, she lived under more stress than many high-powered executives. For the year and a half before the stroke Evelyne had been plagued by headaches, but attributed them to eyestrain. She had lived on extra-strength aspirin until her body finally took over and shut itself down.

She had always thought her marriage was invincible until her illness. That was when she learned what type of man Rick truly was. His request for a divorce left her in a state of shock, as did the realization that almost all of his assets were in his company name. He refused to settle a decent amount of money on her, his list of assets having been drawn up in such a way that he appeared to be a pauper. Evelyne knew he was not.

21

Luckily her attorney was sharp and unwilling to back down from what promised to be a dirty battle, and was able to win her more money than she would have gotten if it had been left up to Rick. What saved her was her habit of keeping a meticulous appointment book over the years; so her lawyer was able to prove how hard she had worked to further Rick's career from the very beginning and that their house in Malibu had been bought in their joint names and not as a holding by Midnight Records. Thanks to community property laws Rick had had no choice but to pay Evelyne support for the years they had been married. But he hadn't been happy doing it. She had wanted to cry at the thought that he didn't seem to consider her worth very much after all she had done for him.

If it hadn't been for Celia and Brian keeping her sane during that period, she would have gone off the deep end and turned into a recluse. Instead, when the divorce proceedings were over, Celia had dragged her off to New York for a round of shopping and attending plays. After three weeks Evelyne was fed up with the cold weather and loudly demanded someplace warm and sunny as long as it wasn't southern California. Celia came through again and Evelyne was on the first plane to Honolulu with a transfer to Kailua-Kona on the island of Hawaii. The resort hotel was all the brochure promised—large, airy suites, freshwater swimming pool, saltwater pool, eight tennis courts, and a golf course designed for the most avid golfer. But Evelyne wasn't there to play tennis or golf. She was going to lie in the sun, work on her tan, and begin rebuilding her life until she knew exactly who she was.

As she opened her suitcases and began lifting the clothing out, she began to decide on her plan of action. Evelyne wasn't there just to find out who she was, but to prove her own femininity in the most basic of ways.

And to do that she intended to seduce as many men as she could. She hung up clothes that consisted of soft cotton dresses and put away lingerie and bikinis in every color known. Cosmetics no sane thirty-two-year-old woman could do without were laid out on the bathroom counter in careful order.

When her unpacking was finished, Evelyne took off the towel wrapped around her and slipped on a light-weight robe before wandering back out onto the balcony to enjoy the warmth. She ran a brush through her long hair, allowing the afternoon sun to dry it naturally.

Evelyne would have hated to admit to anyone she had no idea on how to go about seducing a man. She had met Rick when she had returned home from finishing school and married him soon after. Although extramarital affairs weren't unusual in her circle, they weren't her style. She was a rarity among her so-called friends, a faithful wife.

She soon reentered the room, deciding a short nap before dinner would bring back her energy. The traveling had left her more exhausted than she cared to admit. Even after all these months her usual energy level hadn't returned.

After he'd had his lunch, Rhyder did some minor detecting to learn the lady's name and then wondered why the name Evelyne Winters seemed vaguely familiar. That was the problem with a lawyer's mind: it had to pick up all the little pieces and put them together in the correct order. But it wasn't his lawyer's half that was interested in the lady. Overly thin women with aristocratic features generally weren't his type, yet there was something about her that fascinated him. Besides, if a guy was setting out to be a beach bum, he had to learn not to be too picky. But he had painfully to admit that she was too young for him. He had outgrown sweet young things after he graduated from law school and realized they rarely had anything intelligent to say.

Rhyder didn't see Evelyne again until he was nursing a late-night drink in the bar that sat on a lava bed overlooking the ocean.

She was now dressed in a skimpy, barebacked dress that skimmed over her body to a couple of inches above her knees. She was also accompanied by a man who couldn't keep his eyes off her low neckline and the way the pendant she wore swung saucily between her breasts.

Rhyder groaned inwardly. Just another broad on the make, he decided, swallowing the rest of his whiskey, preferring to forget that he had been on the make since he had arrived. He just hadn't found a woman that interested him enough to make worthwhile the effort to get to know her better. His instincts weren't generally wrong about a woman, but the way his luck had been running lately he shouldn't be surprised it had happened this time. Still, he decided to stay a bit longer and see what happened.

Evelyne was beginning to wonder if having agreed to a drink with Jerry Hall was such a good idea after all. She had run into him in the hotel's restaurant where she was finishing up a late dinner and asking herself what she should do next. She had thought about walking into the bar but felt strange going in alone. Jerry took care of that point very nicely. Oh, he seemed nice and was certainly amusing, but she couldn't help gritting her teeth every time his hand slid over her knee and up her thigh. When they danced, he pulled her body so close to him she felt as if she were suffocating.

"I'm sorry, Jerry, but it's been a long day for me. I think I'd better call it a night," she apologized, flashing him a false smile after they had been in the bar for about forty minutes.

His face brightened. "Sounds fine to me." He dispatched with the bar tab in record time. He had been a little disappointed that she had only drunk Perrier, but it appeared the evening wasn't going to turn out to be a total loss after all. Evelyne may have looked like the perfect picture of a lady on the outside, but he'd bet she was one hot number in bed. The idea of her squirming under him was enough to quicken his step.

"Hey, what do you say we call room service?" he suggested, wrapping his arm around her shoulders and tugging her close to him during the walk back to her room. "You can put something comfortable on and just relax while we get to know each other better."

Evelyne's head told her she had just heard the perfect opening and she was positive it wouldn't take much to lure Jerry into her bed. The trouble was, the thought of his hands on her bare skin didn't seem at all appealing. Just his hand dipping to squeeze her buttocks was enough to fill her with nausea.

"I've had a long day, Jerry, what with the flight from New York and all, and I really need to catch up on my sleep." She ignored the silent reminder of her restful nap that afternoon. "Besides, I'll be here for several weeks and I know we'll see each other again." She injected a sultry promise in her smile.

Jerry backed her up against her door. "I'll remember that," he whispered, angling his body along hers. His kiss had all the finesse of an ox plowing a field, and Evelyne was positive he thought he was the sexiest man on earth. When his tongue plunged into her mouth, she shuddered with revulsion, but his ego probably insisted it was passion.

"Jerry!" she gasped, tearing her mouth away from his rum-scented one.

25

"That's only the beginning, baby," he promised grandly, covering her breast with his hand. He didn't even notice the nipple didn't peak in reaction. "I'll see you tomorrow . . . if you're sure I can't change your mind about tonight?"

Evelyne shook her head and escaped into her room with a sigh of relief. If she looked she wouldn't have been surprised to see Jerry wander back in the direction of the bar in hope of snaring fresh game.

In the safety of her room she cleansed her face, then slipped on an oversized cotton shirt in lieu of a nightgown. After turning off the air-conditioner she opened the sliding glass door to allow the fresh sea air to enter the room and chase away the stale, recirculated air. For the first time in months Evelyne slept deeply without the need of medication.

The next morning Rhyder was enjoying a breakfast of bacon and eggs when Evelyne entered the hotel restaurant. He watched the hostess seat her at a nearby table, where he had a perfect view of her profile. In navy cuffed shorts and a striped T-shirt with her hair rippling down her back she reminded him of a schoolgirl. Only her lightly curved figure and composed manner revealed her maturity.

He glanced up at the silent inquiry in the waitress's face and nodded his acceptance of a refill of coffee. After the young woman left he continued his perusal of the new diner. She looked familiar to him but he couldn't figure out why. A famous model? No, he never bothered reading fashion magazines, so he wouldn't know a famous model if one sat down next to him. A celebrity or perhaps a celebrity's discarded girlfriend? No man in his right mind would give her up and no one approached her the way they might if she were in films. Oh, well, the answer would soon come to him.

Rhyder sipped his coffee and enjoyed watching a man approach Evelyne . . . or Lady Evelyne, as he had nicknamed her. She certainly had the manner to be royalty. He didn't want to admit it, but he had come to think of himself as her self-appointed guardian in case someone got out of line. Rhyder decided he was right for the job; he might be well on his way to becoming a beach bum, but he still had principles, and that meant not having anything to do with a woman who didn't seem interested in him. At the ripe old age of forty-two he could afford to leave some of the women to the men who didn't mind juggling several at once.

He smiled when the man left after a moment's conversation. The lady obviously wanted to dine alone.

Evelyne should have realized she couldn't keep her identity a secret forever, and the man who had just approached her was proof positive.

The man, Tom Evans, was an aspiring songwriter, and wondered if Evelyne had any influence at Midnight Records to have his songs looked at by someone. He admitted to having seen her picture in *People* magazine several months ago, but mercifully made no mention of her illness or divorce. She swallowed a bitter laugh. Influence at Midnight Records indeed. She had so little influence that she had been lucky to leave the divorce with the clothes on her back. She knew if it hadn't been for her lawyer she might not have been able to keep the Malibu house as part of her settlement. When Rick had talked about keeping everything in the company name she hadn't dreamed that meant even a deed to a house or a car registration and would turn out to be a minus for her. She was surprised he hadn't tried to tatoo Midnight Records's logo on her hip.

Evelyne finished her juice and croissant and gestured for the check. She noticed a man watching her, flashed him a brief smile, then made her way to her room. She told herself she should be grateful all the reasons for the divorce hadn't been made public. She didn't know if she could have handled the speculation that would have come about from such a revelation. How many men found their wives repulsive after they had suffered a life-threatening illness? She had certainly heard of enough women rejecting their husbands for that reason during their recovery from a heart attack or a stroke. She just hadn't imagined the position being reversed. She shook her head to clear her thoughts. What she needed was a quiet morning relaxing by the pool.

Rhyder was stretched out on a chaise longue by the pool when Evelyne appeared dressed in a flame-colored bikini. The three other single men by the pool noticed her and were probably wondering idly how long it would take them to get her into the sack. As it was, Rhyder couldn't completely ignore the signals his own body was sending to his brain. He could sense that the lady was on the make; the trouble was, she didn't seem to know exactly what to do when it came to a seduction.

Little did he know how right he was. Evelyne knew the minuscule bikini showed off her body to its best advantage. She should have realized that men wouldn't just stare at her but would also salivate at the idea of sharing her company for a while. She looked around the pool where men and women reclined on lounges looking like a bunch of fried fish lying neatly on a platter; the newcomers were easily identified by their bright-red skin and the ones who had been on the islands for more than a few days sported dark tans. Several men looked up, more than interested in the packaging. She suddenly wished she had worn a one-piece bathing suit for her first day out. Then she wouldn't feel like something on exhibition. She scanned the empty lounges and who was next to them. A few of the men looked just a bit too anxious for her company. One man had glanced up and then returned to reading a book as if the book were more important than looking at women. He looked to be in his late thirties or early forties, not bad looking if you liked sharp-cut features in a man, and he certainly appeared intelligent. Of course, she'd learned a long time ago that looks could be deceiving. Still, he was someone for her to practice on, and that was what she needed. While she had bantered with men during her marriage, she had always made it perfectly clear that she was happily married and not looking for an affair. Now that she was not so happily divorced, she decided it was time to find out if she had it in her to become a siren.

He looked harmless enough. She could bask in the sun and perhaps even indulge in a bit of light flirting with him, she told herself. She took a deep breath and walked toward the other end of the pool.

Rhyder returned to his book so he wouldn't look as foolish as some of the other men ogling the dark-haired woman. He had to admit she had an excellent figure even if she was a bit too thin, and her face was the kind that belonged in a rare painting. He also knew she would probably pick some young stud who could keep up with all-night sex marathons. He had given them up long ago, knowing as a man grew older his body would only allow him to do so much. He'd wait a few minutes then discreetly lift his head to find out where she had gone.

"Is this lounge taken?"

Rhyder looked up. He had been so engrossed in wondering what man she would pick that he hadn't noticed her walking in his direction and stopping beside the heavy plastic molded lounge next to his. He was surprised to see her standing above him.

"No, it isn't." He inclined his head toward one of the men watching Evelyne with avid interest. "You're going to break some hearts around here, you know."

Her smile was pure sunshine. "Including yours?"

Would she? Rhyder wasn't sure. He also didn't know if he wanted to find out.

"If you don't jump my bones, I can guarantee your safety to a certain degree," he promised. "Rhyder Stewart."

Evelyne dropped down on the lounge and held out her hand. "Evelyne Winters."

When Rhyder took her hand, Evelyne was surprised by the small shock that traveled up her arm. It had nothing to do with static electricity. Judging by the bemused expression in his eyes he experienced the same feeling.

"I'd say you're from the Midwest," she guessed, ducking her head to put on a pair of oversized sunglasses.

"Chicago, and glad to be away from the cold." He grinned. "What about you?"

"Los Angeles," she said crisply, preferring not to say too much. The fewer people who knew her true identity the better. She had already learned she didn't like being known as Rick Winters's ex-wife.

"Los Angeles with a European education," Rhyder hazarded.

Evelyne nodded with a smile. "Very good. Most people think I'm English."

30

He shook his head. "Nope, you're haughty, but not frozen like some of the English people I've met."

She thought how much she could like this man who could never run for the Mr. Universe contest. "You enjoy speaking your mind, don't you?"

"It saves misunderstandings in the long run."

"What kind of occupation can a man have that allows him to speak his mind so freely?" *Oh, please don't let him be a reporter,* she pleaded to herself. That was the last thing she needed just then.

"I'm an attorney," he replied. *For the time being,* he amended silently.

Evelyne nodded. She glanced up when a waitress walked by and stopped to ask if either wished for a drink. Evelyne requested a large glass of grapefruit juice while Rhyder asked for something a bit stronger.

"Perrier last night, fruit juice today. You're not much of a drinker, are you?" he observed, watching her raise her upper body, her breasts straining against the two triangles of flame-colored fabric. He also noticed the way her collarbones jutted out and how the skin stretched tautly over her cheekbones. He wondered if she had been ill and had come to Hawaii to recuperate. Then he noticed the wide white band across her third finger, left hand.

"Newly divorced?" he asked gently.

"You ask too many questions," Evelyne retorted, noticing the direction of his gaze. She hadn't been able to take her wedding ring off until the divorce was finalized. The subject was still too painful to talk about.

"That's the only way I learn anything." He grinned, suddenly looking younger, and the lines cleared from his face.

The tiniest hint of a smile tugged at the corners of Evelyne's lips. She found it difficult to get upset with a man whose smile made her think of a picture she had once seen of a leprechaun.

"The name sounds English but the blarney is pure Irish," she pointed out.

Rhyder shrugged. "My family tree is the original melting pot, but there's probably more Irish in there than anything else. As for you, I'd guess there are more than a few drops of blue blood in your veins."

She leaned forward looking as if she was imparting a very important secret. "Just a few," she confided, then turned her head when the waitress appeared with their drinks. Evelyne took this opportunity to dig out a bottle of suntan lotion and apply it over her shoulders and arms. When she had finished protecting her skin she picked up her glass of juice.

"Why didn't you go to bed with Mr. Hotshot last night? He returned to the bar ten minutes after the two of you left—and I doubt you had a quickie."

Evelyne choked on her drink. It didn't help when Rhyder leaned over and casually slapped her on the back.

"Go down the wrong way?" he asked innocently.

She shot him a look fit to kill as she stood up and scooped up her towel and tote bag. Without saying a word she walked away until she reached another empty lounge. According to Rhyder's watch she was joined two minutes later by a darkly tanned man wearing French-cut swim briefs. He said something that made her laugh and took possession of a nearby lounge, pulling it over near hers. It wasn't long before they appeared to be a very cozy couple.

"Touched a nerve did I, Lady Evelyne?" Rhyder murmured, slipping on his sunglasses and picking up his book. He admitted he was interested in her in an impersonal way, but he refused to admit that those few moments with her stirred him more than any

32

woman had done in a long time. He tried to convince himself that he was too old to indulge in the amorous activities of a lovely divorcée even as he reminded himself that part of a beach bum's duties were to seek out vulnerable women. But Rhyder drew the line at women who obviously didn't know the score. So what was it to be? Was he to be a beach bum who bedded every available woman or would he revert back to boring, quiet old Rhyder Stewart who spent his evenings reading law journals?

CHAPTER TWO

For the next five days Evelyne found more than her
share of admirers. She soon realized and enjoyed the
fact that they were men who saw her as a beautiful
and sensual woman. They were also only too happy to
take their acquaintance one step further. The problem
was, when the time came to say good-night she didn't
have the courage to invite them into her room, much
less into her bed. She thought she would easily be able
to prove to herself she could still make wild love all
night with a man, yet she always backed off before the
situation got that far. What made it worse was that
she couldn't help noticing Rhyder Stewart's observa-
tion of her movements.

Who did he think he was? she asked herself angrily.
After all, she was a grown woman and what she did
and who she might do it with shouldn't concern him.
Not unless he was interested in her himself. She
laughed at the idea. Oh, he wasn't that bad looking,
she conceded silently, and there were quite a few lines
on his face as if he frowned a lot, but she noticed there
were smile lines to counterbalance the others. She noticed there had been a few women on their own who
had approached him, but he always seemed politely to
turn them down. Maybe he didn't like women and was
using her as some sort of subject for a book about
women of the eighties!

One night Evelyne lay in bed listening to the roar of the ocean and thinking of the house in Malibu with the master bedroom that dominated the third floor and the sound of the sea pounding against the sand drifting into the room. How many nights had she and Rick lain there talking over their day's activities and their plans for the following day? How many nights had they made love to those erotic sounds? She pressed her fingertips against her lips in order not to cry out loud.

She knew part of her unhappiness was due to her comedy of errors lately, also known as her attempts at acting like a seductive temptress. Such as when Ron Carter had walked her to her room and let her know he didn't appreciate not receiving an invitation inside for a "nightcap."

She wasn't a tease, she asserted to herself. The problem was, it had taken her this long to realize that she just wasn't cut out for a bunch of meaningless affairs. But there was also something else that frightened her: the off chance that Rick's words were true. What if she did suffer some kind of relapse while in bed with a man? There had been stories about men having heart attacks during sex. What was to say a woman couldn't suffer another stroke the same way? After long deliberation she decided she didn't really have the courage to dispute Rick's statement.

Determined to think of anything but sex she crossed her arms over her head, dreaming of her firm, plump pillow on her bed at home. She wished hotel pillows weren't so flat and limp. Even using the other three didn't prop her up more than an inch.

She half raised her head when she heard the forlorn sounding horn from one of the cruise ships that had stopped in Kailua Harbor and was now leaving. She

35

knew it to be part of a line that cruised between the islands.

Acting on impulse Evelyne jumped out of bed and ran out onto her balcony. Since her room was the second one from the corner, she didn't have a complete view of the ocean and was unable to see the departing ship. She couldn't explain why, but she had to see that ship leave. She glanced over at the next balcony, noticed the room was dark and the drapes were half drawn. With luck the room would be empty.

Evelyne rarely did anything on impulse, but she decided this was the perfect time to begin changing her personality. Gauging the short distance between balconies she swung her leg over the rail and carefully climbed onto the adjoining one. Holding her breath, just in case the room was occupied, she tiptoed past the glass doors until she reached the opposite edge of the balcony facing the ocean.

From there she could see the ship's stately motion through the ocean, the lights flickering as if it were a long white Christmas tree. How many times had she been on a cruise? Four, five times? She went on cruises because Rick liked them, while she became seasick at the drop of a hat. She could only stay on the ship as long as she took enough medication. Funny how some of the memories caught her at the oddest times, yet she still hadn't been able to remember what had happened the week before she became ill. The doctor told her it probably wouldn't ever come back to her. A tiny laugh escaped her lips. If she had known that would happen she might have insulted all the people she couldn't stand and wouldn't remember doing it, and they would have been too embarrassed to say anything to her.

"Don't tell me. You're from the Welcome Wagon, right?"

Evelyne spun around, her hand at her throat, feeling the pulse pounding against her fingertips.

"I—ah—I'm sorry, I didn't think anyone was staying in the room," she whispered hoarsely. "At least I'd hoped no one was." She couldn't help noticing that Rhyder wore only a pair of nylon athletic shorts, probably in deference to his nocturnal visitor. His hair was tousled, the skin on his face creased from where it had been pressed against his pillow. She gestured outward with her free hand. "I wanted to see the ship leave." She winced at the absurdity of her statement.

Rhyder walked outside and over beside her. One last mournful moan from the horn floated over the air as if wishing them farewell.

"An impressive sight," he commented, then looked down at the top of her head, which he ruefully noticed was all too close to his chin. If she wore heels she would stand eye level to him. "Care for a drink?"

Evelyne shook her head. "I'm not exactly dressed for visiting." She indicated her cobalt silk nightshirt that covered her almost to her knees.

"I wouldn't worry about Emily Post finding out about your faux pas. I have wine, a couple of beers, and a few of those wonderful small bottles of liqueur they serve on airplanes," he offered. "I've noticed that you usually drink something a little less harmful, but for the moment you might decide to make an exception."

"I'm not thirsty, thank you anyway." She thought about explaining how she couldn't drink alcohol due to the heavy medication she had taken and the pills she still took to ensure her blood pressure remained stable. But since that usually meant having to discuss her illness, she decided against it. Illness. Funny how she preferred using that word. It made it sound more innocuous, like the flu or the measles.

37

"Then I guess you don't mind if I have something." He disappeared into the dark room and returned carrying a beer can. He popped the top, upended the can, and drank thirstily. "Tell me, have you finally decided you can't qualify as a good candidate for the island slut?"

Evelyne would have slapped his face if he had smirked, but his matter-of-fact tone and questioning gaze took the sting out of his question.

"You sound like my father when you say things like that," she said flippantly.

"Did your ex-husband hurt you so much that you feel compelled to prove you're still a woman?" he asked in a gentle voice, resting his hip on the circular glass-topped table.

She pushed the hair away from her eyes, but the breeze just blew it back again, several strands now sticking to her lips. "You said you're an attorney. By any chance do you specialize in divorces?"

He chuckled. "No, but I should have. I certainly would have been a lot safer." He drank more of his beer before setting the can on the table.

"Why do you act like the outraged father where I'm concerned?" she asked, tipping her head to one side. "You don't even know me, yet you criticize my actions and warn me against the men I've met so far. Why should it matter to you what I do?"

Rhyder shrugged. "Hell if I know. Maybe because no one who looks like you could go on a sex spree without getting hurt. And, honey, you're the kind of woman to get hurt badly."

Evelyne shook her head too rapidly, protesting because deep down she knew he was right.

"If you didn't enjoy taunting people so much you could turn out to be a very nice man." She headed for the railing closest to her balcony.

"Whatever you say, duchess." With an economy of movement Rhyder picked Evelyne up by placing his hands at her waist and easily deposited her on her balcony.

She froze at his unintentional use of Rick's nickname for her. Her eyes blazed flaming darts at him.

"I'll make a deal with you, Mr. Stewart. You stay out of my way and we'll both be happy." She whirled away, prepared to enter her room, but a strong grip on the hem of her nightshirt halted her escape unless she wanted to lose her only covering.

"The least you can do is offer me a good-night kiss. After all, I did let you use my balcony to watch the ship leave." Rhyder's head swooped down and he stole a quick kiss. He released her in a matter of seconds.

Evelyne was too astonished to be insulted by his actions. In the end she laughed. She had to in order to hide the strange feelings coursing through her veins from that brief but compelling kiss. Rick had never had any problem arousing her, but never with such a swift kiss. Not wanting him to know how much he had affected her, she took her time walking into her room.

It was a long time before Evelyne fell asleep knowing Rhyder was lying in the next room. She had thought of going to Mexico instead of Hawaii. She wished she had.

Over the next few days Evelyne was oblivious to the fact that news of her hot-and-cold manner had spread among the single men staying at the hotel. But Rhyder heard all the rumors.

"First you think she's a hot piece and then she turns into a frigid bitch," one man complained as he lay out by the swimming pool one hot and sunny morning.

"No kidding," another agreed fervently. "It took me a while to remember where I had seen her before,

39

but after I remembered I was glad I didn't get her in the sack. Who knows what might have happened there."

Rhyder adjusted his sunglasses, curious to find out what this man knew about Evelyne.

"I always knew she looked familiar," the second man went on to say. "By racking my memory it finally came through. She was Rick Winters's wife."

One man cursed fluently under his breath. "Something happened to her brain, didn't it? I heard somewhere that she tried to stab him with a butcher knife and he left her before something really did happen."

"I heard she tried to shoot him."

"Wasn't it poison?"

Rhyder rolled his eyes. He guessed every scandal sheet in the country had a different story, judging from the crazy bits these guys were offering up. It certainly didn't sound like the woman he had met and spoken with. At least he now knew where he had heard her name before. Rick Winters, the darling of rock music, and his lovely wife who made the news with their parties and his new discoveries.

"She had a stroke," the second man clarified. "Can you imagine what might have happened if you were in bed with her and she went into convulsions or something at the crucial moment?" He absently rubbed suntan oil on his flat teak-brown chest. In a pair of white swim briefs to better accent his tan, he looked like the perfect specimen of masculinity even as Rhyder privately branded him an idiot.

So she had suffered a stroke, had she? It wasn't surprising Rhyder hadn't read anything about it in the newspapers, even though he made his home in Chicago and hers was Los Angeles. Judging from the talk that flowed around him, it had happened around the same time he had been going through his own trou-

40

bles. He hadn't had much time for casual reading then.

Had her husband divorced her because of her stroke? Was he the one to put sorrow in her eyes? In some areas of his life Rhyder didn't have a whole lot of principles, but he would never have willingly hurt a woman the way he suspected Evelyne Winters had been hurt.

He leaned back in the chaise, appearing uninterested in the men's conversation flowing nearby, but hearing and making note of every word. What he heard made him understand why Evelyne acted the way she did. If he guessed correctly he would say that her ex-husband had rejected her in bed and now she wanted to prove to herself that she was still a desirable woman. What better way than to flaunt a string of affairs? It seemed she had forgotten to take into account her own deep sense of morality that wouldn't allow her to go to bed with just any man. His heart went out to her.

Moments later his extrasensory perception picked up a new signal. He turned his head and saw her.

Evelyne couldn't move. She had been looking forward to a morning lazing by the pool, and perhaps indulging in some light flirtation until she heard the three men discussing her. Did they see her as some kind of freak? The pressure in her chest increased until she couldn't breathe. She would have tried to brazen out the situation, but a pair of hazel eyes caught her attention. They were filled with pity! She choked back a sob, wheeled around, and ran off before anyone else could see her shame.

Rhyder swore under his breath. He gathered up his things and headed for Evelyne's room. He knocked on the door and called out her name; he received no reply. Not wanting to fear the worst, while at the same time covering all the bases, he let himself into his own room, dropped his towel and book on the bed, and walked out onto his balcony. In a few seconds he was standing on Evelyne's balcony and peeping through the glass door.

"Evelyne?" he called out softly. Getting no answer he pulled at the door and found it unlocked. He stepped inside.

It didn't take a genius to discover she wasn't there. He did find four empty suitcases stacked neatly in the closet, and an impressive array of cosmetics lined up on the bathroom counter. Rhyder had known his share of women over the years and lived with two, but none of them had ever been this orderly. He left the room via the balcony and quickly showered off the suntan lotion and changed into shorts and a knit shirt.

A tour of the hotel grounds and shops told him Evelyne wasn't there. He then drove his rental car the short distance into Kailua in hopes of finding her there. He didn't know why he was going to so much bother over a woman who didn't want his help, except that after over a week of lying in the sun and frying his brains the mental activity was welcome.

The small town of Kailua boasted plenty of shops for the tourists to spend money, so Rhyder decided to try the clothing and jewelry stores first. He found no sign of her in any of them. Acting as a husband searching for his spendthrift wife, he questioned the sales clerks, but no one had seen her.

Couldn't she do anything the way she was expected to? he wondered, before turning and seeing her at Club 53, a restaurant/bar built along the wharf, the name taken from Don Drysdale's player number during his stint with the Los Angeles Dodgers. The club was known for its sports fans sitting around drinking beer and watching the various games on television.

Evelyne sat in one of the canvas-back chairs facing the ocean, a basket of food and a glass of Coke in front of her. She halfheartedly nibbled on a french fry while staring at the small boats dotting the harbor.

Rhyder sauntered over to the bar, ordered a beer, and walked to Evelyne's table.

"You run away once, you'll never be able to stop," he told her in a conversational tone as he sat down in the chair facing her.

"Go to hell." She had a way of looking through a person as if he weren't there.

Rhyder shook his head in reproof. "I don't think you heard that nasty expression from your nanny during your formative years." He drank deeply of the cold brew.

Evelyne's gaze shot through him like an ice-coated shaft. "If you're in the mood for comparing profanity vocabularies, I suggest you try someone else. I'm not in the mood for trading zingers."

Rhyder silently applauded. She was hurt by what she had overheard, but she wasn't defeated. He reached across the table and snitched a couple of her french fries.

Her eyebrow rose slightly. "If you're hungry I'm sure they'd be only too happy to fix you something."

"Obviously your stroke didn't leave you impaired in any way."

Evelyne whitened. She should have expected such blunt talk from Rhyder, but she hadn't expected it to hurt so badly. "Oh, I don't know. I tend to drool at odd times and I occasionally stoop when I walk as if I have a hump. Of course, other than that and occasional slurred words I'm perfectly normal." Her beautiful face was a frozen mask.

Rhyder nodded, understanding her need for sarcasm. He had seen it enough in the courtroom and even when interviewing prospective clients. He had a pretty good idea that his blunt statements were going to force a reaction from her, and he knew that was the only way to insure she didn't try to retreat into a shell or run away from the truth. After all, he had done a pretty good job of running away from life; he didn't want to see her end up doing the same.

"Did the doctors know what caused it?" he asked in a calm voice. One way or another he was going to get her to talk about her feelings.

She shrugged. "They say it was an abnormal blood vessel I'd had from birth that had broken. They don't feel there will be a repeat, and everything else looks normal. Normal." She gave a hollow laugh. "I'm beginning to think there is no such word."

"I once read somewhere that strokes are even hitting women your age who are in high-pressure jobs," Rhyder commented, now sipping slowly from his beer. "It used to be only the men who were affected, but now the sex doesn't seem to matter."

"I married after I graduated from school, and I never held a job in my life," she protested, as if to argue the fact that there was no reason for her to have been afflicted; as if there had to have been some kind of horrible mistake and it couldn't have happened to her.

Rhyder frowned and shook his head. "But you said it was an abnormal blood vessel. I'm sure some kind of mental pressure affected it."

"The doctor explained to me that even though I didn't work in an office I still held a high-pressure job," she explained in her soft voice. "I was a career housewife. We owned two homes, I supervised two separate staffs, I planned all our social functions and personally supervised those. Not to mention that I had an extremely active daily schedule filled with various

44

appointments. I was not someone who slept until noon and spent the rest of the day lying about the house eating chocolates and reading fashion magazines. I was usually up at six and rarely got to bed before midnight. And because I worked myself so hard, none of my staff ever complained if I asked for a bit more than usual, because they knew I would do just as much as they did when necessary."

Rhyder stared down at his laced fingers forming a steeple in front of him. "And then you fell ill."

She nodded. "I had been suffering from headaches for over a year, but I thought they might be eyestrain. Even my doctor did and suggested I have an eye exam. I always found something more important to do. After a while the headaches became worse, and one night I went to bed thinking I might be coming down with the flu. I woke up in the hospital several days later. There were those who weren't sure I'd even survive. It was almost three weeks before I was allowed home."

"And your husband wanted nothing to do with you after that?"

Evelyne looked at him with eyes brimming with tears. "My dear God, you truly like to hurt, don't you?"

"No, I just want you to get that hurt out of your system."

"I never knew rejection could be so degrading," she whispered, looking down at the scarred, round wooden table. "You would have thought I was some kind of freak. Oh, he didn't use that reason when he divorced me; *incompatibility* sounded much better to his ears. So by one judge's decision he was free of me and managed to keep a good part of his assets too."

Rhyder sat up. "Wait a minute. California is a community-property state. Are you saying you didn't get a decent settlement? After all, that guy must be worth millions."

Evelyne didn't even think of informing him that what had happened to her was none of his business; his question sounded so businesslike. She shook her head. "If you look at his holdings on paper you'd wonder where the next house payment would come from. Just about everything we owned was in the company's name and Rick decided he didn't care to pay me any kind of support. He felt I'd spent more than enough money during our marriage."

Rhyder's opinion of the man was decidedly profane. "Are you saying that after all you had done for him he wasn't willing to give you anything?" He was amazed.

She pushed her basket of food away. "I don't even know why I'm telling you about this. No, he didn't want to give me any money and I was lucky to get what I did. I'm not one of those bitter women who demand the earth when they don't deserve it, but I didn't feel I should come out of the marriage with nothing either."

"So you came out here to heal the wounds and reaffirm your femininity," he guessed.

Evelyne nodded, shamefaced. "I can't even have an affair correctly." She sighed, toying with the straw in her drink. "I probably should have bought some books first to find out the proper way to have one."

He hid his smile. "Why have one?"

"Because I have to prove something to myself," she said fiercely.

"You're alive, you're a beautiful woman, and you've kept at least four men dancing on a string. I should think that's doing well enough," he told her. "Why not just settle back and have some fun?"

She looked at him suspiciously. "What kind of fun?"

"Sightseeing, snorkeling, swimming, driving around the island, trying out a different restaurant every night."

"And I gather you don't think I should do this alone?" Her light sarcasm wasn't lost on him.

Rhyder shrugged. "I haven't done much to see the island either. So why shouldn't we do it together?"

Evelyne sighed. "Why do I feel like you're pulling some con job on me?"

"You know very well I'm not. If anything you're probably suspicious since I must be the only man who hasn't made a pass at you," he replied, an appealing grin lighting his face.

They both knew he lied, because the memory of that short kiss hung between them. If he preferred to forget about it, then so would she.

"That's an excellent reason why I shouldn't trust you," she countered.

"Why is that?"

"Because you may be acting like the helpful gentleman when you're really a lecher in disguise." She leaned back in her chair, triumph written on her face.

Rhyder grimaced. "Lady, I don't really care to chase after young girls anymore. Haven't you been able to figure that out yet?"

Evelyne tipped her head to one side, studying Rhyder as if she had just met him. Oh, the sandy-brown hair with its shading of gray at the temples and along the top was cut shorter than that of most men she knew and had definitely not been styled professionally, but it fit his angular features. He wasn't handsome, nor was he ugly. The lines deeply etched in his forehead and along his mouth emphasized his character, as someone she knew she could trust. If she were asked for her reasons for knowing she could trust him, she would only be able to say that he appeared to be a man who inspired trust in people and he would never betray that kind of confidence.

"Why are you offering your friendship?" She had to admit to curiosity regarding his casually spoken offer.

"Because we're two of a kind," he replied cryptically.

Evelyne sensed that she could try to probe farther into his answer but wouldn't hear anything suitable unless he chose to tell her.

"I didn't rent a car," she offered her last excuse even as she knew she would say yes.

"Then how did you get here so fast?" he demanded, knowing how warm the day was and that she didn't look as if she had jogged into town.

"I hitched a ride into town with someone from the hotel. Since I don't have a car for exploring the island, I guess you're out of luck, aren't you?" she challenged.

"I have one." He shot her last protest down the drain.

Evelyne picked up her knife and carefully cut her hamburger, offering half of it to Rhyder along with a napkin. "It was so huge I didn't know how I was going to eat it all," she explained a bit shyly.

He examined the trimmings. "Onions?"

She smiled, the first real smile he had glimpsed since he'd first seen her. "When I don't have a heavy date I always indulge myself in a healthy dose of onions. I once heard it keeps colds away," she said flippantly.

"Good reason. No one could stand to be near you after they get a good whiff of these." He bit into the hamburger without bothering to scrape the onions off.

"Have you ever been married?" Evelyne decided it was time for her to ask a few questions. For all she knew he could be married with six children and had decided to take a vacation on his own.

He shook his head, pointing to his still full mouth.

After he swallowed he said, "No, and if you want to know why it's because I just haven't found a woman I'd care to spend the next fifty or so years with. Oh, I'm not saying I haven't tried. I lived with two women at two different times in my life and discovered that each of them drove me crazy for one reason or another."

"Such as?" She picked up her half of the hamburger.

He chuckled. "I had only been out of law school for a year or so and felt cocky as hell when I asked a woman to move in with me. She was a stockbroker, and I figured she was the kind of woman I needed. You know, the type dedicated to her own career who would understand if I worked late at the office on a case or forgot about her for a couple days. The trouble was, I was so out of it at times that it took me six months to realize that if *I* wasn't available for her, she would find someone who was. Needless to say I asked her to leave. I didn't try again until about six years ago. This time with a more domestic type. After all, I was getting closer to forty than I liked, and I figured it wouldn't hurt for me to look around for a wife who could make a good home for her hardworking husband. Her name was Lora. She ended up clinging to my every word and worrying if I was more than ten minutes late coming home. She cooked meals like you wouldn't believe, and in the end I gained twenty pounds. That arrangement didn't work out either. That was when I decided I was destined to be the crusty old bachelor, and I've left it up to my younger brother and his wife to carry on the Stewart name. He's done the job admirably. To date they have three sons and two daughters." He had guessed her to be in her early thirties and brought his thoughts to voice. "You don't have any children?"

She ducked her head. "Rick said we always had plenty of time. Now I realize it was because he didn't want any to clutter up his life."

And she did want them, Rhyder thought, finding another reason to hate the unknown man for having refused to give Evelyne what she wanted and quite possibly needed to feel complete. Had she any idea how shallow her life had been? He didn't think so. He dreaded the day when she would realize exactly what her ex-husband had done to her.

"So how does a day of playing tourist sound to you?" he asked, purposely injecting a light note into the conversation.

"Such as?" She slanted a flirtatious glance at him.

"There's a lot we could do. It just depends on what sounds good to you. We could visit the volcano park or see the Parker ranch and drive over to Hilo. There's also the macadamia-nut factory near there. I don't think we'd have any problem finding something to do."

Evelyne offered him a french fry with a dab of catsup on the end. "The volcano park sounds interesting."

Rhyder smiled. "I wonder if anyone has ever called a volcano interesting before. Sounds fine with me."

She smiled back at him. She sensed this man was offering a friendship that few had garnered from him, and she realized it was the kind of relationship she needed just now.

That evening they shared a companionable dinner at a restaurant in town and explored the adjoining area. At eleven o'clock they parted to retire to their respective rooms with the promise to meet for breakfast at seven.

Evelyne had always hated dining alone, and eating meals by herself the past week had enforced that feeling very strongly. Having Rhyder share breakfast with her was an experience she couldn't help but enjoy. His dry wit concerning the other diners kept her laughing throughout the meal.

Rhyder leaned across the table to whisper, "Don't look now, but you're being stared at."

She was tempted to turn around and see who was staring at her but had the good sense not to. "Are you going to tell me who's rude enough to stare at me?" she demanded.

"No."

"Why not?"

"Because I talk better when I've been bribed."

Evelyne picked up her last piece of bacon and waved it in front of his eyes. "Is this a suitable bribe?"

He deliberated. "Along with your banana muffin, yes."

She picked up her muffin, smiled sweetly, turned around, noticed one of her past admirers glaring at her, turned around again, and bit into her muffin.

"And here I thought it was a gorgeous man who couldn't keep his eyes off of me." She worked on her piece of bacon next. "You should have settled for the bacon."

"I never settle out of court for small amounts."

Evelyne laughed. "How can someone who doesn't look the smiling type make me laugh so much?"

"Probably because you're so damned polite you laugh at some of the worst jokes known to man," he retorted, not appreciating the idea she didn't think he smiled. He smiled . . . lots of times. He just didn't want to waste a perfectly good smile on someone who didn't deserve one. Evelyne deserved more than one, and he had no trouble smiling at her, because he hoped she would smile back.

He reveled in the sight of her wearing navy shorts

and a short-sleeved white cotton shirt with navy and bright-green pinstripes. Her slender hands were tipped with a bright rose-colored polish as they gestured delicately while she spoke. Everything she did interested him, and deep down he knew that could be dangerous, because after physical attraction came love, and that was an emotion he couldn't afford to learn more about.

CHAPTER THREE

"Do you know how to read a map?" Rhyder asked, tossing a car-rental road-guide into Evelyne's lap.

"Not exactly," she murmured, opening the pages and trying to make out the meaning of the squiggly lines. "Can't you?"

"I've never been able to make head or tails of these things. I'll trust you to find the park." He switched on the ignition and slipped the car in gear.

Evelyne studied the map, turning each page until she came to the one that showed where they presently were, and kept turning pages until she came to the volcano park. "Do you realize how long a drive it is?" she asked in a surprised voice.

"I asked at the desk and they said to figure on being gone all day." Rhyder pulled out onto the highway.

"It will probably take that long just to get there." She studied the map further, told him to take highway eleven, and sat back to enjoy the scenery.

"Some navigator you turned out to be. One sentence and you figure you've got all the bases covered," he grumbled good-naturedly. "If we end up on Maui it's all your fault."

Evelyne glanced at the map again then looked up. "Since that sign over there says this is the way to the volcano park, I don't think we have all that much to worry about."

For the next hour they traveled through small towns that would have made the visitor think they were on the mainland if it weren't for signs advertising some of the island specialties and stores displaying bikinis and puraus, a colorful sarong type of garment popular with all women. They made one stop for something cold to drink, then continued their long drive. Just when Evelyne thought she wouldn't see the ocean again, the road dipped down and began to parallel the beach, although they only saw miles of lava beds with signs explaining what year the lava had flowed down to the sea.

"It even crossed this road," Rhyder commented, noticing one sign that stated the flow had occurred in 1950.

"I want to take some pictures," she insisted, digging into her purse for her camera.

"Pictures?"

"Yes, of the lava beds." Evelyne finally found her camera. "If this is to be a typical touristy day, then we have to take pictures."

"You can take the pictures. I didn't bring a camera with me," he replied, pulling over to the side. He didn't think a camera suited a beach bum's image.

Rhyder helped Evelyne out of the car and then walked a short distance on the rocky surface. He was astounded at the many colors reflected in what he thought to be stark black rock. Shades of reds and greens were just barely hidden under the surface. He was so interested in observing a tiny plant growing in the middle of past devastation he didn't realize Evelyne had snapped his picture.

She didn't know why she'd taken a picture of him. Perhaps because of the expression on his face as he noticed the small piece of greenery in the midst of a desolate area. It also could have been because she felt

54

like that plant. Her world had crumbled around her for so long that she hadn't been sure she could lift herself out of it. Even her so-called plans for this vacation hadn't worked out. But now this man was taking her in hand to make sure she didn't get in trouble, offering her a friendship she had never known from any other man. Rick had been her husband and her lover, but if she cared to admit it, he had never been her friend. When she thought about it, she could count her true friends on one hand; the rest had been acquaintances from Rick's business or some of the social committees she had worked on. They had dropped out of her life not long after she had been released from the hospital. She had even lost a few people whom she had considered friends, since they didn't realize she was the same person she had been before she had been taken ill.

"Why weren't you repelled when I told you I'd had a stroke?" she asked curiously as they headed back to the car.

Rhyder stroked his chin and tipped his head sideways to look at her. "My father suffered from a stroke five years ago. He wasn't as lucky as you. His speech is still a little slurred if he tries to speak too quickly, and he lost the use of his right hand. But he's a fighter, and he was determined not to let it get him down. There were some people who couldn't handle his infirmity, and he blithely told them to go to hell—he'd see them when he got there." A glimmer of laughter lightened his eyes. "You know what? I don't think he's missed any of them. He had been a foreman with a construction firm and couldn't work, but he could advise, and that's what he's been doing. If he ever felt sorry for himself, no one has ever known it. He never allowed my mother to coddle him. In fact, he'd cuss a blue

55

streak whenever she tried. He's the one who taught me that you can't let the world get you down."

Evelyne shook her head, amazed at the idea that a man who had obviously worked on such a physical level could settle for doing so much less.

"I felt sorry for myself," she confessed. "I couldn't remember anything of the week before I fell ill, and just the idea of not knowing what I did or said was enough to make me want to scream. Oh, Rick was the attentive husband and remained by my side the whole time I was in the hospital. My mother couldn't handle the thought of illness, but she telephoned me every day. I don't think she even yet understands what happened to me." She got into the car and settled herself against the warm seat. She didn't care to explain that her mother was so ill herself she couldn't handle anyone else's problems.

"What about your father?" Rhyder hadn't switched the engine on yet and half turned in the seat.

"He died six years ago." Her small voice told him how much she missed him. "He was Victor King."

His head whipped around. *"The* Victor King?"

Evelyne smiled, used to this reaction when she revealed her father's name to the unknowing. "I doubt there's another one like him running around."

Rhyder whistled under his breath. Victor King and his father, Jason, had been known for creating one of the greatest of the movie empires. The Kings dated their heritage back to Spanish California, and while the money was old and came from orange groves and horse breeding, a young Jason, just out of college, had wanted to invest in a daring venture back in the early nineteen twenties, and moviemaking had seemed the way to go. He built his own studio, and what began as a hobby turned into a large money-making proposition under his skilled leadership. Jason's eldest son, Victor, took over the reins and expanded the business into television when it was still in the experimental stages.

"You were right when you said you didn't have any blue blood," he told her. "Honey, it's pure California gold."

Evelyne shook her head. "None of the King children were ever allowed to be spoiled or made aware of their wealth."

"I bet you wore designer diapers."

She rolled her eyes. "You can usually do better than that. If it will make you feel any better, I did have an English nanny." But she knew that her father did dote on her. His first two wives hadn't blessed him with children, and when his third wife gave him a baby daughter he vowed she would never do without. Evelyne, named after his grandmother, had everything a child could ask for, but according to the King tradition she was not allowed to be spoiled. When she reached the age of fifteen, she was sent to an exclusive finishing school in Switzerland where young ladies were groomed to enter high society.

Evelyne had graduated with a degree in languages and returned home only to meet Rick Winters, then a rising promoter in the rock music industry, gave him her virginity a week later, and married him the following month.

Victor hadn't been happy that his only daughter had married someone in the music business; he had always considered them all idiots. But Evelyne was still his daughter and he would always stand by her decision, beginning with the largest wedding Brentwood had seen in years.

Evelyne was just relieved her father hadn't seen the dissolution of her marriage. She knew he would have gone after Rick with a vengeance and probably used every resource at hand to ruin the younger man.

Evelyne wouldn't have wanted that. Not that she considered Rick's leaving her fault, but if he was so weak he couldn't continue standing by his wife in her time of need she didn't want him. Now, Rhyder was a different story. She doubted he would have left her even if he hadn't experienced this before with his father, because it was just part of his nature. She dubbed it his "big-brother complex."

"I bet when you were a small boy you'd bring home dogs with hurt legs and cats who had been run over by cars," she said unexpectedly.

He glanced at her quizzically. "What brought that on?"

"You did, didn't you?" Evelyne curled her legs under her body and leaned against the door, after making sure it was locked.

"Are you comparing yourself to a wounded cat?" Rhyder asked.

She shrugged. "I guess so. You certainly wouldn't have bothered with me otherwise, would you? You never looked at me the way the other men did." She couldn't fathom why she was pressing him this way.

"Probably because you're too young for me or I'm too old for you. Take your pick." He silently cursed himself for remembering that he had indeed looked her over and found out that she had everything in the right places.

"If you're collecting social security, you're certainly well preserved," Evelyne commented lightly.

"If that's a polite way of asking me my age, I'm forty-two."

"Ten years isn't all that much," she countered. "My father was twenty-seven years older than my mother, and she never complained." Evelyne remembered how much the delicate woman had loved her hard-driving husband, but she had never been able to move in the mainstream as easily and her way to cope had been to withdraw until she soon had no life of her own.

"How old is Winters?" Rhyder asked abruptly.

Evelyne knew what he was trying to do. "Thirty-five, and we were married for ten years." Her throat filled as she began remembering happy and love-filled incidents from those ten years.

Rhyder sensed her swinging emotions. "I admit I've never been in the situation you were in, but I've helped several friends through it, and they say it only gets better with time."

"That's what my friend Celia said." She sighed. "And she should know, she's had four husbands and is now working on number five. But I'm determined not to put a blight on a day you've been so nice to plan for me. Why don't you tell me more about yourself? All I know is that you're a lawyer, you live in Chicago, and have a father who was in construction before his stroke. What kind of law do you specialize in?"

"Probate," he explained. "I share office space with two men I went to law school with."

His words were a bit too clipped to Evelyne's ears. "You don't like to talk about your work, do you?"

He smiled thinly. "Let's just say that one night when I get blind drunk I might tell you more about my practice." What was left of it, anyway. One of his partners had called him late last night to see how he was doing and Rhyder had spun a tale of sun, sand, and women, but he knew Ken Marshall hadn't believed him. He knew Rhyder only too well, and Rhyder's story of planning to remain in Hawaii as a beach bum didn't wash.

"You can't remain lazy, Rhyder," Ken informed him. "It's not part of your nature. Before too long you'll be raring to return to work."

"What work?" he had retorted. "This trip was made

thanks to a recent inheritance. It may not have been much, but it was enough to pay my expenses out here. Sure, I probably should have stayed back there and fought my way back again, but, hell, Ken, I have to do something for myself. And this is it. If necessary I can always find a rich woman to live off," he quipped.

"You idiot, if there were any rich women there they'd be hunting down the twenty-year-old studs, not forty-year-old relics like you," Ken said bluntly, not seeing the joke. "Look, you made a common mistake any of us would make. You never had any idea that Debra would sue you for bad advice. If Winston had filed the suit in time, she wouldn't have learned that she could sue you for giving her bad advice and you wouldn't have practically lost your shirt. No matter what you say, you still have your practice, and at least you didn't lose your car."

Rhyder cursed and Ken laughed.

"I'm glad you haven't lost your sense of humor," Ken teased.

"I see no sense in coming back, Ken, so why don't you just lease out my office to the first sucker that comes along?" Rhyder suggested.

"You'll be back once you start going crazy from doing nothing. See you later, buddy." With that Ken rang off.

Rhyder didn't believe him, but knew Ken always did what he wanted. Time alone would tell his friend that he had no plans to return to Chicago to take up a faltering law practice.

He had made a mistake. Little did he know when he had given a "friend"—Rhyder could no longer even think of her as a lover—an attorney's name for a suit she wanted to file the favor would almost ruin his career. The man had been on the verge of a nervous breakdown and failed to file the paper work by the deadline, which meant that Debra Parker's case had been thrown out of court. Since the attorney lost his own business, Debra took another friend's advice and sued Rhyder for referring her to an unreliable lawyer. He ended up losing his house and a great many of his assets to pay off the court settlement. Fed up with the legal system and women in general, he had taken off for Hawaii in hopes of turning into a bum. What he had forgotten was that his natural energy level wouldn't allow him to lead a lazy life.

Then, too, meeting Evelyne had made some changes in his plan. Before he knew what was happening, he was acting like some idiot camp counselor planning field trips in order to keep her out of the kind of trouble she couldn't handle. If he wasn't careful, he'd next plan a sing-along around a campfire! he thought disgustedly, pulling a bit too hard on the steering wheel and inadvertently guiding the car toward the other lane before he realized what he was doing.

"Did someone drive past us at the speed of light and cut us off?" Evelyne asked curiously, wondering what caused the stern expression and anger in Rhyder's eyes as he jerked the car back into the proper lane.

"No," he said curtly, keeping his eyes on the road.

Deciding something was bothering him and she should leave him alone, she sat back to study the scenery, which wasn't the lush green that the other side of the island boasted. This area showed signs of past volcanic activity, the ground a dusty tan or gray with little signs of vegetation, and what there was sparse and dry looking. She wondered if they had somehow landed on another planet and thought back to some of the science fiction books she had read. Their surroundings certainly would have fit in from what she saw around her.

"Are we pouting?" She finally broke the charged silence around them.

A glimmer of a smile creased Rhyder's face. "Not exactly, but it's probably close," he admitted. "You're pretty good at getting people out of bad moods."

"I've always lived with people who lived and worked intensely. I learned at an early age how to defuse a difficult situation," Evelyne explained matter-of-factly. "It looks so stark out here, doesn't it?"

He nodded. "It's no wonder the astronauts come out here for training. The layout certainly looks like something from another world."

"I was thinking that too. I once read a science fiction book set on a planet that sounded very much like the way it looks here," she said, leaning over to adjust the air-conditioner. It seemed the farther they traveled the hotter it got. The problem was, the small car couldn't seem to keep up a good speed and put out enough cold air at the same time.

"How about a quick side trip to the black-sand beach?" Rhyder asked, noticing a sign at the side of the road.

"That sounds fine with me. I've always heard about it, but never got to see it."

"Didn't you once say you've been here before?" He steered toward the turnoff.

Evelyne nodded. "Except we stayed in Waikiki to check out the local talent. Anytime we went somewhere, it was to check out a new band or singer he had heard about."

Rhyder frowned. "I thought he owned the company."

"He does. But he began it by searching for new and unique talent, and he can't get out of the habit of doing it himself." That was when she realized that, in the ten years they had been married, they had never taken

62

a real vacation; only side trips to look for new talent. Why hadn't she ever noticed it before and complained? Was it because Rick had always found ways to keep her occupied or unaware of what was really happening? Now that she was separate from him and able to stand back and view him objectively, she could see how selfish he had been toward her in some ways. No wonder she had unlimited charge accounts and a great deal of freedom; they kept her from complaining about the times he promised to take her somewhere, only to disappear for a couple hours to check out a nightclub. "Here I thought we had wonderful vacations, and we really never had a true one," she murmured, looking down at her hands lying in her lap.

"You're working on a poor-little-rich-girl act, and I'm not going to allow you to feel sorry for yourself. I'm not going to coddle you either," Rhyder said firmly, reaching out to take hold of one of her hands and shake it in order to catch her undivided attention.

"Aren't lawyers supposed to coddle their clients and sympathize with them?" she asked lightly.

"You're not my client." He placed her hand back in her lap.

Evelyne looked down at her hand that felt so warm. A slight tingle had begun at her fingers and worked its way up her arm at Rhyder's touch. How could a man who apparently had no more interest in her than he would in a plant generate such feelings in her? She was finding herself wondering what a real honest-to-goodness toe-curling, lust-filled kiss would be like and how his hands would feel on her bare skin. That all-too-brief kiss he had given her that night on their respective balconies had set her to thinking about him more as a man and less as a nuisance who had seemed determined to ruin her vacation.

They rode on in silence and soon turned and drove

up a road flanked by greenery that contrasted sharply with the desolation they had driven through earlier.

They drove up to the Kilauea visitor center and wandered through the park's station that displayed vivid color photographs of volcano eruptions and paintings of the same, a seismograph that registered earth tremors and other antique equipment used to gauge the volcano's moods. They also sat through a short film that explained the history of volcanoes and viewed volcanoes from all over the world. After the film they gathered up a map of all the craters and wandered back to the car.

"Our best bet would be to follow the Chain of Craters Road," Evelyne said after studying the small map.

"That sounds fine." Rhyder unlocked the car doors and turned on the air conditioning to cool the warm interior before they got inside. "It's hard to believe it's winter when you look around here. Back home I'd be freezing my buns off."

Evelyne couldn't resist walking behind Rhyder and taking a careful look at said anatomy. "That would be a pity, wouldn't it?" She smiled sweetly and slid onto the car seat.

Rhyder shook his head, muttering about smart-aleck women. He glanced at the map, then decided that the signs would be enough for him to find his way. During the drive up the trail they both noticed the abrupt change from a green rain-forest to raw, desolate craters. They stopped at several, Evelyne taking pictures and pointing out the steam escaping from vents in the bottom of the craters. She was again reminded of some of the science-fiction books she had read and mentioned it out loud.

"I would have taken you for a classics fan," Rhyder commented as they returned to the car.

"I read anything and everything," she replied.

64

"Usually it depends on my mood. Sometimes I'll curl up with romance books and then suddenly turn to spy thrillers. Another time I'll alternate between mysteries and historical novels. If nothing else I can admit I'm well read. I didn't use to have as much free time to read as I do now. That's one of the few pluses that came with the divorce." She turned in the seat to face him. "What do you like to read?"

He grinned. "Would you believe law journals?"

"What? Do you mean you never read for pleasure?"

"I never had that much free time, and when I did I spent it catching up on my reading," he admitted.

"If you had so little free time, how did you manage to take a vacation?" Evelyne remembered how Rick worked hard, but never overdid it, claiming that was the sure way to a heart attack. It was ironic that she was the one who had ended up in the hospital suffering from a stress-related illness.

Rhyder's features looked a little pained. "I had no problem taking the time off," he said, his voice sounding harsh to his ears.

"Rhyder." He thought how musical her voice sounded. "You certainly listened to my problems. I hope you realize you have the same privilege. If something's bothering you I'd be only too happy to listen."

"As I said, if I get drunk enough one evening we'll have that talk."

Evelyne couldn't help wondering what bothered Rhyder so much that he didn't want to talk about it. She remembered that he had made some flippant remark that he was there to become a beach bum, and silently wondered if something had happened in Chicago to make him leave. Could he have lost an important case? Or something worse? Although she wasn't sure what could be worse than that. Since he didn't specialize in criminal law she didn't think that he could have played a part in an innocent man's being condemned. All she knew was that he had been wonderful to her and forced her to give up her self-pity and bitterness, and she wanted to do the same for him.

They stopped at the overlook near the Halemaumau crater and got out to take the path for a closer look. Evelyne stooped down and felt the ground. It was warmer than the sun alone could make it, and she laughed. As they walked they noticed four or five flat rocks piled on top of each other.

"A perfect way to find out if an earth tremor is happening," Rhyder told her. "If the sulpher fumes become too much for you, tell me and we'll go back. Some people can't handle them. You also tell me if you get tired."

"I'm perfectly healthy," she informed him tartly.

"Don't get so sensitive," he chided, tapping his forefinger against her nose. "Perfectly healthy people can collapse because of the fumes or find walking over rocks more than they can handle." He took her hand when they reached one hazardous area and didn't bother releasing it.

"And here I thought I was past the hand-holding stage," he murmured, then shook his head when Evelyne looked at him inquiringly. He didn't see any need to repeat his whimsical words.

Evelyne would occasionally stop and examine the lava rocks, entranced by the varied colors running through the stone. She even had Rhyder take a picture of one particular rock she held. He teased her again about acting too touristy, and she retorted she was there to have fun and if he was going to keep her from having a series of one-night stands, then he would just have to settle for her acting like a typical tourist. What she hadn't expected was that an elderly woman would overhear her statement and spear her with a chilling

66

glare as if to say one's perversities shouldn't be revealed in public.

"Darling, you shouldn't make jokes like that." Rhyder told her in an endearing tone. "People just don't understand that strange sense of humor of yours." He turned and presented the woman with a smile filled with charm. The woman just harrumphed and walked toward her husband standing a short distance away.

"And here I didn't even think you had a sense of humor." Evelyne turned on him, her hands braced on her hips.

He shook his head. "I don't have one. I just say what I feel. I can't help it if it's funny sometimes."

She flashed him a quizzical look as he took her hand and directed her on. The smell of sulpher surrounded them, and Evelyne was convinced her clothes would always carry the heavy smell. As they looked over the crater with its numerous steam vents and an appearance of devastation, they were awed with the power before them. Evelyne was surprised by the show of plant life; tiny white flowers could be seen among the craters and lava beds. The smell was enough to convince them to leave after only a short time.

They continued the drive around, passing the volcano observatory, and by mutual decision left the park to explore further. Instead of heading back the way they had come, Rhyder suggested driving along the Hilo side of the island and stopping at a macadamia-nut factory along the way.

The drive gave them another view of the island and a trip to the macadamia-nut factory showed them how they were processed for canning, the making of macadamia brittle and chocolate-covered macadamia nuts. Evelyne ordered some nuts to be sent to friends and bought a few cans of nuts and some of the brittle to take with her. Rhyder also ordered some to be sent to his parents and a box of nuts coated in assorted glazes to be sent to his partners. He reminded himself he hadn't talked to his parents since the night he had arrived and made a mental note to call them that evening. He turned around, watching Evelyne stroll through the visitors' center. He had a good idea his father would adore her, and to be perfectly honest he wouldn't blame him. Not only was she lovely, but she was the kind of woman any sane man should hang on to. Too bad her husband hadn't realized the mistake he'd made.

After they left the factory, they drove into a small town where Rhyder got gas and they debated whether to eat or not. They decided to wait until they reached Hilo. There they found an excellent Chinese restaurant and filled themselves with sweet-and-sour pork, fried rice, and various vegetable dishes.

During dinner Evelyne learned a little more about Rhyder's practice, that he had belonged to a health club for over a year and had only gone once, and his only vice manifested itself during football season, when he could be found in front of his television set every Sunday afternoon and Monday night. He took his phone off the hook during the Super Bowl so he wouldn't be disturbed. His favorite food was pizza and he hated to shop for clothes for himself. If he had his way he'd let his mother shop for him, but she had told him long ago he was on his own and could do his own shopping. While he talked a great deal about himself he never really said all that much of a personal nature. It wasn't that she expected him to discuss past loves, but she did wonder more about him than about his favorite sport, television show, and color. She knew if she probed further he would only retreat. He wasn't the type to confide in anyone, even an emotionally wounded woman who had probably confided in him more than she should have.

"Rainbow Falls," Rhyder announced as they drove out of the large city.

"What?"

"That sign there points to Rainbow Falls," he repeated. "Let's have a look."

"Aren't you afraid you'll get lost if I don't have a map for us to follow?" she taunted.

The trip was longer than the sign intimated, but they finally reached the parking area for the falls. Two paths were designated, and they decided to take the scenic route that took the visitor past two sets of falls. The path was steep, and Evelyne found she needed Rhyder's help at times to keep her balance. She also discovered new muscles in her legs against the strain of walking almost completely downhill. When they came to the first set of falls, they stood out on the concrete platform and gazed at the blue water falling downward to end in white froth and huge ripples.

"How beautiful," Evelyne murmured. She had turned to say something to Rhyder when she slipped on the damp concrete and would have fallen if he hadn't grabbed hold of her arms. Rhyder looked down into her eyes, and she realized he was letting his guard down to look at her finally as a woman.

"Rhyder," she whispered, unable to stop herself from lifting her face a fraction of an inch more.

He took a deep breath and looked up at the sky as if seeking his answer there before looking back at her. After their dinner Evelyne had applied a rose-colored lip-gloss, and it was tempting to kiss it all away, but he knew he couldn't do it. Not if he wanted to keep his sanity. He had enough problems in his life without adding her to the list and hurting her in the process. His emotions would have given in and he would have kissed her if the sounds of people approaching hadn't cut in.

"We'd better go," he said harshly, dropping his hands and turning away.

Evelyne stared after him, feeling as if she had been slapped. Then she stepped off the platform before anyone arrived. For the remainder of their walk she made sure not to need any of his assistance. She also hoped their ride back to the hotel would be mercifully short.

Unfortunately it didn't turn out that way. They still had a couple hours of driving to do, and when they did arrive at the hotel, Evelyne was curled up, fast asleep.

Rhyder looked down at her, seeing the vulnerability written on her sleeping features. He knew he had hurt her at the falls, but he'd had to.

"Evelyne," he spoke softly so as not to startle her when she awoke. "We're back at the hotel." He shook her shoulder gently.

She opened her eyes slowly, the pupils looking vaguely unfocused for a moment before she recognized her surroundings. She smiled at him until her memory brought back what had happened at the falls; then her smile disappeared.

"Evelyne, I'm going to do something totally out of character for me," he murmured, just before brushing her lips with the softest and sweetest of kisses. While he wanted nothing more than to pull her into his arms and explore every inch of her mouth, he wasn't going to. When he pulled back his head he found her smiling at him.

"Rhyder, I don't think you're the old codger you try to make me believe you are," she whispered, pressing a quick kiss on his lips before reaching behind her for the door handle. "Good night." She got out of the car and headed for her room without a backward glance.

"Oh, hell," he muttered, watching her walk with a graceful sway of her hips. That was when Rhyder knew his life would never be the same again.

CHAPTER FOUR

Through the days of her divorce proceedings Evelyne had suffered from nightmares. Since arriving in Hawaii she had been blessed with dream-free nights; unfortunately her bad dreams came back that night. Since she had doubted she would sleep deeply, she had taken a sleeping pill only to become helpless to rise above the horrors of her dreams when they visited her.

The dream never changed. She was dressed in a black flowing gown that swept around her ankles, and her dark hair streamed down her back. The floor was very warm against her bare feet and the hallway she found herself in was filled with closed doors. Out of each door came bizarre screams calling her name. She ran down the hallway to escape the sounds pounding her ears. Evelyne covered her ears, but she couldn't shut out the screams. After she ran down the seemingly endless hallway she found a door slightly ajar, with no sounds within. She crept inside the silence and found something worse. The other nights, before her brain could fully comprehend the contents of the room, she had awakened, but the narcotic effects of the pill wouldn't allow her to surface this time. She stood in the doorway and saw people she had known, but who didn't resemble human beings anymore. She did the only thing she could; she screamed.

"Evelyne! Evelyne, baby, wake up!" The voice entering her dream wasn't loud, but soft and insistent, demanding that she leave the horror behind. She felt as if her entire body were being shaken to bits, but it still took a while for her drugged senses to fully awaken.

She opened heavy lids and looked up at Rhyder's face, taut with a tension she had never seen there before.

"Oh, Rhyder!" She sobbed, throwing herself against him. His arms circled her shaking body and absorbed her tears and her fear.

He hadn't been able to sleep, and while sitting on the balcony, allowing the soft sea air to flow around him, he had heard her whimpers and guessed she was having a nightmare. At the first scream he had vaulted over the railing onto her balcony and run into her room, grateful she kept her door open at night. He'd looked down at her unfocused eyes and instantly realized she had taken a sleeping medication. It had taken him long, scary seconds before he was able to awaken her.

"Don't worry, you're all right now," he soothed, stroking her back with shaky hands. What had caused a nightmare of such magnitude? She was trembling so violently, her words were incoherent.

"It was so terrible, Rhyder," she moaned, hugging him even more tightly. "They wouldn't stop screaming and I couldn't get away from them, and when I did I entered a room. . . . All the people in there. They looked dead but they weren't! And they walked to me . . . they put their arms out to me . . . I screamed . . . I couldn't wake up—I couldn't do anything when they touched me!" She shuddered with revulsion. "I couldn't wake up!"

"Calm down, Evelyne, I'm here, and no one is going to harm you," he assured her, closing his arms around

73

her even tighter. He was going to ensure that no de-
mons came to haunt her again. "Now I want you to
open your eyes and look around so you can see you're
in your room and safe." He felt her immediate with-
drawal. "I won't let go of you. I promise."

She shook her head. "You don't understand. The
dream will come back."

That caught his interest. "You've had it before?"

"Yes." Her voice was muffled against his bare chest.
"But I took a sleeping pill last night and it usually
doesn't happen when I take one. This time it did, and I
couldn't wake up. It was as if I wasn't meant to wake
up . . . ever!" Her voice rose to an hysterical level
which Rhyder's murmured words immediately
calmed. He noticed the small plastic bottle sitting on
the nightstand and reached out to pick it up. Thanks
to the moonlight streaming through the window he
was able to read the label and discovered that the pill
was strong enough to knock out a horse. He swore
under his breath. What kind of doctor gave these to a
woman who shouldn't have a drug so powerful?

He loosened his grasp and edged away. "I'm not
leaving. I just want to get you something cold to
drink." He got up from the bed and headed for the
small refrigerator, taking out a can of juice. He poured
it in a glass and dampened a washcloth before returning to the bed. He set the glass on the nightstand
and proceeded to run the cloth over her face before
handing her the juice.

"Evelyne." He paused, unsure how to phrase the
question, and also afraid of what her reply would be.
"Did—ah—did what happened earlier cause your
nightmare?"

She stared at him, unable to understand what had
brought about the question. Then it dawned on her.
"No, Rhyder," she hastened to reassure him. "This

has happened to me before. And for some reason it's always the same dream."

"Is your ex-husband a part of it?"

She shuddered to recall any part of it, but she could remember that a decaying Rick had been present in that dark room. "Yes," she whispered, bending her head to sip the cold juice and wet her dry throat. She lifted shimmering eyes. "I don't want to be alone, Rhyder. I'm so afraid that if I go back to sleep I'll have the dream again. There were times when I'd question my sanity because no person in their right mind should have such a horrible dream. I never told anyone about it."

Rhyder took her back into his arms. "I'll stay." He wondered if she realized that his staying would play havoc with his sanity? but he knew he couldn't leave her alone, not when she needed him so badly. Besides, he had always been a sucker for women's tears, he admitted wryly. He settled her back beneath the covers and stretched out on top of them, keeping one arm around her body. He gritted his teeth when she snuggled up even closer, her arm draped across his waist.

"It's been a long time since I've slept with anyone," she murmured, closing her eyes, feeling safe enough to go back to sleep. "It feels nice."

"Same here." His dry voice indicated something else. That it was not only a while since he had slept with a woman, but just as long since making love to one. With a very desirable woman cuddled up so trustingly against him the ironic situation didn't help his libido any. Her body was curled up so closely to him, he could smell the soft fragrance of her skin and hair. He figured that alone could set off enough men. After all, he had seen the casualties around here from the first week she arrived at the hotel. Now he could understand why they were so eager to make love to her.

He couldn't remember any woman who stirred him the way she did. He had to remind himself that she'd just had a great scare and he would be the worst kind of man even to think about making love to her. At least she had finally calmed down. He admitted to himself that he wasn't sure what could have happened if she had gotten herself too upset and he helpless to know what to do. He lay back against the remaining pillow and closed his eyes, although he knew it would be a long time before he fell asleep.

Evelyne slept deeply after that and didn't awaken until midmorning. When she opened her eyes she looked around convinced that all of it had been a dream, including Rhyder appearing in her room and comforting her. She would have believed it, too, if it hadn't been for a splash of color on the table near the television set. She climbed out of bed and walked over to the table to find an orchid of the palest lavender gracing a sheet of paper.

> Evelyne,
> I put the DO NOT DISTURB sign out so you could sleep as late as you wished. I'll be out by the saltwater pool if you need me. If you're interested in some lunch I'll meet you at the coffee shop at one o'clock. Just take it easy and I'll see you later.
> Rhyder

If it hadn't been for the matter-of-fact wording of his note, she probably would have died of embarrassment at the memory of not only of disturbing his sleep but of pleading with him to stay with her. She felt extreme gratitude for his tactful handling of the situation. She remembered the nights Celia had stayed with her during the beginning of the divorce and how they stayed up nights talking because Evelyne was too

76

afraid of going to sleep and dreaming. Yet even though Celia was her closest friend, Evelyne had never revealed the contents of her nightmare to her. So why had she told Rhyder about it?

Looking at her watch she decided against going down to the saltwater pool and thought about writing some postcards to a few of her friends. Evelyne did walk out onto her balcony and scanned the area by the saltwater pool looking for Rhyder. When she finally found him there sprawled on his stomach, she silently willed him to turn over. Several moments later, as if answering her mental call, he rolled over and looked directly up at the sixth floor. Evelyne managed to smile and nod her head. Seeming to understand that her nod meant she would meet him for lunch, he inclined his head and lay back down.

She returned to her room for a quick shower and stood in front of the mirror to apply a light coating of makeup. She noticed with satisfaction how her skin glowed a pale gold against the thick white towel wrapped around her still damp body. Evelyne's skin didn't tan easily, and she was glad to see that her careful regimen had paid off. After rubbing a scented body-lotion all over her skin, she dressed in khaki shorts, a boat-necked pale-pink and soft-green striped cotton shirt and leather thong sandals. In deference to the heat she coiled her hair on top of her head.

Standing in front of the bathroom mirror Evelyne placed her hands on the counter and leaned forward. She had to admit she looked better than she had in a long time. Her face didn't look as pinched as it had when she first arrived, and there was even a trace of serenity in her eyes that she couldn't remember having seen for a long time. After all, how could a woman look calm with the schedule she'd had? This was the first time in years she had had days on end with nothing specifically planned, and she had to admit she like it. For once, Evelyne only had to worry about herself, and she was rapidly learning it wasn't such a bad deal.

Evelyne went downstairs to the shop to purchase postcards and stamps. She chose a comfortable chair in the lobby and began writing out the cards. Some of them were easy to write because she only had to say the most superficial things. When she came to a card for Celia she found herself nibbling on the end of her pen and wondering what to say. Should she mention Rhyder? Should she mention her harebrained scheme that hadn't taken off? Now that she had time to think it over she was grateful that she hadn't had the nerve to take any of those men into her bed; she wasn't sure if she could have lived with herself afterward. She smiled, remembering how Rhyder had stayed with her last night and never thought of asking her for more. He gave her the comfort she needed and made sure she had nothing to feel embarrassed about afterward. He was a very rare man in this world of every man for himself.

Evelyne slipped the pen out of her mouth and suddenly began writing. She wasn't going to say anything about him to Celia, because she just might decide to fly out and look Rhyder over for herself. Since the divorce she had become Evelyne's self-appointed guardian angel, making sure no one would take advantage of the broken-hearted divorcée. She was positive that Evelyne couldn't think for herself, and since Celia was a veteran of the divorce game, she was determined to keep an eye on her friend. Frankly, that was the last thing Evelyne had needed. If it hadn't been for Brian, Celia probably would have insisted on coming with Evelyne.

"It appears you've kept yourself occupied." A familiar voice drifted over her head.

She looked up to find a grinning Rhyder standing over her. Did he realize how different he looked when he smiled? He didn't look as stern or unyielding, and she wished he would smile more often.

"Is it one o'clock already?" she asked, surprised when he held out his wrist and showed her his watch. Evelyne tucked her pen in her small bag and stacked her postcards together.

"Did you finish them?" he asked. "If not, I can wait."

"They're all done," she replied, standing up. "Besides, I've just discovered how hungry I am."

Evelyne wasn't joking when she said she was hungry, something she hadn't truly been in weeks. She ate a large crab salad and iced tea in no time and topped it off with a large piece of coconut pie.

"What would you like to do now?" Rhyder asked cheerfully, glad to see the previous night's disturbance hadn't affected her appetite. "We could go into town and hit the video arcade or roam through the shops. We could drive up to that coffee mill and look around, if you're interested."

"What I'd like to do is remain lazy and just lie out by the pool," she informed him. "Rhyder, I don't need you to act like a camp counselor who feels he has to keep me so busy I won't have time to get into trouble. The more I thought about that crazy scheme of mine the more I knew I couldn't have gone through with it. I'm just glad I didn't end up in a situation where I could have been raped because an angry date felt I owed him something." Her delicate features reflected the distress she felt at the idea.

Rhyder's face darkened at the thought of a man touching Evelyne in a threatening manner. He knew if any man tried such a thing he'd probably break the guy's face. He was astounded at his violence, since he had never been much for brute force. He always believed in talking out a problem and never resorting to fists. Now he wondered if there weren't times when a good right hook would be a much better solution.

"That sounds pretty good to me," he agreed readily.

"Rhyder, you're acting like a bodyguard and you don't need to do that," she protested. "If there's anything special you want to do, please, don't let me hold you back."

"Evelyne, I've spent more winters than I care to count in Chicago—which isn't known for its warm weather," he explained. "Right now I'm more than content to spend as many hours as my body allows in the sun baking the chill out of my bones."

She laughed, shaking her head in amazement. "You always try to make yourself older than Methuselah, while there's only ten years between us. You sometimes act as if you could be my grandfather. I don't know why you want to be that way with me." She stared into his eyes as if to imprint her words on his brain.

How could she explain to this man that he was already turning into a good friend in the same way she considered Celia? There certainly had been few close friendships in boarding school, because there was so much competition between the girls as to whose parents had more money and who had the higher social status. Evelyne had had no use for it. All she had wanted was to do well in her studies and return home with her degree. Some of the girls had blamed her disregard for social status on her casual California upbringing, but that wasn't it. They were also envious that her good manners and regal bearing were ingrained instead of drilled into her as with so many of the girls. It was the fact that she could look and act the part of royalty without being aware of it along with slightly exotic looks which caught people's eyes, especially men's.

Evelyne's disregard for social status also came from having met people from all walks of life, thanks to her father's business. Whether they had been gofers or highly paid film stars he always treated them the same. He never put up with prima donnas and backed up his words, which meant his films were quality because they were produced by the best and the most loyal. She was only sad that the studio stock had gone public not long before her father's death and it wasn't the same there anymore. Now King Studios only cared about profit-and-loss statements, not whether the film was one to be remembered down through the years.

"Maybe I act this way because you scare the hell out of me," Rhyder said gruffly, looking out to the waves flowing over the black lava bed their table overlooked. At that moment he found it easier to look at the ocean than at Evelyne's face. He hated the idea of betraying any weakness, and the fact that she kept him off balance so often was a definite weakness!

Evelyne's eyes widened at his admission. "Rhyder, you're frightened of *me?*"

"We don't have to let the whole world know about it," he grumbled, glaring at her. Although her voice hadn't been loud, he was positive that everyone there had heard her words.

She leaned back in her chair thinking over his revelation. She hadn't thought he was the kind of man to be frightened of anything or anyone, much less imagine she was the kind of woman to unnerve him. The idea bothered her. She only wished she knew why it did. Afraid to look into his face and find something there she couldn't understand, she kept her eyes downcast.

"I think I'll go up and change," she said a bit too

81

nonchalantly as she rose from her chair after settling her bill. "This time I'll try the saltwater pool. It doesn't seem to be as crowded."

Rhyder remained in his chair and watched Evelyne leave the coffee shop. He castigated himself for having revealed his feelings. As an attorney he was well aware the last thing to do was show any weakness to the opponent, and right now he knew Evelyne was the most dangerous opponent he could have. If he wasn't careful she could very easily take possession of his heart.

When Evelyne reached her room, she collapsed in a chair before her legs should give out from under her. She knew she was lucky to have made it to her room without mishap. Rhyder's confession had been a surprise to her and reminded her he was much more than a casual holiday companion.

The kiss the day before hadn't been a surprise, but her reaction to it had been. After the other men's kisses had left her cold, it was a shock that just the brief touch of Rhyder's lips could invoke such strong feeling in her. She also knew she had to fight those feelings because before long it would be time for Rhyder to return to Chicago and she to Los Angeles to begin her new life.

Suddenly determined not to let Rhyder bother her she pushed herself out of her chair and proceeded to change into a bathing suit, this time a cobalt-and-black-striped maillot cut high on the hips and low in the back. She twisted her hair up on top of her head, stepped into a pair of matching nylon athletic shorts, and rummaged for her rubber thongs to protect her feet from the hot cement and sand. Picking up a canvas tote bag that held a towel, a book, her room key tucked away in a hidden pocket, and suntan lotion, she left her room choosing to take the stairs instead of waiting for the elevator to arrive at the sixth floor.

She wasn't surprised to find Rhyder already by the pool, his lean body stretched out on a pale-yellow lounge. She also wasn't surprised to find the lounge next to him empty. There weren't very many people by this particular pool, since most preferred to frequent the freshwater pool with its readily available bar service.

"For someone who's afraid of me you don't seem very worried about my sitting next to you," she murmured, flipping her towel out over the warm plastic and stretching out on it.

He opened one eye then the other and half sat up, glancing around at the six other people present. "I've always heard there's safety in numbers, so I don't think I'll have to worry about my virtue here." He flashed her a cocky grin.

Evelyne slipped on her oversized sunglasses, took out her suntan lotion, and smoothed it over her legs, arms, and shoulders before digging out her book. Once settled comfortably on the lounge she opened her book and began to read.

Rhyder wasn't about to believe her studied air of nonchalance and turned his head away so she couldn't see his smile. She wasn't too happy with him, that he could figure out all too easily, but he'd just let her stew for a while. The hot afternoon sun would mellow her out soon enough.

Evelyne forced herself to concentrate on her book, and she was soon able to do so, since the plot was riveting enough to hold her attention. Of course, that didn't mean she would remember any of the details later on, but she could certainly put on a good show of reading. Surprisingly it wasn't long before she forgot her surroundings as she turned page after page. She might have forgotten to turn over if something ice cold hadn't been pressed against her foot. She shrieked and looked up to find Rhyder standing beside her holding two cans of Coke.

"I thought you might appreciate something cold to drink," he told her, holding out one of the Cokes.

"Thank you," she replied softly, her fingers circling the can. Rhyder had already lifted the pop-top, so all she had to do was tip it upward and drink deeply.

"Thank you. I hadn't realized I was thirsty until you brought this." She carefully set the can down in the sand and watched Rhyder do the same before walking away.

"I'm going in the water. Want to come?"

"Yes!" She sat up quickly and rose to her feet, ready to follow him.

He turned around and looked down at her bare feet. "Put your thongs on first," he advised. "You're not going to be wading in your typical cement pool here, and if you're not careful you could cut your feet on a sharp piece of lava rock." He waited until she'd slipped on her sandals and started toward him.

Rhyder helped Evelyne down the lava steps and into the water.

"It's cold," she protested, starting to inch back, but his restraining hand wouldn't allow her to go very far.

"Only because your skin temperature and the air around you are warm." He continued to move slowly. "Keep going, you'll feel better in a minute."

Evelyne wasn't too sure about that. She found it difficult to walk with the thongs on, but she admitted that they were protecting her feet from the rough bottom. She looked down and laughed as tiny fish swam around her legs.

"Rhyder, look!" she called, tugging on his hand.

"Aren't they pretty? It's just like walking in the middle of a tidal pool."

"That's what the hotel obviously planned," he answered, engrossed in watching her almost childlike pleasure.

Pretty soon Evelyne felt confident enough to move on her own when the water reached almost waist level. She made a face when Rhyder held up a sea slug that looked like nothing more than a brown blob. They continued around the perimeter of the pool inspecting the many inhabitants and exclaiming over the fish that had no fear of their human visitors. It was well over an hour later before they made their way back to their loungers. Rhyder went to the snack bar for more Cokes, and they enjoyed their cold refreshment while drying off under the hot afternoon sun.

"Want to try one of the restaurants in town for dinner?" Rhyder asked, mentally deciding Evelyne's one-piece suit was just as sexy as her bikinis in the way it molded so lovingly to her slim body.

"Perhaps you should have a night to yourself," she suggested. "I'm feeling a bit tired and thought I'd just order something in from room service."

Rhyder eyed her sharply, looking for pinched features and colorless lips, but found nothing. "Are you all right?"

She could easily guess the reason for his question. "I'm just fine, thank you. In fact, my health has probably never been better," she replied testily. "It's just that I didn't have a lot of sleep last night and I thought I'd take it easy. That would give you some time to yourself. After all, you should have a chance to meet some nice women, and without me you'd have a much better chance."

"All right," he agreed a bit too readily. "I think I'll go in and take a shower. See you later."

Evelyne watched Rhyder gather up his towel and book and amble off toward the hotel.

"It wouldn't have hurt him to make some kind of protest," she mumbled, picking up her own things.

Evelyne did order her dinner from room service, and while the mahi mahi and rice pilaf she had was excellent, she learned she wasn't in the mood for her own company. Pretty soon she was pacing the width of the room. She tried every television program, along with the cable movies showing. Nothing appealed to her.

Finally deciding solitude wasn't meant for her after all, she applied some makeup, hurriedly changed out of her red silk kimono and into a dark lilac skirt that buttoned up the side and a matching scoop-neck sleeveless crop-top that barely grazed the skirt's waistband. As she left only a few buttons on the skirt fastened, a good portion of leg and thigh were revealed as she walked, along with a couple inches of trim midriff if she lifted her arms. Evelyne looked at her reflection in the full-length mirror bolted on the bathroom door and decided it was just the outfit to wear for an evening out. She didn't bother to see if Rhyder would care to go with her, since she figured he might have already gone out. She checked her purse to ensure that she had her room key and money with her. Then she left.

Evelyne began her evening in the hotel bar, met a very nice man named Lloyd, who had just arrived that afternoon, and sat at a table for well over an hour listening to him talk about the chain of hardware stores he owned in the Southwest. Though the conversation was far from fascinating, she wasn't bored as she listened to a life that was totally opposite to the one she had lived. She heard about Lloyd's love for horseback riding, his weekends camping and occasional trips to Mexico. He told her this was his first trip to Hawaii and he intended to live it up to the fullest. Evelyne guessed his plans for a fun-filled vacation in the Islands when he stared into her eyes before his gaze wandered hungrily yet discreetly down to her breasts. She looked up when the band returned from their break.

"Shall we dance?" she asked lightly, standing up and holding out her hand.

While Lloyd wasn't the best dancer Evelyne had been with, he certainly wasn't the worst. It wasn't long before she was laughing and thoroughly enjoying herself. She ended up with a different partner almost every song, but that just seemed to be part of the fun. By now she wasn't thinking about a man as a prospective bed partner but as a dance partner and a nice way to spend the evening. One thing Rhyder had done was make her see the truth that she couldn't indulge in a series of short-term affairs without losing her self-respect in the bargain.

Evelyne smiled brightly and threw herself into the music. If she began to feel a little tired after a while, she shrugged it off and continued to dance. She might have kept on as long as possible if it hadn't been for a restraining hand on her arm. She looked up into Rhyder's dark, angry eyes.

"Do you mind?" Lloyd demanded, not appreciating all the men who were attracted to the woman he hoped to end the evening with.

"The lady is recovering from a serious illness and really should be resting," Rhyder told him in a harsh voice, gently pulling on Evelyne's arm.

"Sick? She sure doesn't look sick to me," Lloyd retorted as they edged away from the dancers.

"I am perfectly able to take care of myself," she

tersely informed Rhyder, trying to pull her arm away without much success.

"Is that why you're so pale and seem to have trouble catching your breath?" he asked.

Lloyd studied Evelyne a bit closer and seemed to agree silently with Rhyder's diagnosis. Then he carefully edged away from the couple. Seeing his intent she could only throw him a look filled with disgust. She already knew she would have to deal with Rhyder soon enough.

"I'll—ah—I'll see you later, Evelyne," Lloyd muttered, finally making his escape.

Evelyne threw off Rhyder's hand and marched out of the bar. His long strides allowed him to catch up with her without any trouble, and he walked beside her without saying a word. He sensed this was not the time to say anything, if he wanted to keep his head where it belonged. They stood side by side in the elevator for the six floors, and Evelyne stalked out of the small car and down the hallway to her room. She rummaged in her purse and dug out her key, hoping to get inside before Rhyder could catch up with her again. She should have known better. He appeared at her side and grasped her hand, easily taking the key out of her fingers.

"Evelyne," he began.

She held up a hand. "Don't say anything, Rhyder," she warned. "I don't want to hear about your concern for my health or any other asinine reason you had for coming after me the way you did. Who do you think you are for doing such a despicable thing? You had no right to drag me out of there as if I were some errant child! You're not my father or my husband. My father always made sure I went to parties he prescreened, and even Rick only attended functions that were business oriented. Don't you realize I wanted to have some fun on my own? No one has ever let me do anything on my own before. I've always had someone around to protect me. Now I really don't have anyone, and it's time to learn to be on my own. I can't do that if you decide to go into your Saint George act." Her voice was kept low in deference to the other guests, but it was no less emphatic. At the same time her words suddenly struck a chord deep inside her. Had she really had all the freedom she thought she'd had? Or had Rick merely concealed from her his careful monitoring of her activities? Come to think of it he had always asked about her day's activities and would make suggestions whether she should attend a particular luncheon or not. Was it his way of keeping control of her life? The idea left her nauseous. She turned away and fumbled with the door lock.

"I came by your room earlier in hopes you might like to go downstairs for a drink," Rhyder explained quietly, noting her distress, but not the true reason behind it. "I can understand if you want to think I was interfering, but I didn't go down there to spy on you. I wasn't sleepy and decided to go out for an hour or so. I saw you dancing, and you looked unusually pale. I was afraid you were overdoing it and only wanted to help."

She shook her head not just to him but to clear the tears from her eyes. Evelyne entered her room and closed the door. Rhyder didn't try to detain her. She sank into a chair and buried her face in her hands. She thought she had had a wonderful loving husband, but now that she stood back and thought of him objectively, she realized Rick was a manipulator in the pure sense of the word. If Evelyne had a free and loving marriage it was only because Rick wished her to. The more truths she figured out the more distraught she became. She was beginning to see just how much of a victim she had been in her marriage. She didn't feel as strong in mind and body as she thought she was, and the realization hurt a great deal.

CHAPTER FIVE

Evelyne did something that night she hadn't done in quite a while; she cried herself to sleep. And as she cried, she took a long hard look at herself and the man she had lived with for ten years.

She had always thought of herself as a strong person, a woman who could handle any situation that came along. But it had turned out that she couldn't handle her own life. When Rick had filed for divorce she wasn't sure if she would ever be able to pick up the pieces. Evelyne, the Rock of Gibraltar, the woman everyone could count on, couldn't even decide what to eat or what to wear. The woman who made snap decisions couldn't take hold of her own life. The more she cried the more she realized she was crying for the fraudulent life she had lived. And she cried because the life she had known was gone and she didn't know how she was going to survive on her own once she left the Islands. Mostly she cried because the fear she had ignored for the past few months had finally made its way into her heart.

When she awoke the next morning she had a raging headache and her throat felt itchy and swollen. Looking at herself in the mirror told her the brutal truth when she saw blotchy cheeks and puffy eyes. She deemed herself not a pretty sight and soaked a cloth in cold water, pressing it gently against her face. She groaned when she heard a knock at the door. Tossing the cloth in the sink she went out to the door. She didn't need to look through the peephole to identify her early-morning caller.

Rhyder's slight grin disappeared when he saw her face. "You really know how to make things hard on yourself, don't you?" He sauntered inside her room and headed for the chair.

"Come in, why don't you?" she asked sarcastically, allowing the door to close.

"I came to see if you'd like to go on the glass-bottom-boat cruise," he commented, settling in the chair. "That is, if you can get your face back to normal instead of looking as if you'd just gone ten rounds with Rocky. Of course, you'll need to do it before the end of the day."

Evelyne's eyes blazed. She slid open the closet door, extracted clothing, and pulled underwear out of a drawer. The door slammed behind her as she entered the bathroom. It wasn't until she stood under the shower that she realized the motivation behind Rhyder's taunts. In his own acerbic way he had gotten her angry enough at him in order to forget her own troubles. She laughed softly. If she didn't mellow too quickly she just might throttle him.

They only had time for a light breakfast before the next cruise left to sail along the coastline. It wasn't long before Rhyder regretted his idea of getting Evelyne out in the fresh air. A little over an hour later he assisted her off the boat and into the car.

"You still look pretty green," he told her as they drove back to the hotel.

"I feel green," she groaned, laying her head back.

"You once mentioned you've been on several cruises. Didn't you get seasick then?"

Evelyne nodded slowly, afraid too much motion

92

would find its way back to her stomach. "The ship's doctor and I were always on a first-name basis before the ship left the dock."

"And yet you were willing to go on that cruise with me, knowing you'd get sick? Why did you do it, Evelyne?" Rhyder couldn't believe she had blithely gotten on that boat knowing she was prone to motion sickness. He was curious to know why she hadn't told him about her problem instead of suffering silently for almost an hour. If he hadn't noticed her abnormally pale face, he wouldn't have sensed how badly she felt; she hadn't said one word of complaint. When he first met her he had seen her as a flighty woman who was concerned with only herself. Now he knew better. Evelyne Winters was endowed with a very tough constitution; she had to be with her past history. The trouble was she just didn't know it yet.

When they reached her hotel room, Rhyder insisted that Evelyne lie down while he ordered hot tea and crackers from room service.

"Believe me, this is nothing compared to the way I felt on the larger ships," she said weakly, rolling carefully over on her side to watch him move around the room. "Rhyder, you're a very nice man to take care of me like this, but I'm beginning to feel funny about you acting as if you're a member of the family. I admit I haven't shown good judgment since coming here, but I can't rely on you helping me out for the rest of my life. After all, it won't be very long before I'll be returning to Los Angeles, and I'll be on my own then."

Rhyder's movements stilled for a split second. How could he tell her he didn't like to think of her being on her own? He certainly didn't want to admit that she had come to mean something to him. Not when he was the guy who didn't want any entanglements in his life and this woman was the kind who had invented the word *commitment.* While she resembled a delicate Victorian cameo, he knew she wasn't the kind to resort to vapors the way her ancestors had when life grew unbearable. So far she'd always come out fighting.

When the tea and crackers arrived, Evelyne obediently drank the strong brew and nibbled on two crackers before Rhyder would allow her to sit up. She agreed wholeheartedly that she was unable to do more at the moment. As a past master of combating seasickness she knew the worst thing she could do was to attempt to sit up too soon and suffer the consequences.

Rhyder sat on the edge of the bed with one arm braced over Evelyne's legs as he leaned forward. "You've got some color in your face," he commented, unable to ignore that most of that color was due to a very lovely blush. "How are you feeling?"

She stared into his eyes, for the first time noticing flecks of gold and green in the irises. "How can you practice such a cold-hearted profession as law when you have those beautiful eyes?"

He smiled. "You say the damndest things at the oddest times."

Evelyne shook her head. "I don't think it's all that strange. The lawyers I've met always seem to have beady eyes, set close together, and they look cold. You're not that way at all. You're warm and friendly, and I doubt you work just for the money."

Rhyder placed his fingers across her lips. "Sorry to disillusion you, honey, but for about fifteen years I did nothing but work for the almighty buck. I wanted the Mercedes, the large house, and an impressive stock portfolio, and my hard work gave me everything I wanted. The trouble is I found out that material goods can disappear all too easily." There was no rancor in

94

his tone, only a resignation that she hadn't heard before.

"This is a rude question, but you're broke, aren't you?" she asked softly, tracing the harsh line of his jaw with her fingernail. "That's why you've made all the jokes about living here as a beach bum, isn't it? Something happened in Chicago that forced you to lose everything and you came out here to recuperate, just the way I did."

He raised an eyebrow. "Do you realize that's the first time you've admitted the true reason for your being here?"

Evelyne braced her hands next to her, using them to push herself up into a sitting position. "I have to start being honest with myself or I'll end up lying my way through the rest of my life. I've decided I don't want to live that way." She smiled ruefully. "I faced a lot of truths last night, Rhyder; about me, about Rick, about life in general. Men are going to be uneasy about me because of what had happened, but I can't let that upset me. Rick liked me to wear trendy clothing and makeup, but sometimes those new looks weren't me. He enjoyed the idea of having a wife who could cope so well with his hectic life-style, but he never stopped to think that there might have been evenings I would have preferred spending a quiet evening home instead of sitting in a smoky, loud nightclub listening to a new band or singer. I was his perfect wife, but when that blood vessel broke, I was rendered imperfect and he couldn't handle that." The expression in her eyes was sad with the memory of a night filled with angry words and tearful pleas. "Or perhaps I should say he didn't want anything that wasn't whole and beautiful in his house and his life."

Rhyder pulled her into his arms and cradled her against his chest. "As far as I'm concerned you're about as perfect a woman any man would want," he murmured, brushing his mouth across her forehead. "Don't worry about what anyone else might think. I like you just the way you are."

Evelyne closed her eyes, smiling at the different sensations between his slightly rough voice in her ears and the feather-light touch of his lips on her skin. She moved her face just enough so that his mouth settled on the corner of hers. Rhyder stiffened, drawing his head back slightly to look down at her.

"You're not feeling well." His voice was hoarse.

"Tea is an excellent cure," she murmured, raising her eyes to stare into his. "And I doubt you'd use my brain hemorrhage as an excuse to reject me. I need to know that a man wants me. You don't care who I am or about my looks. You're probably the first man to look inside of me and still want me." Her smile quivered. She was fully aware she could be letting herself in for rejection, but she knew she wanted to feel his lips on hers again, and she doubted he would touch her that way unless she gave him the go-ahead. "If you don't understand what I'm talking about, I'll be only too happy to put it in writing for you."

He remained still for a few moments, studying every centimeter of her face. "You look as if you belong in another era," he murmured, speaking more for his own benefit than hers. "I picture you with your hair up, wearing a Victorian gown with elbow-length gloves and an ostrich-feather fan." His hand brushed a stray hair from her forehead and lingered near her lips that were moist and slightly parted. The tip of her tongue appeared to flick at the ends of his fingers. That was Rhyder's undoing. Groaning, he bent his head and took Evelyne's mouth in a kiss that left her mind spinning. He gave her no chance to resist as his tongue plundered the soft cavern and sought out every corner.

His tongue dipped in and out of her mouth in a leisurely manner that left her aching for more intimate contact. Her arms crept up around his shoulders and clung to him as he nipped at her bottom lip and drew it gently between his teeth into his mouth.

"Rhyder," Evelyne moaned, feeling her body slipping downward as he eased her back onto the bed. She ran her hands over his back and slipped under the hem of his loose cotton shirt to caress the slightly rough skin.

Her head wasn't the only one to spin. Rhyder learned it was a mistake to kiss Evelyne, because he found out he didn't want to stop at just that. He wanted to go on inhaling the exotic fragrance of her cologne mixed with her own natural scent. He wanted to map out every inch of her skin with his hands and lips. He wanted to make love to her in every way possible until she could think only of him. He wanted to be completely selfish and never let her out of his sight. He wanted it all; he wanted everything she could give him, and in return he would give her all that she would ever need.

He pressed his hand gently over her breast, feeling the tiny cotton-covered nub thrust up against his palm.

"I want to see you," he said roughly, pulling her shirt up. "No bra." He smiled wickedly.

"It's too hot to wear one," she replied breathlessly, taking his hand and placing it back over the taut nipple. "I like to feel your hands on me, Rhyder." She pushed her hand under his shirt in order to find his male counterpart. It hardened under her ministrations. She rose up and covered it with her mouth, her tongue moistening the cloth covering the male nipple. But as he continued to touch her, she discovered she couldn't concentrate on anything but the incredible sensations he caused in her body.

Rhyder's mouth suckled gently on her nipple while his hand kneaded her other breast until Evelyne cried out with joy as molten fire coursed through her veins.

"So sweet," he muttered against her breast. "You taste like fresh honey. No one should taste this good. I could keep this up forever and never get enough of you."

Evelyne wanted to tell him how good he made her feel. It had been so long since a man had touched her intimately, and while she had been a passionate wife she had never known anything like the sensations he gave her by just using his mouth. His hand swept over her from chest to knee and back up, stopping to rub the cotton fabric of her shorts against the juncture of her thighs. Her hips rose and fell under his gentle probing and she could feel the warmth flood through her body.

"Rhyder, I can't take much more," she gasped, reaching out to grab hold of his hands.

"I'm giving you pleasure." He easily evaded her grip as he continued to rub his palm against her in seductive circles.

"But you should have it also." Her hand passed over the zipper straining against the masculine bulge. Her fingertips moved up and down in a knowing fashion that left him breathing raggedly.

"You first." He found the hem of her shorts and crept upward to find the silk of her panties and under them to search out her femininity. His exploration found her moist and receptive. "I want you to have all you deserve."

Evelyne breathed deeply as sanity struck her with a vengeance. "Rhyder." She knew she had to tell him even as her body screamed for release and his own had to be begging for fulfillment. "I don't—I'm not—the doctor couldn't put me back on the pill." She blinked the tears from her eyes.

Rhyder was undaunted. His knowing touch didn't pause as he continued to draw her to the brink. It wasn't long before Evelyne felt the heat flow rapidly throughout her body, starting with the spot between her thighs and radiating outward. It had been a little over a year since a man had touched her, and it didn't take long before she felt the convulsions heralding her climax. She cried out his name, arching upward against the pressure of his hand before she fell into a tailspin. Rhyder immediately gathered her into his arms and spoke softly to her until she caught her breath. Even after her respiration returned to normal, her body still felt heavy but satiated; for now.

"I'm sorry," she murmured. "You didn't—" Her eyes fell to his thighs.

"But *you* did," he corrected with a smile, keeping a possessive hand against the soft curve of her stomach. "Besides, I don't normally carry any form of protection with me." He placed his lips against her damp forehead. "Just out of curiosity, how did you plan to handle all these affairs you expected to have if you didn't bring anything with you?"

Evelyne's face reddened. "That just goes to show how much of a novice I am at this, doesn't it? I guess I expected the man to . . ." Her voice dropped off as she realized how bad her idea had been.

Rhyder shook his head. "Very bad planning, lady. Haven't you heard of Women's Lib? Protection is part of the woman's job too."

She sighed. "I was on the pill before, but I couldn't go back on it because it tends to raise the blood pressure, and that's the last thing I need right now," she confessed. "At the time I didn't think I would ever

99

need anything. I was pretty bitter about men. I feel so guilty about you. If I had had something now, you wouldn't be left feeling frustrated."

Rhyder rolled over on top of her. "Evelyne, you don't have to worry about me. I'm not some kid who can't handle the sexual demands of his body. This time I wanted to give to you. To remind you that there's absolutely nothing wrong with a woman being given pleasure if she's in the proper man's hands." He smirked, earning a punch in the shoulder.

"That was a very bad joke," she informed him.

"I thought it was pretty good, myself."

"Now I know your sense of humor is a bit strange."

"And your body is beautiful." He looked down at her bare breasts, pleased to see the nipples harden in response to his gaze. How could he explain that just touching her made him feel warm inside? She made him feel emotions he had thought died years ago. Each day he came to know more about her and every bit he learned scared him more, because she was not a woman to flit from man to man. She was the kind to need a home and man to take care of her. Oh, it wasn't necessarily that she couldn't take care of herself. He knew she was still feeling vulnerable from her divorce, and that was natural; but he figured she hadn't learned that she could easily stand on her own two feet. The trouble was, part of him wanted to be there when she did need someone to lean on. How could he want that when he was determined to be Hawaii's best beach bum? He had no place in his life for a woman, so why did he keep on thinking about her as more than just a prospective lover?

Evelyne lay quietly taking in what had just happened. She hadn't imagined that a man would put a woman's needs over his own. She should be embarrassed over what had happened, but she couldn't; he made her feel like someone very unique. He knew about her illness but thought nothing of allowing her to drown in sexual pleasure. Admittedly it wasn't the full lovemaking she desired to share with him, but it did take the edge off her sexual appetite. After almost nightly lovemaking with an insatiable husband and enduring a year's celibacy, she hadn't realized just how much she missed a man taking her to the edge and beyond. At the same time she had to remember that this was a vacation and things happened during holidays that wouldn't ordinarily happen if she were back in Los Angeles. By remembering that she just might be able to get through what was obviously the beginning of a love affair, without too many scars. She turned, burrowing her face against the curve of his shoulder.

"We've both just taken another step, haven't we?" Her words were muffled against his skin.

He nodded, even though he knew she didn't see him. " 'Fraid so."

The sensuous brush of her tongue against his shoulder sent shock waves through his system, along with a very disruptive stirring in his lower body.

"You don't sound very happy about it. Is it because you still think you're too old for me?"

Rhyder considered her question before answering. "That's part of it, yes, but there's more to it than age. Whether you want to admit it or not, you're really looking for husband material. I'm about the worst bet any woman could end up with."

She laughed softly and shook her head. "I can't believe you're saying that after hearing the horror story that was also called my divorce." She sat up, ignoring his mock look of pain at her moving away from him. "You have to realize there are a great many men who aren't going to want me because of my stroke." She paused, her head tipped to one side, a tiny smile curving her lips. "I can't believe I'm finally admitting what happened to me. Maybe I'm growing up after all."

Rhyder lifted himself up on one elbow. "If you think a man wouldn't fall in love with you, you've got another think coming," he informed her in the abrupt tone she soon learned not to like. "You're a lovely woman and have a lot to offer a man. If he turns you down he isn't worth having, and that's what you'll have to remember." He peered at her. "You look a bit pale. Are you feeling all right?"

"I'm just fine and dandy," Evelyne retorted sarcastically. "I hate people who think I'm going to kick the bucket just because I look a little pale."

Rhyder grinned. The return of her temper meant she was feeling more than fine. Damn, she was more woman than even she probably realized she was. He knew they would make love in the very near future, but he still wondered if it was a good idea. As a lawyer he was used to arguing more than one point of view, and his mind was doing it then. He knew he was rapidly losing the battle. He knew if Evelyne wanted an affair he would give her one, because he would make very sure that they parted as friends when it was over. He could certainly put off turning into a beach bum for a couple of weeks. She would also be good for a man who had developed a cynical outlook on the world lately. While she could have turned into a very bitter woman over what had happened, she hadn't. She had been hurt, yes. Hell, any woman would have been devastated over the turmoil created in her life, but she had also picked herself up and worked to begin her life over. Maybe they needed each other and fate had stepped in to enable them to teach the other to trust again.

The new twists in their relationship were still fragile

when they went out to dinner that evening. They chose to dine away from the hotel at a restaurant built like an old-fashioned ranch house. They feasted on huli chicken, a special barbecue dish, french fries, and decided on cheesecake for dessert.

"At the rate I'm going I'll be leaving here ten pounds heavier than when I arrived," Evelyne confessed as they left the restaurant.

Rhyder looked down at her dress with the solid-color knit bandeau top and the handkerchief hem skirt of a bold print. "I don't think you'll need to worry for at least twenty pounds. If you ever start getting chipmunk cheeks, I'll be sure to advise you to cut down on starches."

"Chipmunk cheeks?" She laughed. "Now you're making me think of Chip 'n Dale."

"It's certainly better than having elephant legs," he commented in a low voice, inclining his head toward a heavily set woman walking with her husband into the restaurant.

Evelyne rolled her eyes. She waited by the car door as Rhyder unlocked it. "Your jokes are getting worse. It must have been those two mai tais you had before dinner."

"They left me feeling pretty mellow." He walked around to the driver's side of the car and got in. "Any suggestions of what you'd like to do?"

She shook her head. "I'm not really in the mood for dancing or even walking through the shops."

"Want to see what's playing at the movie theater?" He steered the car down the steep driveway to the highway.

"As long as it isn't a western." She went on to explain, "When I was fifteen my father made practically nothing but westerns, and I spent so much time at the studio watching them being filmed that I couldn't watch one for years after that. There are times when I still can't handle looking at one. It was like eating candy; if you eat too much you become sick, and you don't want ever to look at another piece again."

"Then why did you go to the studio so much?" he asked curiously.

"Because my father wanted to make sure I'd never want to become an actress," she replied. "After I starred in the school play during my freshman year, he was convinced I would want to major in theater arts. He decided the best way to show me how hard the work was was to see how films were made and how hard actors worked in their craft. I didn't have the heart to tell him that I'd only taken the part in the play because I most resembled the character, and it took a lot of fast talking by the teacher who directed the play to convince me to do it. I was petrified on opening night, and to this day I don't know how I managed to walk through it without making a major mistake."

"And your father felt that he'd proved how difficult acting was?"

Evelyne nodded. "He was pleased with his idea, and I was happy that I didn't have to go to the studio anymore."

"Why didn't you just tell him you had no aspirations to become an actress?" he questioned, slowing down as they reached the movie theater.

"Because he would have thought I was only saying that to make him happy. Many of his colleagues' children were anxious to break into acting, and he naturally decided I was the same."

"No, I doubt you're like anyone else in the world," he murmured, pulling into the parking lot and steering the car into a slot.

Evelyne listened to his words and knew there was a

hidden meaning in them, but sensed this wasn't the time to decipher them. She looked up at the marquee, but the title didn't mean anything to her. "Have you heard anything about this movie?"

He shook his head. "Shall we give it a whirl?"

"Why not? Who knows, we might be watching next year's Academy Award winner," she said lightly.

Inside the lobby they stopped off at the snack bar and decided to share a medium size container of popcorn and a package of Junior Mints.

"For two people who claimed they were stuffed after dinner, we're doing pretty good with the junk food," Rhyder joked as they walked down the aisle and selected seats. Once seated Evelyne handed Rhyder his Coke and he set the container of popcorn between them. The theater darkened and the screen lit up with upcoming previews.

It wasn't long before Evelyne guessed that the movie wouldn't be the next year's Academy Award winner. If anything, the film would easily qualify for a film erotica award. It may have been rated R, but the hidden meanings in much of the dialogue were definitely X. While she usually didn't care for erotic movies, this one had a light comic touch that she enjoyed.

Rhyder didn't agree. He felt that every piece of sensual dialogue was directed at him. When an explicit love scene appeared on the screen he shifted uneasily in his chair to ease the ache in his lower body. The more he watched the more he wanted to take Evelyne back to the hotel and make love to her. He glanced at Evelyne a few times, but she didn't seem to be as much affected by the love scene. He shifted his position again. The trouble was, there was no relief to be found. He looked down at his watch until he could read the numerals. It had only been forty-five minutes! He wasn't sure he would survive.

Evelyne may have looked calm and collected on the outside, but she wasn't so cool on the inside. The witty repartee between the main characters was really nothing more than verbal foreplay, and it was soon having a very noticeable impression on her. She could feel her blood warming, the way it had when Rhyder had touched her that afternoon. Her breathing felt labored and her nipples hardened until the sensitive nubs felt the abrasion of the knit fabric rubbing against them. She fanned a wad of napkins in front of her face.

"It's a bit warm in here," she whispered when Rhyder looked at her curiously.

He smiled, not letting on that he knew exactly why she felt warm. He casually rested his arm behind her shoulders, his fingertips just touching the edge of her breast. He wasn't surprised when Evelyne later moved in her seat until she was a little closer to him.

She leaned over to whisper during one particularly energetic love scene between two of the minor characters. "Can a man really do that?"

"Only if he's a pretzel," he whispered back. "And what makes you think I would know?"

"You're always telling me that you're so much older than me. That must mean you've been dallying with the opposite sex a great deal longer than I. I assumed you would know most positions known to man and perhaps a few not known." She swore she could feel his breath against her cheek. Was he going to kiss her?

Rhyder didn't kiss Evelyne, but that didn't mean he wasn't thinking about it. He just wasn't going to indulge in some teen-style fumbling in a movie theater when there was a perfectly comfortable bed in a hotel room waiting for them. When the movie ended, he decided he would drive to the nearest drugstore and from there they'd go back to the hotel, where they could recreate a few of the scenes from the movie.

Evelyne sipped her Diet Coke in hopes it could cool her blood. No such luck. She silently vowed if she saw one more love scene she was going to turn in her seat, rip the clothes from Rhyder's body, and have her way with him.

Both of them heaved a silent sigh of relief when the movie finally ended. Rhyder couldn't imagine ever spending a longer two hours. They left the theater with the small audience and walked to the car left in a darkened corner of the parking lot. They didn't say anything as they got into the car and sat staring out the windshield at the other cars leaving the lot.

"I want to make love to you," he said quietly, still not looking at her. "I could blame it on the movie, but that would only be ignoring what I really feel." He turned in the seat to face her. "In fact, I'd like us to go back to the hotel and spend all night and maybe even a good part of tomorrow in bed together."

Evelyne's answering smile was pure sunshine. "I think that sounds like an excellent idea. I'll even provide a DO NOT DISTURB sign for the door."

Rhyder's laugh was brief but filled with happiness with her decision. He leaned over and pressed a hard kiss on her lips. "I don't dare try any more or we'll never leave here. First I have one quick stop to make." He switched on the engine and almost stripped the gears in his eagerness to leave. Searching his memory for the location of the nearby shopping center, he pulled out onto the highway and headed for the drugstore he knew to be there. During the drive he kept one hand closed around Evelyne's, squeezing her fingers periodically.

Evelyne felt a bubble of happiness well up inside. While the movie hadn't been the best, she was certainly going to remember it fondly! After all, it was the nudge that Rhyder had needed. She silently damned every red light they encountered; there seemed a great deal more of them than usual. A few times she could hear Rhyder curse the traffic lights for turning red at the wrong time, and she agreed with him. There weren't many cars on the road, and while the thought of running a red light wove through both their minds, the idea of receiving a traffic ticket dampened the idea.

What seemed like hours later Rhyder pulled into the shopping center's parking lot and headed for the drugstore. He stopped in an empty space in front of the store and stared at the bright-green CLOSED sign hanging on the door. Suddenly he felt as if he had been sucked into a vacuum. How could this be happening to them?

"For a world who supposedly loves lovers, we're not receiving our share of luck," he muttered, slapping the steering wheel with the flat of his hand.

"What do we do now?" Evelyne asked, looking helplessly at the store and only seeing the CLOSED sign that suddenly seemed to have grown ten feet tall.

Rhyder turned to her, a rueful smile on his lips. "What we do is settle for a couple of cold showers, since I doubt I'll be able to find what I want in the hotel's gift shop."

CHAPTER SIX

Fifteen minutes later they stood in front of Evelyne's hotel room door.

"It looks as if we're not meant to be together," she murmured, looking down at the ground.

Rhyder blew out a breath of exasperation. He took her key out of her hand, inserted it in the lock, and pushed the door open. He propelled her inside and closed the door behind them. "The last thing I want you to be is pessimistic," he said harshly, gripping her shoulders none too gently. "Neither of us planned for this to happen, and tonight we happened to be caught up short. I'm not usually an impulsive person; I'm known to plan everything I do well in advance."

"And I certainly wasn't part of your plans."

He shook her just enough to regain her attention. "You're right—you weren't part of my plans and I wasn't part of yours, but that was days ago. All that has changed now. I'm going to my room to take a shower before I change my mind and hope your calendar is on the right side."

Evelyne looked far from happy. "I haven't been very regular since I was taken off the pill." She sighed with regret. She looked up with surprise to hear Rhyder chuckling.

"Naturally," he said dryly, bending his head to drop a kiss on her forehead. She stared at him with pleading

109

eyes. "Oh, no, we'll wait until there won't be any worry. That's the last thing you need right now, since you're still working to regain your health."

She smiled. "Do you realize that at a time like this most men would think more about themselves than about my health?"

"I'm not most men," he reminded her. "Sleep well. I'll see you in the morning." He let himself out of the room, and a moment later Evelyne heard the sound of the neighboring door opening and closing.

"Sleep well?" she asked herself with a wry smile. "It would be easier if he told me to sleep standing on my head in the middle of an earthquake!" She headed for the bathroom to take an extremely cold shower.

All things considered, Evelyne slept well that night, though Rhyder wasn't as lucky. He spent the hours until dawn pacing the length of his room and staring at the wall facing Evelyne's room. He wished he still smoked. He also could have opened a bottle of beer in hopes the alcohol would slow his libido down, but he doubted anything would do that but making love with Evelyne. Funny, he hadn't truly thought about that until recently. Not until he'd learned just what a wonderful lady she was. It had been difficult to meet a woman he didn't mind being with most of the time, but she had so many facets to her personality that he never failed to learn something new about her each time they talked. He wondered what she was going to be like as a lover. He had an idea he wouldn't be disappointed. The trouble was, thinking about her in his bed only brought about that now familiar ache in his lower body. He sighed, headed for the small refrigerator, and withdrew a much needed bottle of beer. Maybe he'd drink two if he thought it would help him sleep.

The moment Evelyne woke up the next morning she

knew there were things she had to do. She first called Rhyder and explained she wouldn't be meeting him for breakfast, since she had some errands to run, and no, thanks, she wouldn't need him to act as chauffeur. She next ordered breakfast from room service, made several telephone calls, and dressed while waiting for her meal to arrive.

Rhyder ate his breakfast in the coffee shop, wondering what Evelyne might be up to.

"I see you've gone where no man has dared go before," one of the men Rhyder remembered seeing with Evelyne at the beginning of her stay said with a touch of sarcasm.

Rhyder put down his coffee cup and took his time looking up. "You're maligning the lady's name and I wouldn't advise you do it again," he said quietly with the force he had been known to use in the courtroom.

That didn't stop Jerry Hall. "Look, it's none of my business if you're putting it to her, but I'd sure worry about her going into convulsions or something when you're on that high," the younger man advised brashly.

Rhyder stood up. He may have been shorter by a couple of inches, but his aura was definitely more powerful. Jerry backed down, surprised that Rhyder was so angry over his words.

"Okay, okay." He held his hands up in self-defense. "You can't blame some of us for wondering, since you didn't show any interest in the lady at first. I just hope nothing happens while . . ." He noticed the dark look in Rhyder's eyes and backed off a few more paces. "All right, I get the message, but it's your funeral." He turned and walked away.

Rhyder was tempted to label Jerry with the appropriate title, but he knew it would give him only temporary relief. He returned to his breakfast even though

111

his appetite had greatly declined. Finally he finished his coffee, paid the bill, and took his leave.

Evelyne's errands took her longer than she'd anticipated, and she didn't get back to the hotel until early afternoon. She had barely stepped inside her room when a knock sounded at the door.

"Where the hell have you been?" Rhyder demanded, sweeping past her.

"Please, do come in," she said mildly. "Did you have a nice morning?"

"Aren't you going to answer me?" He spun around, his hands braced on his hips.

"No."

"Why the hell not?"

"Because you haven't asked me politely." Her serene smile was almost his undoing.

Rhyder gritted his teeth. He raked his fingers through his hair and turned his back to her. "I was worried about you." His voice was so low she almost didn't hear him.

She stared at his back. Her teachings ran strong that she never act thoughtlessly toward another person. "I'm sorry," she whispered, holding her hand out in supplication. "I wouldn't ever dream of hurting you."

Rhyder spun back around, saw her hand, and reached out for her, pulling her toward him. "You said you'd be away only a couple of hours, and I had no idea where you'd gone. For all I knew, you could have gotten ill or something." His words were muffled against the heavy silk of her hair.

Evelyne's hands feathered over his back. "I didn't realize it would take me so long," she replied.

He exhaled a deep breath. "Are you hungry for lunch?"

"A salad would be wonderful," Evelyne admitted. "Why don't we go swimming afterward?"

He nodded, finally relaxing with the knowledge she was safe and sound in his arms. "Sounds like a good idea to me."

By the time they reached the coffee shop, Rhyder was feeling and acting more like himself. Inside he cursed himself up one side and down the other for having allowed his feelings for her to show so openly. He wasn't supposed to care for her more than he had any other woman he'd been acquainted with. But then, he was quickly learning that Evelyne wasn't like any other woman he had ever known.

Unaware of his tumultuous thoughts Evelyne seated herself at a small table overlooking the ocean and glanced at the menu the hostess had handed her.

"The fresh fruit salad looks good," she commented, looking across the table at Rhyder. "What about you?"

"What?" He looked up, his eyes hazy from his speculation. "Oh." He quickly studied the menu. "I'll probably have a steak sandwich."

Evelyne wrinkled her nose. "A steak sandwich? Rhyder, you're in the tropics now. Look at all the fresh fish offered."

He shrugged. "I'll still stick with the steak sandwich." He looked up and gave his order to the waitress. After she left he turned back to Evelyne. "Did you have a nice morning out?"

She thought about her errands and wasn't entirely sure how to answer. "Yes." There, that was safe. He'd find out her secret soon enough, and there was no reason to go into it just now.

He gritted his teeth. Why all the secrecy? "Did you go into the village?" He couldn't understand his need for finding out her destination.

Evelyne nodded, grateful for the waitress's intervention when she placed tall glasses filled with iced tea in front of them and moved away.

"What did you do this morning?" she asked brightly.

"I tried to pretend I was lazy."

"Isn't it difficult to pretend to be lazy?"

"Harder than I thought it would be."

Evelyne nodded. For a while Rhyder acted as if he had gotten over his sulks, but he didn't really appear to have done. She sipped her iced tea to hide her smile. She remembered one of her teachers once saying men acted like small boys even as they grew older and supposedly wiser. Rhyder was obviously a successful attorney, which meant he had an excellent education, spoke of his love for plays and concerts and the few travels he had taken, but if he didn't understand something he would grow angry, cool off, but never forget what had caused his displeasure. She first thought of humoring him but knew if he guessed her reason he would not be happy. She decided it would be best to ignore his disgruntled mood.

It was easier once their food arrived. Evelyne looked down with pleasure at her fruit salad, lightly sprinkled with coconut. She'd only had a small breakfast and found herself very hungry. She picked up her fork and speared a pineapple wedge first, then tried a small piece of melon. She pushed a stray lock of hair away from her face and silently wished she had tied it back or pinned it up. In this heat, that had turned out to be the best method for her hair. A few times hairdressers had suggested it be cut, but she acknowledged openly she was extremely vain about her hair and only had the waist-length tresses trimmed every few months.

"What will you do when you leave here?" Rhyder's

114

abrupt question brought her back down to earth with an alarming thud.

Evelyne shrugged. "I don't really know," she replied softly, toying with her fork. "I guess I should sell my house and look for something smaller. Houses in Malibu are at a premium, so there would be no problem getting a good price for it. After that maybe I'll try to find a job or something. My best bet is to take it all one day at a time." She knew she would also visit her mother at the expensive sanitarium she had been living at for the past seven years. Luckily her father had set up a trust fund to pay all the costs, since it was very likely her mother would die there. In the beginning they had called Amanda King's problem a nervous breakdown. Now it was called "retreating from life." "When you get down to it, I'm not all that sure what I'll be doing," she concluded with a sigh.

Rhyder nodded. "You don't seem happy at the prospect of selling the house."

"It's on the beach, and I always felt more myself there than at the house in Bel-Air," she explained. "But it's very expensive to keep up and much too large for just myself."

He couldn't see her living alone for very long. A man would come along who didn't give a damn about her past medical history and carry her off. He only hoped she would be luckier in love the next time around and find a man who would truly appreciate her. He didn't doubt that her ex-husband had loved her, but he wondered if Rick Winters's own interests had come before his love for his wife during their marriage. Rhyder told himself he better stop speculating about what Evelyne's life would be when she returned to Los Angeles and worry about how his own messed-up life was going to be straightened out.

After lunch they walked back to their respective

rooms with the idea of meeting by the saltwater pool in a half hour. Evelyne didn't need much time to change into a patchwork-style bikini and matching cover-up and twist her hair up on top of her head in a loose knot. When she walked outside to the small lava-edged pool, she found Rhyder already stretched out on a lounge and a towel draped over the one next to him. He glanced up and gestured to the other lounge to let her know it was for her.

"I picked up a couple of cold drinks for us," he informed her, gesturing to the two frosty cans anchored in the sand under the front part of his lounge. He picked up the can of sugar-free lemon-lime soda, popped the top, and handed it to her. "And make sure to put lotion on. It's hotter than usual today."

Evelyne nodded. She reached into her tote bag and drew out a brown plastic bottle of suntan oil. Unscrewing the cap she poured a small amount into her palm and allowed her body heat to warm it before smoothing it carefully over each leg. When she'd finished there, she worked on her midriff, chest, and arms.

Rhyder's mouth went dry at the unconscious erotic grace of her movements. Each time her hands moved over another part of her body, his own palms itched to mimic those caresses, except he would draw them out more and eventually work his way under the small pieces of fabric she called a swimsuit. The more he watched the more he wanted the chance to touch her bare skin. Finally, in an act of desperation, he pushed himself off the lounge, muttering that he was going for a swim.

Behind the cover of her oversized sunglasses Evelyne watched Rhyder walk away. She sensed he was just a bit perturbed watching her apply her suntan lotion, and the idea that he was disturbed left her feeling pretty good. After the problems they had encountered over the past few days, she wouldn't have been surprised if he had dropped her fast. Funny, if she had met him a year ago she probably wouldn't have given him a second glance. She was usually uncomfortable with the serious types, but now that she knew Rhyder better, she was aware that he did possess a sense of humor, however dry it may have been. She also discovered that he wasn't much of a drinker, no matter how much he talked about it, and he was a true gentleman. A somewhat old-fashioned gentleman at that. Her lips curved with a knowing smile. Had he realized that the old-fashioned gentleman was warring with the lusty man? She wondered what a nice blend of the two would be like. She wasn't going to think that he might necessarily prod her into bed that night; not after last night's catastrophe. She certainly couldn't blame him, since she hadn't been all that much help. While she couldn't have stood the idea of any of the other men she had met so far making love to her, she knew the thought of Rhyder doing just that was an entirely different story. In fact, she was looking forward to having him as her lover.

She lay back and closed her eyes, feeling the sun beat down on her. A lot had happened to her in the past few months, and she knew she wasn't emotionally out of the woods yet, but she knew Rhyder had been a big help in getting her back on her feet.

Rhyder was doing a bit of thinking as he explored the shells, and the fish swimming in the pool. Last night had seemed an opportune time for making love, and he knew it wasn't something he could casually mention to her the way he might ask her to dinner. She had been sheltered during her lifetime even if she didn't see it that way. For someone who had survived the emotional turmoil of a divorce and lived with a man who was news for the tabloids at least once a week, she didn't seem to know as much about men as she should have. At the same time there was a quiet maturity about her that many women in their fifties and sixties didn't have. She was such a contradiction of the other women he had known that he found out something new about her almost every day.

It had been quite a while since he had thought about planning a seduction. Many of the women he had known were pretty straightforward, and he admired that in a woman because it showed she knew what she wanted and went after it. He remembered how Evelyne had decided she wanted to indulge in a series of affairs, and how they hadn't worked out because deep down she wasn't meant to have them. Oh, no, he was determined that the only affair she was going to have while in Hawaii was with him—just as soon as he figured out how to broach it without sounding like some besotted fool asking her to jump into bed with him. He glanced over at her lying on the chaise with one leg slightly bent at the knee. Did she realize what that bikini did for her? Even if she didn't, he certainly did! He knew it only emphasized the areas he wanted to know better. That brief morning in her bed was only a taste of what he wanted more of. And he would have more; just as soon as he figured out how to approach her.

As time passed Evelyne was feeling bolder. While Rhyder swam in the small pool and appeared deliberately to stay away from her for the next hour, she was busy plotting out the evening in the same methodical way she had planned so many parties and dinners.

Not long after he'd returned to his chaise, Evelyne announced she was feeling a little tired and was going up to her room for a nap. Rhyder glanced at her sharply.

"Are you feeling all right?" he demanded, checking her face to see if it looked unnaturally pale or if her eyes appeared cloudy.

She nodded. "Just a bit tired. A nap will fix me up just fine," she assured him, laying a hand on his arm. "Shall we just have dinner here?"

"All right," he agreed. "I'll come by for you at seven."

Evelyne smiled. "All right. I'll see you then." She gathered up her things and headed for her room. That gave her plenty of time to put her plans in action.

By six forty-five Rhyder was dressed in lightweight beige slacks and a short-sleeved cotton shirt of pale blue that emphasized his eyes and deep tan. He started out the door, stopped, and walked back to the dresser to pull open a drawer and withdraw a small packet which he pushed into his slacks pocket.

Just in case, he told himself, walking back to the door and this time closing it behind him.

When Evelyne opened the door in reply to his knock, he was surprised to find her wearing a semi-sheer caftan of a deep-blue silk, with her hair hanging in loose waves down her back.

"If you're running late, I can come back." He couldn't move his eyes away from the alluring sight of her body shadowed by the gauzy fabric or ignore the erotic scent surrounding her.

"I'm not running late." She smiled and stood back. "Come in."

That was when Rhyder saw a table set up in the middle of the room with a warming tray standing next to it.

"I thought it would be much nicer if we had a quiet dinner up here," Evelyne murmured, leading him to the table. "Would you like to open the wine?"

119

Rhyder looked at her quizzically, unable to ignore the fact that with her wearing high heels she was now eye level with him. He may have preferred petite women once upon a time he decided, but taller women weren't so bad. "You're not supposed to drink alcohol."

"No, but that doesn't mean I would deprive you." She presented him with a glowing smile. "I took the privilege of ordering for both of us. I hope you don't mind."

He nodded, still occupied with the sultry figure standing before him. He allowed Evelyne to seat him and watched her take the opposite chair. She held up her glass of Perrier.

"To a lovely evening," she said softly, lifting the glass a fraction higher.

Rhyder smiled and repeated her toast. He looked into her eyes, which appeared smoky and mysterious from her artful use of makeup. Even her skin held a luminous glow he didn't remember having seen before, and her perfume seemed to reach out and grab him by the throat.

He had no idea of the time she'd spent in the hotel's beauty salon having her hair conditioned and blown dry, her skin pampered with a special facial, and a manicure and pedicure added to her afternoon of beauty preparations. When she returned to her room, she had showered, rubbed a scented body lotion into her skin, and spent a great deal of time with her makeup so she would look natural and seductive at the same time. Judging from Rhyder's stunned reaction when she opened the door, Evelyne knew she had done an excellent job.

"What made you think of our having dinner up here?" he asked once he had regained his voice. Even a quick gulp of wine didn't help his equilibrium. He had a sneaking suspicion that his idea of seducing her had been taken out of his hands.

Evelyne took the covers off their salads and placed one of the chilled plates in front of Rhyder. "I asked for their house dressing."

"And our main course?" He knew what his idea of a main course was, but he was going to stick to the rules. For now.

"Mahi mahi, baked potatoes, and coconut pie for dessert." She ticked off the items on her fingers.

Rhyder decided it was safer to concentrate on his salad rather than on the light scent of Evelyne's perfume wafting into the air. With the muted sound of the ocean waves crashing against the rocks, it was all too easy to imagine them as the only people left in the world.

During dinner they talked about any topic that came to mind, always skirting the real issue in the back of their minds; the ultimate conclusion to the evening.

"If I got you drunk enough, do you think you'd talk more about your life in Chicago?" Evelyne said lightly, refilling Rhyder's glass.

"Wine has never given me more than a fuzzy head, so I'm afraid you're out of luck." He grinned. "What would it take for you to spill all your secrets?"

"Considering I feel that I've already done it, it's a rhetorical question. But if someone wanted truly to bribe me, the best method would be to present me with a double hot fudge sundae with real whipped cream and plenty of crushed peanuts on top," she replied without hesitation.

Rhyder almost choked on a crouton. "A hot fudge sundae?" That was not the answer he'd expected.

Evelyne nodded. "Chocolate was a bad word during my childhood because I had a nanny who believed it

121

corrupted innocent young girls. I always asked her how it corrupted girls, but she never answered me. She probably knew she couldn't give me a legitimate reason. And once a girl reaches her teens she's afraid to touch chocolate for fear of pimples. I was afraid to have any for fear of putting on weight. My dream is to gorge myself on the largest sundae I can make and enjoy every sinful bite."

"You'd probably end up pretty sick," he predicted.

"But it would be worth it!" she insisted, leaning forward as if to make a point. "There's always a food that's pretty well forbidden to us, and that makes it all the more enticing. For me it's a hot fudge sundae." She stood up and picked up her salad plate.

"With me it's butter toffee peanuts." Rhyder leaned back as Evelyne took his empty salad plate away and replaced it with the main course. "I can buy a large bag and they'll be gone in an hour, so I just don't buy them unless I've had a hard day at the office and feel I deserve them."

When their meal had ended, Rhyder pushed the tray into the hallway under Evelyne's direction and walked back into the room. There was no pause in his movements as he strode toward her and gathered her into his arms.

"I've been wanting to do this all day," he muttered. "Even when I was so angry at you because I didn't know where you were, I wanted to kiss you."

"Then what's stopping you?" she tempted huskily, tipping her head back.

Rhyder groaned and bent his head to capture her mouth in a possessive kiss. She tasted of coconut and coffee and a sweetness that was all her own. The more he explored her mouth with his thrusting tongue, the more he wanted her. His hands slipped down her back and cupped her buttocks, drawing her up against his hips. His respiration grew ragged as he realized she was wearing hardly anything under the caftan.

"You're driving me crazy, lady," he rasped before tugging at her lower lip with his teeth and pulling it back into his mouth to gently suckle. He discovered that the caftan boasted a row of tiny buttons down the front, and he was soon working his way down them until he freed a breast. "So sweet," he murmured, nuzzling the pale globe of flesh until it began to swell under his searching lips.

Evelyne closed her eyes, her hands at the back of his head urging him on. "Don't stop," she pleaded, digging her fingers into his scalp.

"Honey, I couldn't stop if I wanted to." He turned his head to pay equal attention to her other breast. By the time he'd finished, both dusky rose nipples had blossomed under his loving. Even as he nipped the sensitive skin, he continued unbuttoning the caftan until it dropped off her shoulders to her waist.

Evelyne dipped her head to trace her tongue around the shell-like shape of his ear and to dip it inside. She chuckled softly when she felt his tremors under her touch. To make sure the feeling wouldn't go away, she continued nibbling her way around the ear to the lobe. There she would soothe the tiny hurt with the wet ministration of her tongue.

"You're beautiful," he muttered.

"So are you."

"Your breasts are like ivory satin, do you know that?"

"Your skin reminds me of rough silk, so cool and comforting." She kissed his nape.

"You're making me sound like a quilt." He laughed roughly, pushing her caftan off her completely. He breathed sharply when he found her wearing only a tiny pair of blue French-cut bikini panties with a ribbon tied saucily on each hip. "Talk about a present." He fingered one of the ribbons.

Evelyne drew him up so she could unbutton his shirt and push it off his shoulders. She splayed her hands out over the heated skin of his chest, her fingers tangled lovingly amid the hair that narrowed down into his slacks. She smiled, whispering to him how she could feel his heart pounding under her fingertips. Rhyder suggested she do all the exploring she cared to do. Evelyne fumbled for a moment with the belt buckle, but soon that was undone and the zipper lowered, the slacks pushed to the carpet. She smiled at the slim-cut boxer shorts he wore.

"And here I thought you'd have a very sexy pair of briefs on." Her tongue flickered out to tease a flat brown nipple until it hardened.

Rhyder touched one of the ribbons but did nothing to untie it just yet. Instead he pulled her upward and nearly bent her head backward under the force of his kiss. His tongue slid easily into her mouth and explored every sweet, dark corner.

"I don't think I can get enough of you," he told her in a hoarse voice.

"Nor I of you." Her tongue darted out to caress the lower curve of his lip and inside to slide along the smooth surface of his teeth.

Rhyder shuddered and pulled her into his arms. A few steps forward for him and backward for Evelyne sent them falling onto the bed. He pulled her onto him. One hand cupped the back of her head and brought her face down to his for searing kisses that left her weak and trembling from the force.

She could feel her body yielding to his, her blood running faster through her veins and the warmth flowing slowly downward. She adjusted her body until her hips lay fully against his and she could feel his arousal against her thigh.

Not wanting to rush it, they kept kissing and caressing each other, but the kisses lengthened and their hands kept returning to special areas with unbearable ease. Rhyder rolled over, pinning Evelyne under him and moving his hips against hers.

"Evelyne, I have to get something out of my slacks," he said when he realized he couldn't wait any longer.

She smiled and shook her head. "I've already taken care of everything."

Rhyder frowned and would have questioned her more, but her fingers had surrounded him and she began to guide him into her. Feeling her close around him, he knew there was no going back. With a groan floating up from his chest he thrust into her and waited until her legs wrapped around his hips before thrusting again . . . and again.

"Velvet," he said huskily. "You're like warm velvet that covers me so perfectly."

She raised her head to kiss him. Her eyes were heavy lidded and bright with passion as they began a journey that transcended time. At first they were able to time their movements slowly, but as the needs of their bodies caught up with them the thrusts were deeper and faster and she arched up to keep him within her as deeply as possible.

Evelyne closed her eyes feeling something well up inside her. This emotion was new to her, and she knew this was a lovemaking she hadn't experienced before. It wasn't long before she felt the tiny explosions in her body move upward until they reached her brain. Her lips parted and a cry escaped to be swallowed by Rhyder's marauding kisses. When she felt herself spinning outward, she felt Rhyder follow her directly. He collapsed on top of her, his mouth moving against her breast before he rolled to one side and pulled her with him.

"Now are you going to tell me why you're so confident you're safe tonight?" he asked in a conversational tone.

CHAPTER SEVEN

Evelyne smirked. "That's easy. I went to see a doctor today," she explained. "After all, there's more to prescribe than the pill, you know."

Rhyder shook his head to clear it. "Since you claim you're not a very good liar, what did you tell him?"

"I told him the airlines lost part of my luggage and I'm on my honeymoon," she said proudly.

He fell back against the pillow and laughed. "And here I went to the drugstore first thing this morning." He chuckled.

"Really?" Evelyne giggled, rolling over on her stomach. "Rhyder, we both had the same idea!"

He nodded. "It appears so." He grew thoughtful. "Did you explain to the doctor about your medical problems?"

"Yes," she replied. "This isn't harmful to my health. And my blood pressure checked out normal."

"I doubt it would now."

"You don't have to act so smug about it." Evelyne playfully punched his shoulder.

He pulled her up against him, aligning her perfectly along his body. "Considering I'm ready to do more than talk about it, I'd say I have a lot to be smug about." He nipped her lower lip lightly before pressing down even harder.

Evelyne moaned softly and curved her arms around

his neck. "Then I guess we should do something about it, shouldn't we?"

By then Rhyder was past talking. He slid easily into her and began thrusting faster and faster until they were both caught up in the fantasy. Time had no meaning for what seemed long, beautiful hours as they indulged their craving to explore each other's body to the fullest.

It was almost dawn when Evelyne awoke. For a few moments she luxuriated in the comfort of Rhyder's warm body curled around hers. One arm lay under her waist and the other across her hips, with one leg nestled intimately between her legs. She listened to the soft sounds of his sleeping before she turned her head. He didn't look as harsh now as he did during waking hours. In fact, although she knew he would hate the comparison, she thought he resembled a little boy curled up in bed with a life-size, very feminine teddy bear!

She carefully disentangled herself from his embrace and hunted in the dark for her robe. When she couldn't find it, she picked up his shirt and slipped it on. She fastened a few buttons and walked out onto the balcony. Looking out over the sea she could see the dark sky beginning to turn a pale gray with hints of pink and orange along the edge. She couldn't imagine a more beautiful sight. She braced her hip on the railing and studied the beginning of the new day. When Rhyder's arms snaked around her waist and drew her back against a bare chest, she tilted her head and accepted his soft kiss.

"Good morning." She spoke softly in order not to disturb the mood.

Rhyder smiled. "Aren't you afraid of getting chilled?"

Evelyne shook her head. "How could someone from

a cold part of the country fear that? In case you didn't notice, I did take precautions against the chilly weather we're having."

Rhyder slid his hands under the soft cotton to warm her bare flesh. "Talk about a good way to shock the neighbors," he murmured, nuzzling the tingling spot just behind her ear.

"I only have one neighbor to worry about." She tipped her head to one side to aid him in searching out every spot. "He's a bit eccentric. An attorney, I'm told; somewhat harsh, but nothing to worry about."

His laughter vibrated against her nape as he proceeded to kiss every vulnerable inch. "Honey, if I were you, I'd worry about him a lot."

Evelyne turned her head to kiss him. "I'm sure there are much better things to do than worry about the neighbors."

Rhyder twisted her around and picked her up in his arms. "There's something more important in my mind that we can discuss. What would you say we go inside to delve into this much further?"

"Mmm, sounds like an excellent idea," she said throatily, snuggling up to him as he carried her into the room.

"You're right, you shouldn't gain another ounce or I'd never be able to pick you up."

"Rhyder!"

It didn't take him long to soften her cry of outrage to one of supreme satisfaction.

The lovers didn't surface again until late morning. Luckily Rhyder had thought enough at dawn to put out the DO NOT DISTURB sign and they were able to lie in bed and talk about anything that came to mind.

Rhyder learned about Evelyne's tenth birthday party that had been held at the family estate with one hundred children attending. There had been clowns performing magic tricks and pony rides, but what she most remembered was Johnny Maxwell pushing her into the fish pond and ruining her brand-new dress.

"But I got even with him," she explained. "I poured punch down the front of his shirt."

"This does not sound like the proper little lady graduate from an exclusive Swiss finishing school," Rhyder said.

"Occasions like Johnny were few and far between. When I misbehaved, my mother explained to me how I was hurting her by acting that way. I couldn't bear to hurt anyone, and that usually brought me to my senses."

Rhyder combed his fingers through her hair, enjoying the feel of the silky tresses spilling out over his hands. He could see her eyes clouding with memories of the past and wanted her to regain her usual exuberance.

"I guess you're growing hungry for food," he commented when the sound of her stomach grumbling seemed to echo between them.

Evelyne blushed. "It is past lunchtime."

Rhyder climbed out of bed and reached for his clothes. "Why don't we both freshen up and we can go into the village to eat?"

"All right." She sat up in bed, not embarrassed that the sheet fell to her waist.

He turned around and groaned at the lovely sight her bare breasts made. "Ordinarily I might suggest we shower together, but for the sake of our sanity and our stomachs, I think I'll go back to my own room. Will a half hour be long enough?"

Evelyne raised her arms over her head in a lazy stretch. "Better make it forty-five minutes. I think I'll soak in the tub instead of taking a quick shower."

Rhyder nodded. "Then why don't you knock on my door when you're ready?" He walked back over to the bed and dropped a kiss on her lips. "You're too tempting for your own good," he murmured, before taking his leave.

Evelyne's grin was just like the cat's who'd caught the canary. She couldn't remember ever having felt as satisfied as she did then. Rhyder had been an incomparable lover. He had begun their loving gently, not because of her previous illness, but because he knew she hadn't been with a man in almost a year. The fact that a deep passion soon entered into their lovemaking told her how much he had given of himself, and she doubted he had done that with too many women. A tiny part of her felt guilty that she felt more after one night with him than she had after so many nights with Rick. But she reminded herself that Rhyder wanted her, and Rick didn't. She finally got up and went into the bathroom with the idea of soaking in a hot tub for a while to relax some muscles that hadn't been used in quite a long time.

It was closer to an hour before Evelyne tapped against Rhyder's door. She barely had time to take a breath before he opened the door, pulled her inside, slammed the door shut, and trapped her against the wood panel for a searing kiss.

"I missed you," he said huskily, rubbing his hips suggestively against her pelvis.

"You're making an admission you may be sorry for later," she murmured, covering his chin with tiny kisses and moist flicks of the tongue.

"I'll claim to the court that I was under duress by the plaintiff." He did a fair share of his own nibbling.

"And I'll accuse you of perjury, counselor."

"Hmm, you learn fast." His eyes closed as he sa-

131

vored her taste to the fullest. "At the rate you're going you'll have your law degree in no time."

They might have ended up on the bed if Evelyne's stomach hadn't started growling again.

"Okay, I get the hint," Rhyder laughed, moving away. "We better get out of here before that hungry stomach of yours wages a full-scale war on me for not feeding it."

As they drove into Kailua Village, Rhyder realized he was more relaxed than he had been in a long time. In fact, he couldn't remember ever having felt as good as he was feeling now. He knew he had Evelyne to thank for that.

He began to wonder if she would truly be all right when she returned to Los Angeles. Or would she end up finding a man like her ex-husband and living the life she had practically been thrown out of? Could she take that kind of pressure again? He wanted to laugh at the irony of it. For a man who was determined to become a beach bum and live out his days on the Hawaiian Islands, he was doing an excellent job of worrying about someone other than himself. If he wasn't careful he'd begin thinking about returning to Chicago, his practice, and all the problems involved. He wasn't sure he wanted to enter that rat race again. He wasn't sure the work was all that rewarding, and he felt he sometimes worked for the wrong side of a suit, but he had been too used to going where the money was. He knew Evelyne was planning on leaving next week. He wondered if he could persuade her to stay another week. Oh, not because he wanted her to stay for him, oh, no, this was so she could better equip herself emotionally for her return to the fast lane of L.A.

Evelyne was doing some thinking of her own. She had already thought of Rhyder in more intimate terms than she should have allowed herself to, and after last night she was afraid she would count on him even more. If she had a shred of sanity left, not to mention common sense, she would take the first plane back to Los Angeles. Well, she decided, she never had been too smart for her own good. Her departure at the end of next week would be too soon as it was. Rhyder was right, she wasn't casual enough to handle one-night stands. She almost wished she had made up an excuse not to have lunch with him.

Rhyder parked the car, and they mutually decided to eat at Hurricane Annie's. The rustic restaurant was situated in the middle of the Kona Inn shopping village, and sitting on the patio they could hear the cheerful sounds of the birds, including the distinctive shrieks of cockatiels, which were caged in a nearby dress shop. They were hungry enough to splurge on barbecue ribs with a beer for Rhyder and a large glass of iced tea for Evelyne. She eyed his glass with longing.

"I never drank that much before, but when you're not allowed to drink at all it's amazing how good all forms of alcohol look to you." She sighed, digging into her ribs with gusto. "I look at the mai tais, the Blue Hawaiis, and Caribbean Sunsets, and I wish I could have one tiny sip."

"But you can't," he reminded her with a soft smile.

"At least it won't always be like this." Evelyne brightened up. "I'd like to say I'd go on a real binge when I'm off the medication, but I know I won't. I've had exactly one hangover in my life and I wouldn't care to suffer through another."

"Then you've got much more willpower than I do," Rhyder told her. "I've had more than my share of hangovers, and I always seem to forget about them when I indulge. I always end up suffering the next day, swearing I'll never do it again. Naturally I conveniently forget my vow next time around."

Evelyne wiped her sticky fingers on a napkin. "I guess that's a lesson you just don't want to learn, is it?"

"I'm stubborn that way." Rhyder looked down at his glass. "Would you like to fly over to Kauai tomorrow morning and drive out to see Waimea Canyon?"

Her face lit up. "I've always wanted to go there. I had thought about doing that while I was here, but I'll admit I didn't want to go alone."

"When we get back to the hotel I'll call the airline and make our reservations."

Evelyne hesitated. "Rhyder, I'd like to pay my own way. You've paid for most of the meals, and it isn't fair for me to expect you to continue doing that."

"All right," he agreed, guessing her need for independence and respecting it.

After lunch they walked around the shopping village. Rhyder waited patiently while Evelyne wandered through the dress shops and tried on more dresses than he imagined any woman had the energy to do. Considering all the clothing she tried on, she bought little; only a short cotton jumpsuit, a sundress in a colorful bold print, and three T-shirts. She also insisted on buying Rhyder an aloha shirt in a bronze print, even though he privately wondered when he'd ever have the nerve to wear it. Then he remembered he was supposed to be a beach bum and decided the shirt was perfect for his new image.

They stopped at a bakery for Cokes and pastries before returning to the hotel. They parted long enough to put on their bathing suits and take a swim in the freshwater swimming pool to work up an appetite for dinner.

As the evening progressed, Evelyne wondered how

it would end. Though she had been bold the night before in initiating their lovemaking, she wasn't sure she could do it again. They drove back into town for dinner and dancing along with a stop at Club 53 for late-night drinks and listening to the talk around them. Since a lot of locals enjoyed the popular club, they heard the fishing stories and legends. And all the while they sat together, Rhyder didn't let go of Evelyne's hand for a moment. He seemed happy lacing his fingers through hers and rubbing his thumb over her inner wrist. A couple of times she laid her head on his shoulder and smiled up at him as naturally as if she had done it for years. The first time it happened, he experienced the jealous thought that she might have been used to doing this with her ex-husband. Then he saw the luminous quality in her smile and the egotistical part of his nature doubted she would ever have looked at any other man the way she looked at him. The more beers he consumed the more positive he was she had treated no man the way she treated him.

"Time for all sexy girls to be in bed," he whispered in her ear just before closing time. He stood up and pulled her out of her chair, draping an arm around her shoulder.

"You're drunk," she teased, curling her arm around his waist.

"Just enough to leave me happy with the world, and that doesn't happen all that often." He guided her out of the bar and across the street to the car. During their walk he stole a few badly aimed kisses, much to Evelyne's amusement, especially when one loving peck landed on her eye.

"Perhaps I should drive," she suggested.

"I'm not that drunk," he argued.

"No, but you're a bit too loose to trust behind the wheel." She searched through his pockets for his keys.

"Hey, honey, at least wait until we reach the hotel," Rhyder said a bit too loudly.

Evelyne glared at him when a couple nearby laughed at his remark, but he merely smiled and allowed her to keep on exploring his jeans pockets.

"Where are the keys?" she demanded, holding out her hand after realizing she was only arousing him. He was right when he said he wasn't all that drunk. "I want them now, Rhyder."

He flashed her a lopsided grin and slowly brought his hand out from behind his back. The keys dangled from his fingertips. Evelyne snatched them away and unlocked the passenger door, pushing him none too gently inside.

"If you had asked me in the beginning, I would have given them to you," he told her, watching her pull the seat up a bit and insert the key in the ignition.

"Then why didn't you give them to me when you knew very well they weren't in your pocket?"

"Because you didn't ask me for them."

Evelyne muttered under her breath, started the car, and backed out of the parking space.

"What did you say?" Rhyder asked curiously.

"Nothing you'd care to hear." She pulled out onto the main road and drove toward the hotel. Once there she found a parking space not too far from the building that housed their rooms and parked the car. She practically shoved Rhyder out of the car and walked around to meet him. She told herself she should be glad he was a happy drunk and that he was really appealing in a little-boy way right now. She was still determined to remain stern so he wouldn't think he could constantly wrap her around her finger.

"Hey, baby, my place or yours?" Rhyder leered,

sliding his arm around her shoulders and drawing her against his side.

"I doubt you would be acting this way if you weren't drunk," she commented, wrinkling her nose at the beer fumes coming her way. "And I'm sure you're going to regret your cute ways tomorrow."

"I never regret anything. Nor am I so drunk that I don't know what I'm saying," he said, too gravely for one who was definitely a few sheets to the wind. He steered her to the waiting elevator car. Evelyne was relieved there was no one else to witness Rhyder's affability.

"Please, hold the door open!" Evelyne's heart sank when a woman's voice rang out.

Rhyder lurched forward and pressed his finger against the OPEN button. His eyes almost bugged out when an extremely buxom blonde ran into the car and bumped into him. Evelyne was just as stunned to watch someone defy the laws of gravity as a bright-yellow tube-top was stretched to its limits and a pair of tiny white shorts barely covered the lower part of a slim torso and revealed a pair of legs that seemed to go on forever, only to end with red-tipped feet in a pair of high-heeled sandals.

"Never fear, we knights of the realm would never leave a damsel in distress behind." Rhyder swept his arm across his body in a theatrical bow. Evelyne silently calmed herself. She couldn't believe what she was hearing. "What floor, pray tell, milady?"

The blonde woman smiled, revealing pearly white teeth Evelyne would swear on her life were capped. "Whatever floor you're going to."

"For you, madam, I would gladly take us to the moon." Rhyder couldn't seem to keep his eyes from the straining tube-top that looked as if it would give up the ship at any moment.

"Uncle Harry, don't tease the lady." Evelyne knew it was time for her to speak up. She affected a sickly smile. "After all, it is way past your bedtime, and Dr. Forest insists that you have as much rest as possible." She turned to the blonde. "The poor man has suffered so much lately." She lowered her voice. "His wife left him only six months ago because he couldn't . . . well, you know." She lifted her eyebrows to emphasize her story and inclined her head toward Rhyder.

The blonde glanced at Rhyder and noticed his glassy-eyed countenance. Her eyes wandered a bit lower, then up again. She quickly pushed the button for the next floor and got off as soon as the doors slid open.

"What was wrong with her?" Rhyder asked, momentarily recovering from his stupor.

"We arrived at her floor," Evelyne said serenely, easily guiding him out of the elevator when it reached their floor, and leading him to his room. "Now, this time *you* give me your room key."

He sighed, leaning back against the wall next to the door. "You're really not very much fun, you know." He dug into his jeans pocket and handed the key to her.

Evelyne's lips tilted upward before she could recover and replace it with a stern expression. She opened the door and pushed him inside. After flipping on the light switch she escorted him into the bathroom. Rhyder sat on the commode lid while she turned on the shower and adjusted the temperature.

"Strip," Evelyne ordered.

His face lit up. "For you, anything."

She shook her head. "Oh, no, I don't intend to have a sex fiend who'll pass out at the wrong moment. I want you to take a shower first. Now, off with the clothes." She remained where she was until he was divested of his clothing. It took all of her willpower not to reach out and touch the lean body she already had come to think of as hers. She hated to admit that the chesty blonde had given her a few jealous twinges, even though she doubted Rhyder would have looked at the woman if he had been sober.

"Hey, this is cold!" he shouted when he stepped into the tub under an icy stream of water.

"It's the fastest way for you to sober up," she told him, gathering up his clothes left on the floor and folding them neatly before leaving them on the counter.

Evelyne wandered back into Rhyder's room and headed for the small refrigerator. She opened the door to find a few green glass bottles nestled inside. She smiled at his thoughtfulness and withdrew one. She took a glass, filled it with ice, and poured a good measure of Perrier into it. She sipped her drink as she walked over to a chair and sat down.

She was leafing through a magazine about the island's attractions when Rhyder walked out of the bathroom wearing just his jeans. She looked up pleased to see that his color had returned to normal and he walked with a steadier step.

"I see we're back to our old self again." She smiled.

"Thanks to your idea of a shower," he grumbled, rubbing his head with a towel. "I could have turned into a Popsicle in there."

"No way. Alcohol doesn't freeze."

Rhyder glared at her as he dropped into the chair opposite her. He picked up her glass, drank, and grimaced.

"This stuff tastes terrible," he groaned, setting it back in front of her.

"It's an acquired taste, like avocados," Evelyne explained.

"I hate avocados." He got up to retrieve a can of Coke out of the refrigerator.

Evelyne watched him with a look of amusement in her eyes. "You're really something when you're tipsy. Lovable, in fact."

Rhyder winced. "Do I gather that you were talking about that blonde with the big bo—that blonde?"

She nodded. "She looked at you like you were a freshly made French pastry and she couldn't wait to bite into you."

"She was definitely not my type." His eyes raked over her with alarming thoroughness. "I'm more into thoroughbred stock."

Evelyne stood up and reached behind her to unbutton the loose top that skimmed her waist. When it dropped, she wore only a lacy wisp of a bra. Just as leisurely she unfastened her shorts and allowed them to fall to the floor. "Such as this?" she asked huskily.

His head felt very heavy as he nodded. "Definitely blue ribbon."

Evelyne walked over to Rhyder, nudged his legs apart, and took two paces forward until her knees lightly bumped the denim-covered juncture. She braced her hands on the chair arms, leaned forward, and brushed a kiss across his lips. She was surprised to find them tasting of mint instead of beer.

"Very nice," she murmured, moving her lips back and forth against his.

"Show me nicer."

The tip of her tongue appeared to bathe his mouth with her taste. First she outlined his lips, then ran it across the center before darting inside. Growing more daring by the moment Evelyne raked her fingernails over his chest, lingering on the tiny nipples nestled among the still-damp golden-brown hair before moving downward. Her lips tasted his ear before trailing

140

along his jaw and down to his shoulder, until she reached the tiny nub that she blew on with her cool breath.

Sensing her need for dominance Rhyder kept his hands on the chair arms with a willpower he hadn't known he possessed. He smelled her perfume surrounding him in a sensual cloud and endured the touch of her mouth along his collarbone and down to his chest. He felt her fingers teasing the denim fabric away from his waist and delving beneath to tantalize him with short strokes guaranteed to drive a man insane. He groaned, arching his hips upward against the light touch that brought him such heated pleasure.

"Are you inviting me to have my way with you?" she asked with faint laughter in her voice.

Not bothering to reply, Rhyder splayed his hands out over the tempting curves of her buttocks and brought her even closer to him. His mouth fastened hotly against hers, his tongue plundering her mouth to bring her taste back into his. He snaked one arm around her waist, tipping her off balance into his lap. The teasing was finally over. He dispensed with her bra, knowing he needed to feel her skin fully against his. He groaned appreciatively when his hand fitted perfectly over her small, well-formed breast. His thumb teased the nipple and it swelled even more under his caress. She moaned in his ear, shifting her body.

"I wouldn't suggest you try too much of that until we're in a more comfortable position," he said hoarsely, one hand slipping under the lace of her panties.

"Then you better get us over to that bed as soon as possible," she whimpered, sinking her teeth into his shoulder as a not too subtle reminder of the extent of her arousal.

"Whatever the lady commands." Rhyder stood up with Evelyne in his arms and carried her over to the bed. Smiling into her softened features he eased her onto the counterpane and followed her down. It took a bit of maneuvering, but they were able to unfasten and push his jeans off without too much trouble. By the time they finished their labor, they were laughing.

"You shouldn't wear such tight jeans," Evelyne teased, running her fingernail across his hip, feeling his shudder from her touch.

"I should have dried myself off completely before putting these damn things back on," he grumbled, tearing her panties off with undue haste. "At least there wasn't any problem with these things." He laid his hand over that portion of her throbbing for his possession. "And there certainly isn't any problem with you."

"Do you realize what those words truly mean to me, Rhyder?" she asked in a low voice, placing her hands on his shoulders. "I'm a whole woman again, and I wasn't truly sure I would ever be one. You helped me find that part of myself."

He nuzzled the tender skin of her throat. "I figured if you were such a lady on the outside, you'd have to be a regular witch in the bedroom. At least that's the way the saying goes."

"I could have turned into a cold-blooded witch," she thought to tell him.

"No, not you." His fingers insinuated themselves into her femininity to seek the warmth he knew to be there. "Not when you have a mouth that begs to be kissed." He matched action to his words. "And skin pleading to be caressed. I sensed you would be like this." His fingers delved farther until her body writhed in a plea for all of him. "Are you prepared?" he asked hoarsely.

142

She nodded, watching Rhyder's head move downward. As his lips found the tender skin of her inner thigh she realized what would happen next. He nipped the skin lightly, then nuzzled his way up. His tongue flickered out, bringing her to the brink, then retreated to allow her a brief respite. Each time she felt the mists leaving her brain he began his subtle torture again until Evelyne wasn't aware of anything but the pleasure of Rhyder's seeking lips. He kept it up as long as possible, until he knew he had to have her. He slowly moved up, feeling her hands roam over the damp skin of his back and down to his buttocks.

"You're mine," he said roughly.

"Yes," she sobbed. *"Yes!"* She cried out again when he lifted her to him and entered her with little effort.

Again and again he plunged deeply into her until she didn't know where one ended and the other began. Rhyder's hand cupped the back of Evelyne's head, bringing her face up for his kiss. They kissed wildly, as if there would be no tomorrow, and their twisting bodies were further proof that they made love as if they would be parted at dawn.

Rhyder whispered dark love words to Evelyne, told her of his fascination for her body and his appreciation of her beauty. He did all but tell her he loved her, not realizing that was exactly what his body was doing as he first slowed the rhythm until she couldn't stand it any longer, then sped it up as she cried out to him at that mind-shattering final climax. When it finally came, they fell among the shower of stars together, lost in the fires of their passion.

Rhyder lay back, keeping Evelyne close to him as he tried to regain his breath. His lungs hurt from the effort, but he considered the pain more than worth it after the pleasure he had given and received.

"It gets better every time," he mused.

"You sound as if that's unusual," she said sleepily.

"For me it is," Rhyder said under his breath.

Evelyne wasn't sure what to say. She knew he hadn't been a monk, but she couldn't imagine he had never experienced such beauty before. Certainly she hadn't, but then she had only one other lover to compare with.

"One night," she began hesitantly, but deep down she felt she had to say it, and if she didn't say it now it probably would remain in the deep recesses of her brain forever. "Rick and I had attended a party. He didn't drink very much, but I always felt he had indulged in something else that night. By the time we arrived home it was three in the morning and I was dead on my feet and had to be up at six. Rick was wide awake and ready for sex." She found she couldn't even call it lovemaking anymore. "I wasn't and I told him so, but he had other ideas."

Rhyder propped himself up on his elbows. "He raped you?" He thought killing the man wouldn't be punishment enough.

She shook her head and said quietly, "No, but he knew exactly what buttons to push. I felt so used when it was all over. I told him no and he still went ahead, figuring he could get me in the mood. That was the first time I felt more like his possession than his wife and lover. I couldn't forgive him for a long time. What hurt most was that he refused to see my side of it when I tried to talk to him about it later."

Rhyder exhaled a deep breath. "While I get turned on just looking at you, I hope that you'll remind me of this story if I ever try to talk you into making love when you aren't in the mood."

Her lips curved into the smile that made him want to kiss her mouth. "I don't think I'll have that problem when I'm with you. I get some pretty erotic ideas all my own."

Rhyder pulled the covers away and draped them over them. His arm stayed around her shoulders, her head nestled against his collarbone.

He suddenly chuckled. "I forgot to call the airlines to make a reservation."

Evelyne made a drowsy sound. "We can either take a chance tomorrow or go the next day. I'm in no hurry, are you?"

Why did her question bother him? Was it because he wanted to pack their days together with every memory possible so she would never forget him?

"No, I'm in no hurry," he said quietly.

CHAPTER EIGHT

Luck was with the lovers. Rhyder and Evelyne easily made the first flight to the Lihue Airport in Kauai. Not caring to tempt fate too far they made return reservations to the Keahole Airport. They rented a car, studied a map, and set out for the Kaumaulii Highway.

"I don't think it will be too easy for us to get lost here," Rhyder commented, noticing the signs posted for the Waimea Canyon.

Evelyne looked around. "It's so green," she murmured as the Toyota zipped along the road.

"And it seems to be much quieter," he replied.

As during their trip to the volcano park they passed through small towns and an occasional view of the ocean on their left.

It took them a little over two hours to begin climbing the winding road that led to the canyon that rivaled the Grand Canyon in Arizona for beauty. Evelyne remarked on the rich red earth surrounding them and insisted on stopping a few times to take pictures. Rhyder obliged her by posing with the high walls of the canyon behind him and then suggested she pose for him.

When they reached one of the lookouts, they were finally able to see the true beauty of the canyon even with a fine mist lying over it like a pale-gray sheer fabric shrouding the earth. They walked up a set of stairs that led to a higher point and looked around them with awe. Stray wisps of Evelyne's hair whipped around her face from the strong wind as she lifted it in silent prayer to the elements surrounding her. Rhyder looked at her, doubting she had ever looked so beautiful. He reached out to touch her shoulder and turn her toward him. He grabbed hold of her braid, his fingers digging into her nape to hold her head still, but he needn't have worried that she'd move away. His face descended until their lips were a breath apart.

"Do you mind if I kiss you here in front of God and everybody?" he whispered.

She shook her head. "If we can't do it here, where can we?"

Rhyder bent his head and told her exactly where he would like to do it and what he would like to do. Evelyne laughed, twisting her head away from him.

"That isn't what I was talking about and you know it," she scolded.

Anything else she was going to say was interrupted by his mouth covering hers in a searing kiss. His hands molded her against him until they were one except for their clothing separating them. When they heard sounds of other cars pulling into the parking area, they reluctantly parted.

"Being I don't know how many miles from the hotel can be very painful at times," he said, breathing deeply to bring his body back under control.

"Yes." She rested her forehead against his chest.

"Evelyne, don't say that word just now," he groaned, gently pushing her away from him. "We'd better get on with our sightseeing."

They toured the rest of the canyon, viewed the many falls dotting the island, took a picture of the Sleeping Giant, a mountain outline that resembled a

147

man's reclining figure, and drove to the opposite end of the island to Hanalei, the shoreline used for the movie *South Pacific* and known for the wet caves.

"Ugh," Evelyne shuddered as she viewed the interior dripping with condensation and covered with a heavy moss. "This would look more appropriate in a horror movie."

"Not unless there are bats," he said, peering further inside.

"Bats!" she cried, stepping back.

"There are no bats," he assured her, turning around and grabbing hold of her hand. "Come on, I'll show you."

She shook her head. "This is as far as you'll get me to go. Besides, I don't think we should go in too far." She looked around fearfully.

Rhyder nodded in the murky darkness and walked back out with Evelyne. After the dim light of the cave the bright sunlight almost blinded them for a moment.

He glanced down at his watch. "If you want to see the Fern Grotto, we probably have just enough time before we catch our plane."

"All right. As long as there aren't any wet caves."

Evelyne was happy not to find any wet caves. Befitting the name, the open cave was covered with low hanging ferns and was a popular spot for weddings. That wasn't a word she thought highly of after her one bad time with matrimony. She decided to hope that her time with Rhyder would give her the strength to return to Los Angeles. If a nice man came along, she wanted to be able to handle an affair with the right amount of casualness without giving up her heart in the end. She only hoped Rhyder wouldn't spoil her for other men—although she'd once thought she wouldn't be able to make love with another man after Rick and she had certainly overcome that obstacle.

Their flight home was uneventful, and after a stop for an early dinner they returned to the hotel. Neither of them wishing to do anything strenuous that evening, they spent several hours sitting on Rhyder's balcony, sipping drinks and staring out over the ocean.

Not feeling the need for words Rhyder picked up Evelyne's hand and placed it on his thigh. There wasn't anything sexual in the movement; he just wanted to know she was there with him not just physically but mentally.

"When do you leave for Chicago?" Evelyne asked in a small voice.

"Probably in about fifty years."

She turned her head. "Are you saying you're going to be living here?"

"That's it."

Evelyne shook her head in denial. "But what about your practice?"

"My practice is shot to hell." His tone was bleak rather than bitter.

She squeezed his fingers. "Is that the subject you said you'd have to be drunk to talk about?" She wondered if he would talk about it now even though he had only drunk two whiskies and they had only relaxed him a bit.

Rhyder nodded. "Now I suppose you want a further explanation."

"Only if you want to talk about it."

He sighed deeply. "I don't know if it would make things easier."

"It helped me when I talked," Evelyne said softly, still staring at his profile. "I hadn't really talked about Rick and me with anyone except my friend Celia, but she had trouble understanding because she took men with a grain of salt. She's had so many husbands and

149

lovers she would need an appointment book to keep track of all of them."

Rhyder chuckled at the differences he pictured between the two women. "Sounds like a busy lady."

"Busy? That's an understatement." She flashed him an impish grin.

He stared long and hard into her face. "What do you say we leave all this tropical splendor and go inside?"

"That sounds like an excellent idea."

They turned the lights off in the room and left the sliding door open to allow the soft ocean breeze flow around them as they got into bed.

"Um, that feels so good," Evelyne murmured sometime later, a breathy sound threaded through her voice.

"Does it feel as good here?"

"Uh-huh."

"How about here?" His hands moved over another sensitive area of her body.

"Definitely."

"I think I found another spot."

"You certainly did." She could have lain there and purred under his knowing touch.

"Is it the same here?"

"Oh, yes. You're a master with your hands."

"So I've heard."

A low moan escaped Evelyne's lips, her hips undulating under his exploring fingertips. "Don't stop now," she pleaded.

"I wasn't thinking of it. Not yet, at least."

She moved sinuously under his hands. "I think I'm in heaven."

"You look like you are." He chuckled, lifting his hands.

Evelyne rolled over. "I told you not to stop," she pouted.

"Honey, I've been rubbing your back for the last hour and you'd allow me to continue for the rest of the night. Fair is fair. I rubbed your back; now you can rub mine."

She sat up, her bare breasts pearly in the moonlight filtering into the room. "All right, but you can expect a back rub I doubt can be equalled by any other woman."

And she did just that.

The next day they had a picnic lunch packed up and decided to drive out to the Black Sand Beach for a day of sunbathing and privacy.

"It looks like something out of a science fiction movie," Evelyne stopped to pick up a handful of the sand and filter it between her fingers. She looked around at the stand of palm trees bordering the beach area.

"It's just lava crushed to the consistency of sand over the years," Rhyder replied, dropping their towels and picnic basket. He looped an arm around her neck and pulled her close. "Don't worry, if any strange little men with gills and purple feet appear, I'll protect you."

She made a sound of disgust and stood back. "Very funny." She frowned. "You didn't used to have a sense of humor. What happened?"

He shrugged. He didn't want to admit he was just as surprised by the lightening of his attitude as she was. He had been a joker and life of the party while in college and law school, but somehow that left him as the years passed and he had to work hard to establish his practice. When he met Evelyne he wanted to make her laugh more than anything, because her laugh was the same thing magic was made of. Except how could he explain that to her without her thinking he was ready for certification to a mental ward? "I guess it just feels better than frowning and acting as if fun were a sin. No wonder they say laughter is the best medicine around."

Evelyne sidled up to him and clasped her arms around his waist. "Sometimes I think you're the best medicine I could have."

He wrapped his arms around her and held her close to his heart. "The same here," he said quietly in her ear. "The same here."

In an effort to lighten the mood between them, Rhyder picked Evelyne up and carried her out to the edge of the water.

"Rhyder, not this way!" she squealed, kicking her legs.

"No problem, just hold your breath and it will be over before you know it," he assured her, walking out until the water was almost waist high. Lifting her as high as he could, he suddenly loosened his hold and she dropped into the softly rolling waves.

Evelyne surfaced, sputtering curses at Rhyder and swearing to get even as soon as she caught him. He made sure she had to work hard to catch him, and when she did, he held her by the waist and dropped down, smothering her mouth in a kiss she was helpless to reject. By the time they drifted to the surface, they were breathing hard from more than just lack of oxygen.

"You're lucky that I've never been one for making love in the ocean," Rhyder informed her in a raspy voice, urging her legs to wrap around his waist. He rubbed his pelvis suggestively against hers.

"Then it's a good thing I'm with an attorney who could defend our case if we were arrested for indecent exposure," she crooned, combing her fingers through the wet silk of his hair.

Rhyder dropped her back into the water. "I think it's time we both cooled off."

They indulged in a water battle that ended in kisses and the decision that they'd better walk back to their towels before the situation threatened to boil the water.

After feasting on mineral water, fresh fruit, teriyaki chicken, two different kinds of salads, and delicate pastries, Evelyne stretched out on her towel and closed her eyes. Rhyder remained awake, content to watch her sleeping figure.

He was afraid to tell her how worried he was about her. He knew she hadn't slept well the night before, and the faint lavender shadows under her eyes were proof. He didn't tell her that he was aware when she had crept out of bed in the middle of the night and sat in a chair on the balcony watching the ocean. He wanted desperately to know what she was thinking, but he doubted she would tell him if he asked her. That didn't stop his brain from thinking the worst. Could it be her health? Or was she not looking forward to returning to Los Angeles? He had once asked her why she didn't stay with Celia for a while, but she explained that the woman traveled between the two coasts and Evelyne wasn't fond of the cold weather in the East, where Celia's main house was. He knew something was bothering her, and he just wished he knew what it was so he could make it better for her.

He cursed under his breath and rolled onto his back. He couldn't allow himself to feel more than desire for Evelyne, because a stronger emotion usually led to the sort of ties he couldn't give her. She had been hurt enough by her ex-husband; she didn't need to have him inflict more pain on her. In time his own eyes drifted shut and he floated into a light sleep.

It couldn't have been twenty minutes before Evelyne awoke. She twisted onto her side and propped her head up on her hand, watching Rhyder sleep. She smiled. Did he realize that he had the cutest snore? It wasn't loud enough to bother anyone, just a soft exhalation of breath with the tiniest catch in the middle, but it was still a snore. It was also a strangely comforting sound.

Time was running out for her, and she wasn't sure if she was ready to face the outside world just yet. By coming here she had retreated into an element that had a fantasy touch to it. Here, nothing was real, and she could do whatever she wanted and not worry how it would reflect on the person she had been. The trouble was, she wasn't sure who she truly was. Shaking off her bleak thoughts she sat up and rummaged through the cooler for the bottle of mineral water. She poured the rest of it into her glass and leaned back on her elbows, sipping the cool liquid to soothe her parched throat.

"You look like you're posing for a fashion magazine." Rhyder's rough voice sounded sleepy as he rolled over.

She shook her head as she looked down at the briefs to her sea-blue bikini. "My thighs are too heavy."

"Your thighs are just right—as is the rest of you," he argued mildly, stroking said part of her anatomy.

"You're just prejudiced." She turned her head and smiled at him.

"No, I just know good woman flesh."

Evelyne groaned. "You make me sound like a horse."

"Only the best, darlin', only the best." He shaded his eyes with his hand and looked out to sea. "It looks as if a storm might be heading in. We'd better get back to the hotel."

She nodded and stood, gathering up her belongings.

During the drive back Evelyne felt a sense of foreboding, as if her life wasn't going to be the same again. She hadn't felt this way since the night Rick had refused to make love to her and left the house, filing for divorce soon after that. She only hoped the feeling had nothing to do with Rhyder. She didn't want to lose him just yet.

Rhyder was experiencing a few of the same unsettled feelings. He was sorely tempted to turn the car around and drive in the opposite direction as fast as he could in order to protect Evelyne from some unseen force that threatened to hurt her. He tried ascribing his feelings to the storm rumbling inland but knew it was just an excuse. He'd have to wait and see what was going to happen and keep a close eye on Evelyne. She had come a long way since she had first arrived in Hawaii, and he didn't intend to see her slide backward.

The cloud of despair surrounded Evelyne until she thought she would suffocate. When the car pulled into the hotel parking lot she blindly gripped Rhyder's hand.

"Evelyne, what's wrong?" he asked sharply, sensing her desperation.

Her head made a faint movement indicating she didn't know. "I'm not sure. I just feel as if something very bad is going to happen and I have no power to stop it." Her voice sounded as if she were on the verge of tears.

The moment the car was parked, Rhyder turned in the seat and pulled her against him. "Nothing is going to happen to you as long as I'm with you," he insisted fiercely, burying his face in her hair with its tangy scent of the ocean. With that statement the velvet chains binding him to her tightened even further. He knew he couldn't leave her now. If it came down to it, he'd just have to turn into a California beach bum instead of a Hawaiian one.

By mutual decision they left their towels and the cooler in the car until later. They walked slowly toward the building with the intent of reaching their rooms as soon as possible.

"Mrs. Winters?" A man's voice rang out.

Pure instinct prompted Evelyne to turn around. A man in his mid-thirties ran toward them, and she saw him as the threatening force she had worried about earlier. Only her strong will kept her from shrinking against Rhyder.

"What do you want?" she asked tersely, immediately guessing he was not a member of the hotel staff.

"I'm Elliot Hayes with the *L.A. Times,*" he replied. "It's taken some time to track you down."

"Why have you bothered?" Evelyne demanded.

"To find out your reaction to your ex-husband's remarrying."

The shock engulfed Evelyne like a cold wave. She searched deep down for the strength not to falter under the man's knowing gaze and his pity. She wanted to cry out that she didn't need his sympathy.

"Why can't you leave her alone?" Rhyder rumbled.

Elliot looked at him curiously. "What are you to Mrs. Winters?"

"I'm her attorney," he said sharply. "She's still recovering from her illness and doesn't need reporters digging up any more dirt to harm her with."

"That's not the way it is," he denied. "I've always tried to give her a fair break, even if the other papers didn't. I did the same when it came to stories about her father and mother, although a lot of writers preferred looking for the dark side of their relationship."

A faint smile touched Evelyne's lips. "Now I remember. You were the one who tried to visit me in the hospital, weren't you? If I remember correctly, you sent yellow roses to me."

"It didn't get me in to see you for an interview, but I hope you enjoyed the flowers."

She turned to Rhyder. "He wrote a very sweet note accompanying the flowers that he wasn't out to crucify me but to tell the truth about my illness. I believe we talked on the telephone a week later."

Elliot nodded, giving a grim-faced Rhyder a wary eye. "I'm flattered you remembered me."

"You were the only one to think about printing the entire truth." Evelyne felt the tears filling her eyes and refused to give in to them. "To be honest with you, Mr. Hayes, I didn't know my ex-husband had remarried. When did it happen?"

Relieved that he wasn't going to be thrown out, he dug into his jeans pocket and handed her a newspaper tear sheet. The headlines of the entertainment page told it all. Rick had married a singer who had signed with his company two years before.

All of a sudden she realized that seeing the words in black and white didn't bother her. She knew she was finally free of Rick's influence and the past they had shared. She chose her words carefully so they wouldn't be misconstrued.

"I hope he and Kayla will be happy," she said quietly, handing the tear sheet back to the reporter. "Other than that I don't know what you would want me to say."

He nodded. "You've always been straight with me, so I'd like to give you some advice. If I could find you, others will, and they won't be content with a one-liner for a reply. They're going to want as much dirt as they think they can get, and they'll stick around until you give it to them or they'll bend the rules to write the story they figure the readers will want to see." He glanced at Rhyder again. He guessed by the protective stance of the older man he was more than just her attorney. That was one piece of news he would keep to himself for the time being.

Rhyder muttered a crude expletive under his breath when he saw Evelyne's face pale.

"How much do you want to keep Mrs. Winters's whereabouts secret for a while?" he demanded.

"Not a cent." He grinned cockily. "But if the time comes, how about an exclusive about how you've coped with your stroke and a divorce right on top of it? It might help other women who've been in the same situation."

Evelyne smiled and held out her hand. "You have a deal, Mr. Hayes. And I thank you for being so considerate. After all these years of dealing with the media, it's unusual to find a reporter who still has some scruples. I'm sure it's helped you go far in your profession. When I feel ready to talk, you can be assured I'll contact you. It's a shame you had to come so far for your story."

"Are you kidding? I intend to take a few days off and look around." He gazed off in the direction of the pool with a few bikini-clad beauties stretched out on the lounges.

As soon as he could, Rhyder ushered Evelyne up to her room. Only when the door was closed behind them did he breathe a sigh of relief.

"Do you trust him?" He walked over to the telephone and picked up the phone book.

"Yes. He was very kind and understanding when I was ill." She dropped into a nearby chair.

"He's pretty well on his way to falling in love with you."

Evelyne looked surprised at Rhyder's harsh tone. "And you sound jealous."

"Damn right." He found the page he was looking for. "Where's your airline ticket?"

"Why?"

"Because you're going to have to make some changes if you don't want some hard-nosed reporters running you down. You may trust that guy, but I don't."

Evelyne picked up her purse and dug into a zippered pocket until she found her travel folder. She withdrew her ticket and handed it to Rhyder. She sat on the edge of the bed and watched him dial the phone, listening to him cancel her ticket and arrange two flights from Honolulu to Chicago for Mr. and Mrs. Rhyder Stewart in two days' time. He broke the connection, dialed another number, and reserved two seats on an early-morning flight to Honolulu.

"What are you doing?" she demanded.

"Just what it seems." He replaced the phone in the cradle. "The best way to get you out of here safely is under a different name. I'm not allowing anyone to harass you."

"But you didn't intend to return to Chicago," Evelyne argued. "You told me that yourself."

"I'm entitled to change my mind." He paced the room, picking up one of her T-shirts here, a skirt there. "We've got a flight to Honolulu first thing in the morning, and I think it would be a good idea if we had dinner in the room tonight."

"No." She wasn't going to have him win every point.

"There may be a reporter already here, lying in wait

for you, and the next one might not be as polite in his quest for his story."

"I don't care. Besides, I can't imagine anyone stupid enough to go against you when you're in your tyrant's mood," she said sarcastically. "You've already re-arranged my vacation without asking me if I was willing to go along with your plans."

"That's correct."

"Then I'll have my say when it comes to where I will dine tonight." She stood straight and tall, prepared for a battle and prepared to win.

Rhyder expelled a sharp breath. He raked his fingers through his hair, wishing he could find an easy way to calm his racing heart. Was he going to have to confess that he had been scared to death for her when that reporter approached her downstairs? That he was afraid she was going to receive the shock of a lifetime? Of course, she may have already done that in hearing her ex-husband had remarried. She claimed she was no longer in love with him, but she might only have been mouthing words while secretly praying Rick Winters would appear on his white charger and carry her off to happily married land again.

"Does it bother you that he's remarried?" he asked with an abrupt change of the subject.

Evelyne blinked. Whatever she'd expected him to say, this wasn't it. "No." Her low voice carried conviction to her words. "He's a part of my past that I won't be able to forget, but I won't sit in the shadows and grow bitter that he found someone else so quickly." She laughed. "Actually, he didn't find Kayla all that fast, since she's been under contract to Midnight Records for two years. The only part of their marriage that may bother me is that he replaced me with a nineteen-year-old rock singer whose idea of giving a party is to buy several gallons of wine, put out

160

bowls of drugs, and blast the house with music guaranteed to bring down the walls. I won't hate her for marrying him, though. I remember meeting her at one of the parties we gave. She's very pretty and bright and will probably turn out to be the kind of wife he wants now." Only the last word came out in a bitter voice. "As for loving Rick, I stopped loving him a year ago when he told me he couldn't make love to me for fear I'd have a convulsion or something as equally disgusting."

Rhyder's face hardened at the thought of her having gone through such abuse. He strode across the room and took her into his arms. "Then he's lost one pretty hot-blooded lady," he murmured, tilting her chin upward with his fingertips. "I've gained with his loss, and I don't intend to give her up." With each word his mouth descended further, until his lips rested lightly on hers. When her mouth began to yield under his, he took swift possession. After their nights of learning each other's bodies, learning how little it took to ignite their desire, they were soon whispering love words and sharing intimate caresses.

"Do you want dinner here or in the dining room?" Rhyder whispered, capturing the side of her neck with his teeth and nibbling the sensitive spot.

She found herself wondering if she had the strength to move away from him to shower and dress, just to walk across to the other building where the dining room was. She drew her head back until she could look up into his glittering eyes.

"First of all I suggest that you go to your room for a nice leisurely shower." She slipped a finger between the buttons on his shirt and etched a pattern against his skin. "Dress in something comfortable." She gazed up at him under lowered lashes which gave her a sultry look. "And return here." She added a dynamic

161

smile. "Then we can walk down to the dining room for a lovely dinner at a table overlooking the sea. After that I'm entirely in your hands."

Rhyder inclined his head in acknowledgement that she had won the round. "All right," he said gravely. "And as you said, afterward you will be in my hands entirely. I suggest you eat a hearty dinner, because you're going to need your strength."

Several hours later Evelyne decided Rhyder's words were an understatement. She also found great enjoyment in putting herself completely in his hands.

The next morning a sleepy-eyed Evelyne boarded the plane with Rhyder in tow. She was so tired she didn't notice that he was studying the people milling about them as if one of them could be a prospective assassin. In his mind a hardhearted reporter more interested in the news than in a person's feelings was the same as a cold-blooded killer.

"We'll be staying at a hotel where I hope you won't be recognized," he murmured. "Too bad you don't have a wig to wear."

She shot him an exasperated look. "I'm not a rock star or famous actress who needs constant guarding, Rhyder." She also sensed that wearing a pair of old but comfortable shorts and a T-shirt style popular in the Islands and her hair hanging in a fishtail braid down her back she would look far from the picture she used to give the press of the woman who wore the most trendy clothing and believed in setting fashion trends instead of following them.

"No, but your ex's name is news, and the vultures are now going after you. I don't want you upset over this."

"I'm not upset."

"Yes, you are. You just don't know it yet."

Evelyne sighed as she settled down in the window seat. She knew a saner person would have fought Rhyder's overly protective manner, but to her it meant that she wouldn't lose him just yet. What she couldn't understand was why he was taking her to Chicago when he didn't care to return there. Why was he going to all this trouble for her? She rested her head against the back of the seat and closed her eyes.

Rhyder noticed her movement and wondered if he should have kept her awake so long last night. He didn't know what had driven him to continue reaching for her in the night, but whatever it was, it had driven her, too, because she had never refused him. Each time he'd kissed her or caressed her bare skin she'd turned to him with a soft cry of joy and given herself up to the pleasure he gave her.

"Are you all right?" he asked softly, leaning over so no one else would hear his words. If any listeners noticed his attentive manner, they would ascribe it to a bridegroom's bewitchment by his lovely bride. In some ways they wouldn't have been wrong, because he was so caught up in Evelyne's spell he couldn't have escaped if he had wanted to.

"Of course, as long as you promise to leave me alone for the flight so I can sleep." Her words were tempered by her smile. "Do that and I promise to tire *you* out tonight. It isn't fair, you know; I'm worn out and you look fresh as the proverbial daisy. And here you worried about being so much older than me. If we keep this up, I'll be the one needing heavy-duty vitamins," she grumbled.

Rhyder chuckled and dropped a kiss on her forehead. "Have a nice nap. I'll wake you when we reach Honolulu."

It wasn't two minutes later that Evelyne fell asleep, her head resting comfortably on Rhyder's shoulder.

CHAPTER NINE

Evelyne surveyed with amused tolerance the large room overlooking the beach. They had finished their dinner an hour before and walked along the shoreline, hand in hand, before wandering back to the privacy of their room.

"A little room in an out-of-the-way hotel," she murmured, turning to Rhyder. "Funny, I never thought of the Hilton as being out of the way."

"It is if someone doesn't think to look at the most obvious, figuring you'd never stay there," he retorted, nettled by her teasing.

Evelyne crossed the room and threw her arms around him. "You're beginning to act stuffy again," she chided. "And you were doing so well at acting like the laid-back individual who didn't have a care in the world."

"I don't want anyone to hurt you, Evelyne," he said seriously, resting his hands against the small of her back. "And I'll do whatever I have to to ensure that."

"I know. I just want you to realize that I've been exposed to the press from the day I was born. There were times when it was livable and others when I wanted nothing more than to crawl away into a hole and never come out. I'll survive again."

"Such as when your mother was hospitalized?"

She rested her cheek against his chest, her arms

linked around his waist. "That was a shock I should have been prepared for, considering her erratic behavior in the past. I felt the same when Rick and I divorced. I didn't care what the media said about me, but I cared so very much what they said about my mother."

"What really happened with your mother?" he pressed gently, sensing her need to talk about it.

Evelyne shrugged. "Who really knows, other than that she had an extremely delicate constitution and couldn't stand the pressure of being in the limelight all the time. When she married my father she was a minor actress who'd gained some excellent reviews in the films she had done, but nothing that would have sent her into instant stardom. Personally I don't think she was truly happy acting, and Dad's proposal was probably heaven sent for her. I understand she had a difficult time giving birth to me and an even worse time undergoing the pressures of motherhood and being the wife of a very influential man. The trouble was, she began believing my father was having affairs and started drinking and taking pills to calm herself down. Unfortunately she didn't have the strength to confront him with her suspicions, and it eventually undermined her health so badly, she had to go into a hospital."

"And he never cheated on her," Rhyder guessed.

"I honestly don't know," she replied. "I hate to say this, but if he did have a mistress, he had an excellent reason, since my mother stopped being a wife to him when I was born. She was afraid of having more children and her religion forbade birth control, so my father slept in another room."

"And it didn't forbid liquor and drugs."

She nodded. "I love my mother dearly and I'm sorry that she couldn't have been stronger for my father, but I knew I couldn't live their lives for them."

"Obviously you inherited your father's strength."

"I think I made my own," Evelyne lifted her head for his kiss. "Now, I do believe I promised you an evening you would never forget. Shall we get started?" The tip of her tongue outlined his lips.

Rhyder picked her up and carried her to the bed. He was determined to hold her to her promise.

The next day was spent exploring the International Marketplace in Waikiki and Kings Village, an old-world-style shopping village situated behind the Hyatt Regency, following which they took a late-afternoon swim. They dined in the hotel in a corner private and dim enough to please the couple.

"I don't know why I feel so tired," Evelyne moaned as they walked into their room. She collapsed on the edge of the bed, kicked her high-heeled sandals off, and lay back, sighing with relief.

"It was probably all the walking we did today," Rhyder replied, stretching out on his back beside her. "Or should I say *you* did today."

She turned her head to face him. "I didn't hear any complaints."

"I didn't have the strength to complain, what with you dragging me all over the place." He clasped his hands behind his head and stared up at the ceiling. "So, what do you want to do now?"

Evelyne mimicked his posture. "I don't know. What do you want to do?"

His body shifted as he shrugged his shoulders. "Wanna play gin or poker?"

"We don't have any cards."

"Oh, right."

"We could walk on the beach," she suggested.

"I just took a shower, and I'll get my feet dirty again. Want to watch some TV?"

166

"I don't think so. Do you want to try the bar here?"

"Nope."

For several minutes they continued lying on the bed staring upward. As if by mutual consent they turned to face each other. The smile curving one's lips was mirrored on the other's as they began undressing without bothering to rise. Clothing was pushed unceremoniously off the bed and they came together with the assurance of longtime lovers.

"Do I gather you don't mind my idea?" Rhyder asked, taking lazy possession of Evelyne's mouth, his tongue tracing the delicate curves.

"Your idea?" She spoke as soon as he allowed her to come up for air. "If I remember correctly I was the first one to begin undressing."

"It really doesn't matter who started it, I still like this much better than playing cards," he said huskily, smoothing his hands over her satiny skin and finding the heart of her femininity with alarming ease. "Do you realize how beautiful you are?" His voice broke with emotion. This was why he wouldn't allow her to leave the Islands without him. He had fallen in love with a woman who he doubted could ever return his love. The pain of his knowledge was so intense, he felt as if a knife had struck him through the heart.

"Rhyder?" Evelyne grew alarmed at the look of agony twisting his features. "Are you all right?" She raised herself up, her hand cupping his cheek only to find it had gone ice cold.

He clasped her tighter to him. "Love me, Evelyne," he begged. "Show me what love should be like."

She smiled. He couldn't have asked her for a better gift. For quite a while she had been wishing to give him something very special and now she could; herself.

Evelyne placed her hands against his chest and

pressed him down onto the bed. "And now you must lie completely still and let me do all the work," she whispered, placing feathery kisses along his jaw and up to his ear. Her tongue darted inside his ear and around the whorled surface.

Rhyder groaned. He wondered how much of this he would be able to stand before he exploded, but he sensed this was important to Evelyne, and he wouldn't ruin her wish for anything. He only hoped he could handle the torture he was sure she would inflict on him.

Evelyne sat back on her heels to gaze lovingly at the male form lying before her. He was all hers! She leaned forward, passing a hand over the taut expanse of his chest, her fingers combing the crisp hair until she reached the nipples. Her lips soon followed the same path.

"Rough silk," she murmured against the skin she dampened with her tongue. "Something so very rare and wonderful."

Rhyder shuddered while Evelyne's lips took one path and her hands traveled another.

"If you're trying to drive me crazy you're doing a great job of it," he rasped, his hips arching up under her light touch that sent flaming spears through his blood. "Honey, I'll give you all the state secrets you want to hear if you'll just finish."

"You don't know any state secrets," she teased, her lips brushing across the flat plane of his stomach before moving downward.

Rhyder moaned loudly. Every bone in his body felt stretched as if he had been put on the infamous rack. He could feel the sweat popping out of each pore and wondered how much more he could take. For scant seconds her lips were cool on him, but they rapidly turned white hot as she caressed him in a way no woman ever had before. Oh, it wasn't the first time a woman had loved him like this, but it was the first time a woman had done it with her heart, not because she felt she should. His arms were flung over his head, his hands gripping the headboard with a strength he wouldn't have dreamed he possessed.

"Evelyne, if you have any compassion at all you'll put me out of my misery *now,*" he grated, his voice a hoarse whisper but enough to catch her attention.

She looked up, flipping her hair away from her shoulder and across his heated skin.

Rhyder doubted he had ever seen her look as beautiful as she did when flushed with her power over him. His irrational side hoped she would never leave him.

Evelyne's smile was pure triumph as she continued weaving her spell over him. She couldn't have imagined ever having such control over a man and reveled in her newfound power.

When she finally slid up over his damp skin and settled onto his rigid masculinity, he gritted his teeth against the pleasurable pain racking his body. Not caring to allow her to continue doing all the work, Rhyder unclenched his hands from the headboard and grasped her hips, but made no effort to take over the rhythm she began. Her head dipped and their mouths met in a frantic duel of tongues and teeth. The musky scent of their bodies blended into an aphrodisiac that was more potent then anything that could be bought. In no time they were oblivious to anything but the needs of their bodies.

Evelyne's breathing speeded up as she raced to the glorious end she knew she would find with Rhyder's help.

"So sweet," he crooned, smothering her face with kisses. "You feel like silken fire around me, Evelyne.

169

Give it all to me. Show me that piece of heaven we've shared before."

Her movements sped up and she was lost . . . lost in the multicolored world she would never forget. Soon Rhyder joined her as their cries echoed in the dimly lit room.

Evelyne collapsed against Rhyder's chest, hearing the rapid beating of his heart under her ear. She couldn't remember ever having felt so sated or in tune with her body as she did then.

"Did I ever tell you how beautiful you are?" he asked softly, combing his fingers through the damp tendrils curled along her back.

She nodded. "But I certainly wouldn't mind hearing it again."

Rhyder tipped his head back, staring at the patterns of light on the ceiling. "When I first saw you in those ridiculous leather pants I thought you had a great-looking tush and a look of touch-me-not."

"I do believe I've made a liar out of you," Evelyne mocked.

Rhyder tapped her on the nose, indicating silence. "I don't consider myself the best-looking guy in the world, but I'm not the ugliest either."

"Hmm, you're in between." She lifted her head to bestow a beatific smile.

He shot her a look of exasperation. "Are you going to let me have my say?"

Evelyne kissed his chin. "Is it important?"

"Yes."

She changed her position until she lay in a neat curve along the side of his body. "Then I promise to listen without any more interruptions."

Rhyder uttered a short laugh. "Judging the length of your promises, I'd better talk fast."

Evelyne dug her fist into his stomach, but not hard enough to cause any harm.

He half sat up, pulling her along with him. "What I want to say is that no one has ever given me what you have—yourself, so unselfishly. I thank you for that."

Evelyne couldn't remember ever having felt so pleased by a man's compliment. Others had told her she was beautiful or intimated she was sexy, but none had meant it as sincerely as Rhyder. A tiny voice in the deep recesses of her heart told her she loved him, yet her brain refused to acknowledge it for fear of a much stronger hurt than she had experienced during her divorce.

Rhyder knew it was time to speak of the past.

"I came to Hawaii to live out my days as a beachcomber because I was sued and lost everything but my kitchen sink." His attempt at levity fell as flat as a pancake.

Evelyne shot up into a sitting position. *"What?"*

He nodded reluctantly. "It's called giving someone bad advice where they lose a lot of money and they sue you for whatever they can get."

"There's more to the story than just that brief statement," she prompted.

Rhyder agreed. "Basically a friend of mine needed assistance with a lawsuit. Since that part of the law isn't my specialty, I referred her to another attorney. I didn't know that he was in the middle of a nervous breakdown and didn't follow through on the paper work."

"Follow through?"

"He didn't file the paper work in time, so the case was thrown out of court," he explained.

"But that isn't your fault!" Evelyne argued. "It was the other attorney's fault."

"In a roundabout way it is my fault," Rhyder replied tersely, hating to relive those agonizing months, but needing to share that time. "You see, she couldn't sue him because he had already filed bankruptcy, since his practice was in such terrible shape. I was the only one left, and she found someone who advised her she could sue me. When the court found in her favor I decided I wasn't too enthralled with the judicial system and decided to take off to see new places."

Evelyne digested this new piece of information about him. She would have guessed anything else might have happened to send Rhyder to the Islands but this.

"Does it change your mind about me?" he asked quietly. "I had to liquidate most of my assets for the settlement, so to say I'm pretty well broke is an understatement."

She shook her head. "I don't remember ever asking you for a credit report, but I still don't understand why you happened to come here."

Rhyder shrugged. "Beats me. I had gone into my office to clean out my desk, much to my partner's disgust, and wandered along a street where I saw a travel poster advertising Hawaii. I decided it would be nice to get away from the cold and I could also get a great view of beautiful women in bikinis." He ducked when she tried to hit him with a pillow.

Guessing the part he hadn't told her, she added, "And you thought you would turn into a beach bum preying on wealthy old ladies."

"Why not? What I don't have in youth I can make up for in experience," he said glibly.

She groaned. "I saw a few of those adorable *young* men hanging around, and they also seemed to have a bit more than youth, my darling. I'm afraid you would have struck out." She stroked his hair in mock sympathy.

172

"The same way you did as a femme fatale?"

"That was a very low blow," Evelyne chided, poking him in the chest. "At least I had an excellent start as one. In fact, I do believe I did an excellent job of seducing one man."

Rhyder stared off into space. "What man did you seduce?"

Her eyes sparkled with devilish delight. "An over-the-hill beach bum."

His answer was a vigorous tickling session that only ended up in a very satisfactory manner. Their sighs mingled with the muted sound of the ocean and the exotic scent of the tropical flowers.

Evelyne awoke just after dawn with the tingling feeling in her bones that all was not right. She rolled over and found the other side of the bed cool to the touch. She didn't call out Rhyder's name, since she sensed he wasn't anywhere in the room. She collapsed back against the pillows, wishing she knew where he was. They were leaving the next day for Chicago. Once again she asked herself why she was allowing him to sweep her off to a strange city—after all, she knew him intimately but still didn't know everything she should probably know.

Too restless to remain in bed any longer she got up to walk out to the balcony and catch a view of the dawning day that would be another beginning for her. That was when she saw him on the beach.

Rhyder was walking along the water's edge, his head down and hands in his shorts pockets. His distant figure didn't resemble the self-assured man who had been planning her days and nights for the past few weeks. Those words struck a chord in her brain. Planning her days . . . just the way Rick used to plan her life. What was happening to her? Was she inadvertently falling into the same trap she had recently gotten out of? Or was she so conditioned to having a man make decisions for her that she couldn't deal with having to fend for herself? She suddenly felt frightened; but then the rational part of her brain reminded her that Rhyder wasn't anything like Rick. What he'd done for her so far was with her best interests in mind, and she resolved to remember that.

Evelyne almost ran back into the room, only to stop short at the sight of the bed with its rumpled covers. A silent reminder of what had happened during the night. She could feel the walls of the room closing in on her and knew she had to get out. She practically ran for the closet and pulled out some clothing.

Ten minutes later Evelyne was walking swiftly along the beach until she reached Rhyder.

"Is something wrong?" he asked, frowning at the idea of her being out alone at such an early hour.

"I woke up and felt alone," she replied candidly. "And when I walked out to the balcony, I saw you here. If you don't care for company, just let me know and I'll go my own way." She felt as if she meant that she would also get out of his life.

"No." His husky voice with a faint catch in it told her all she needed to know. "I couldn't sleep and I didn't want to disturb you, so I thought I'd come out here for a walk." *And sort things out,* he finished silently. He had awakened an hour earlier with the thought that he was rushing both of them into something they might not be able to handle. In order to figure out what to do he had put on some clothes and come out to the beach to walk and think.

Evelyne looked up at him in the dawn light, her hair blowing back from the strong breeze. "Too much, too soon?" she guessed.

He shrugged. "More like I'm doing just what you

said your ex-husband did . . . running your life. I'm not giving you a fair break, am I?"

"No."

Rhyder flinched. "Please don't hold anything back on my account," he said wryly. "I've done some heavy thinking and what I've come up with is, if you'd prefer to go back to L.A. I won't try to talk you out of it."

Evelyne turned away to look out at the gray expanse of ocean. She could see the pale-pink-and-orange dawn feathering over the water's surface. "Is that what you want me to do?"

Rhyder let out a deep breath. He noticed she didn't agree with his idea, but she didn't argue against it either. "We both know it can't be what I want you to do, Evelyne. It has to be your decision."

She continued looking out to sea while looking in at her own feelings. Out of sheer perversity she was going to take her time answering. "I've never seen Chicago, so I guess it wouldn't be a wasted trip." She turned back to face him. "Of course, I'd need to find a place to stay."

He just barely hid his relief. "I think that can be arranged. I happen to know a place that has a great view, large rooms, and the price isn't too bad either."

"What about privacy?"

"That depends on how much you want."

"I'd also like to know there's someone nearby if there are burglars in the neighborhood." She tipped her head to one side, flashing the smile that always headed straight to his gut.

"I believe that problem can be taken care of," he replied, still careful not to give the game away too quickly.

Evelyne nodded. "Then I believe I'll give it a try." She held out a hand. "Let's go back."

Rhyder took her hand, keeping it loosely between

them as they walked up the beach to the hotel. Once inside their room, he made love to her with a violent kind of worship. Deep inside of him was the fear that the day would come when Evelyne decided she wouldn't need him any longer and he would again be alone. He knew there could never be another woman to take her place. When they fell asleep they were still joined, in body and spirit.

The next morning, after packing the rest of her clothing, Evelyne filled a small carry-on bag with warmer clothing and carried her fur coat in preparation for changing clothes once they reached the airport. She knew she had no desire to suffer wearing wool the short distance to the airport, and it would be easy enough to change there.

During the check-in procedure Rhyder experienced a strange feeling in the pit of his stomach. He hadn't thought he would be returning to Chicago so soon. Deep down he knew he wouldn't have stayed in Hawaii forever, because his partner was right; he wasn't cut out for the lotus eater's life. He was too used to being on the go and had found that lying by the pool and looking at bikini-clad beauties wasn't the fun he thought it would be. So now he was escorting a beautiful woman back to his hometown and in his own crazy way protecting her from a life he felt she couldn't handle for the time being. At least he could say that was the reason, and that he wanted to spare her the indignity of being besieged by reporters and anyone else out to hurt her.

"I may as well change now. I'll be back in a few minutes," Evelyne told him after they'd found two chairs near their boarding gate. She picked up her bag and left for the nearest rest room.

Rhyder wandered around the general area and

stopped to scan the newspapers displayed in one of the gift shops. He halted at one of the mainland papers and picked up a copy. After paying for it he sat back down and leafed through the pages. On one he found a color picture of Rick Winters with his new bride, a woman he privately thought belonged in a grade-B movie. While Rick looked pretty normal considering he wore a pair of delapidated jeans and a black T-shirt which only heightened his California blond coloring, Kayla wore a lacy bright-pink camisole top with a skirt that must have been popular in the forties, and black textured hose and high-button shoes. Her flat-black hair couldn't even be called artfully tousled. It looked as if it hadn't seen a brush in the past five years. He uttered a sound of disgust. *This* was what Rick had married after sharing so much of his life with someone like Evelyne? A rose-tinted nail entered his line of sight and flicked the paper.

"When I first met her she was a blonde." Evelyne's quiet voice floated over him like a warm blanket.

Rhyder quickly closed the paper and looked up. Now she looked like the woman he'd first seen. She wore a pair of tobacco-brown wool pants over brown high-heeled boots and a deep-gold silk shirt that hinted of the curves he knew were beneath. Several strands of tortoiseshell beads accented the shirt's collar.

"I don't fall apart easily anymore, Rhyder," she reminded him, taking the paper out of his hand and reopening it. The gentle smile on her lips disappeared as she finished reading the short accompanying article mentioning Kayla's happy pregnancy and the revelation that they also had a child of eighteen months. There was a brief explanation that the first Mrs. Winters was now in seclusion and couldn't be reached for

177

comment regarding her ex-husband's marriage. "That bastard," she uttered forcefully.

"Evelyne, not here," he warned softly, looking around to make sure no one saw her distress or the reason for it. "We don't want any more reporters sniffing you out, and so far that other one seems to have kept his word."

Breathing deeply she carefully folded the paper and carried it to the nearest trash receptacle, dropping it in.

"You can live with someone for years and still not know everything about him," she said finally, after seating herself in the molded chair.

Rhyder took hold of her hand, feeling the tension radiate out from her fingertips. "Let's walk around," he suggested, knowing he had to do anything possible to get her mind off the newspaper story. What he knew would work wasn't possible in a public place, so he did the next best thing. He stood up and pulled her out of her chair. "We still have about an hour before we board."

Evelyne knew he was trying to ease her mind, but his efforts weren't having the desired effect. Even as she looked at posters and picture buttons of Tom Selleck displayed next to hula dolls and boxes of macadamia nuts ready for shipping, all she could think about was Rick giving Kayla the child he denied to her. How could he do such a thing when he knew how much Evelyne had wanted a child? He had always told her when the time was right they would have their baby. That time had never come.

She knew Rhyder sensed her unease and she appreciated his silent support, but how could he know how she felt? While her love for Rick was gone, he would always still hold a tiny place in her heart, and she doubted Rhyder would be able to understand that.

He'd tried to protect her by trying to keep the story from her, even though she would have found out at some time. Better to find out this way than to hear it from a reporter the way she'd heard about the wedding.

"Do you want to pick up a book or some magazines for the flight?" Rhyder asked, breaking into her thoughts.

She started at the sound of his voice. "Yes, that might be a good idea." She walked slowly toward the magazine and book racks. There she chose several fashion magazines and a thick historical romance paperback guaranteed to take her mind off her present troubles.

Rhyder decided he wasn't going to take a free breath until they'd boarded the plane. He was relieved they were flying nonstop and wouldn't have a layover in L.A.

He had noticed the hurt on Evelyne's face when she read the article and wished she could have been spared the misery for a little while longer.

He picked up a few business magazines and a book, then gestured to Evelyne when he heard their flight number announced over the loudspeaker.

They boarded the jet and were directed into first class, where Rhyder ushered her into the window seat. Once seated Rhyder took Evelyne's hand and lifted it to his lips. She fought the tears from crowding her eyes.

"I've wanted a baby for the past seven years," she whispered brokenly, looking out the window to hide her feelings from him. "But Rick kept putting it off."

He hugged her as close to him as the armrest would allow. "Don't blame yourself," he said, feeling her body tremble against him. "He may have married her

179

because she's pregnant." He wanted to retract his words the moment they left his mouth.

"Very true." Her voice was bitter. "And I feel as if the truth about my so-called beautiful marriage is being rubbed in my face. It appears Rick wasn't as faithful as I assumed him to be. Since he was home just about every night, he had to have been very busy to keep her happy too."

They barely heard the cabin attendant's instructions regarding emergency procedures, and as soon as someone came around to take drink orders, Rhyder ordered a whiskey and requested juice for Evelyne. She muttered that she preferred something stronger, but he reminded her she wasn't allowed anything stronger until she'd spoken to a doctor, something he intended to have taken care of as soon as they arrived in Chicago.

The long flight turned out to be uneventful, with a movie they had both seen before, and they spent their time talking softly and reading. All the while, Rhyder was conscious that Evelyne's thoughts were somewhere else, and he silently cursed Rick Winters for having hurt her even further by revealing to the world that his marriage hadn't been perfect after all. It was as if he flaunted the fact that he'd had to find another woman to have his child. Rhyder vowed that if he ever met the man he would personally knock him flat for having hurt Evelyne in every sensitive spot her gentle yet fiery nature held. He was also determined that no man would have that chance again as long as he was around to protect her.

CHAPTER TEN

Evelyne's first impression of Chicago was extreme cold, dark, and gloom. The jet landed at O'Hare Airport in the early morning hours and the tired passengers disembarked through the tunnel into the main terminal. Rhyder kept hold of Evelyne's arm, guiding her downstairs to the baggage carousels, and arranging their luggage to be taken to a taxi.

She stepped outside into the freezing cold, grateful for the warmth her coat offered her. She wrapped the fur closer around her and buried her nose in the collar to keep it from becoming frostbitten. She had remembered the bitter cold she'd encountered in New York, but it was nothing compared to this city that was well known for its freezing winters. She stepped into the warm cab and listened to Rhyder give the driver an address. She sat back with her eyes closed, not wanting anything more than to sleep for the next twenty-four hours. It wasn't long before she slipped into a light doze, where she remained for the balance of the trip to Rhyder's apartment building.

It only took a few words from him to awaken her when the cab parked in front of a large building. Rhyder assisted her out of the taxi and into the building, leaving her in the brightly lit lobby while bringing the luggage in. She was still in a fog as they rode the elevator up.

"It isn't much, but it's been home since I lost my house in the settlement." Rhyder's light words belied his anxious undertone. He unlocked the door and ushered her inside. He reached to one side and flipped on a light. "I'll get the heater started."

Evelyne could feel the chill penetrating her skin and decided to keep her coat on for the time being. She could understand Rhyder's words. There was little to say it was a home. The modern furniture was a neutral color to blend in with beige walls, but there were no paintings on the walls or anything else to distinguish his personality. Her fingers itched to add some color to the room and bring it to life. She wandered over to the window and looked out to see streetlights and what looked to be a river off in the distance. She guessed it to be a beautiful view in the daylight.

"I'll have to call Celia to send me warm clothing," she said, turning around and noticing the small kitchen and an informal dining area set off to one side. "Otherwise I'll freeze to death in a very short time."

"You can't tell me you wore bikinis and sundresses in New York?" he said, walking toward her.

Evelyne shook her head. "I left my heavy clothing with Celia so I wouldn't have to worry about carrying them with me. This way there will be no problem with her sending it to me right away. I can always buy what I need until my things arrive." She ran her fingertips over the windowsill; it was clean. "You have an excellent housekeeping service. I always had to keep after my cleaning woman to make sure the sills were dusted."

Rhyder smiled. "Ah, yes, Mrs. Cats. She swore I'd return when I got my senses back. She told me I was going through a midlife crisis and it would pass just like gallstones."

Evelyne chuckled. "I have an idea she's the perfect

182

woman to keep you in line." She yawned. "I don't suppose you'd care to show me the bedroom?" She gazed in the direction of a narrow hallway.

He took her arm and steered her down the hall. "This first door leads to the guest room, but I have a much better place in mind for you. It's larger and more convenient."

She shot him a sly glance. "Convenient for whom?"

"Me." He steered her toward a closed door at the end of the hall. He held her back long enough for him to flip on a light, then allowed her to enter.

Even here Evelyne couldn't find any trace of the Rhyder she knew. She doubted she would have found it any different before he left for Hawaii. There was nothing more in the room than a double bed covered with a dark-gold spread, a chest of drawers, an easy chair in one corner, and two large closets with mirrored doors. A door leading to a bathroom was set off to one side. She turned around and smiled.

Rhyder approached her until they stood a breath apart. He thrust his hands into her hair on both sides of her face, imprisoning it so that she was forced to stare up into his dark eyes. He bent and kissed her, a long, deep, melting kiss that left her trembling and weak. His mouth left hers to trace a fiery path across her cheek, ending at the lobe of her ear, which he worked with his teeth and tongue until a tiny whimper of desire rose from her throat.

"Answer one question for me," he spoke softly into her mouth.

"What?" She was prepared to tell him anything he wanted to know.

"Is Rick tall?"

Soft laughter escaped her lips. "Six foot three."

Rhyder nodded wryly. "I thought so. Rick is a very tall name." He lowered his face to continue nibbling

183

her lips until they tingled with delight. "I'm taking advantage of you, Evelyne," he whispered heatedly. "We've been on a plane for hours and you're dead on your feet and should rest. The trouble is, when I'm around you I can't think clearly."

"I can't think clearly either," she breathed, resting her forehead against his chest. He was right. While her senses were clamoring for release, her body acknowledged that it needed rest. "You're right. If I weren't so tired I would take you up on your very exciting offer." She shrugged her coat off and laid it over a nearby chair. The rest of her clothing soon followed until she stood nude before him.

"I'll—ah—I'll bring your suitcases in," he said in a choking voice, escaping before his body got the better of him.

Evelyne sat on the bed pulling out the pins that secured the sophisticated knot at the back of her head. She wondered what was taking Rhyder so long, unaware that he was in the living room using deep-breathing exercises to lower his rapid heart rate. The longer she sat there the more tired she grew, until she lay back and closed her eyes. She was asleep in less than a minute.

Confident he could handle the raging demands of his body, Rhyder returned to the bedroom to find Evelyne on top of the bed fast asleep.

"So much for taking the gentleman's way out," he muttered, pulling back the covers and gently placing her on the cool sheets. He reached across the bed to turn on the electric blanket and draped the covers around her bare shoulders. When he felt she was sufficiently covered, he went into the bathroom for a much-needed cold shower. Afterward he climbed into bed next to Evelyne, drew her into his arms, and settled down to sleep.

* * *

Evelyne woke up slowly early that afternoon. It took her a few moments to orient herself and remember the events of the previous twenty-four hours. She lay quietly for a few minutes, then carefully disentangled herself from Rhyder's arms. She noticed he didn't move, proving how deeply he still slept. She headed for the bathroom for a shower and dressed in a pair of cotton slacks and one of Rhyder's shirts she found hanging in the closet. Not wanting to bother drying her hair she braided it wet and secured it with a band.

Evelyne knew it was too much to hope that she would find food in the kitchen, but some coffee, peanut butter, and crackers were enough to take the edge off her hunger. She sat at the glass-and-wood dinette table sipping her coffee and just enjoying her more thorough study of Rhyder's apartment. She found it difficult to imagine he could have been living in this place without having put his stamp on it in any way. Even the kitchen held only the barest necessities in the way of appliances. Obviously he was not much of a cook.

For some reason that brought to mind the woman who had sued him. Had he loved her? Was that why the episode bothered him so much that he would virtually run away from all that he had known? Suddenly the coffee tasted bitter; as bitter as the idea of his making love to any other woman.

"What're you doing?" Rhyder's sleepy voice intruded on her thoughts.

She looked up to see him leaning against the corner of the wall. "Drinking coffee." She gestured to her cup. "Want some?"

He winced. "Nah, it might keep me awake." He turned away and staggered back to his bedroom.

"And a good afternoon to you too." She held up her cup in a toast.

185

It was another two hours before Rhyder reappeared from the confines of his room. Evelyne spent the time glancing over his magazine selection, dry at best, and watching television. She also called Celia to request that her clothes be sent to her right away.

"Does he know all about you?" her friend demanded over the phone after Evelyne told her about her change of location. "Are you sure he's safe? What I mean is, is he respectable? Evelyne, do you honestly know what you're doing going to a strange city with a strange man?"

"Yes, Rhyder knows all about my illness. He's perfectly safe and respectable. In fact, he's an attorney. And I know exactly what I'm doing," Evelyne chanted with a smile. "Celia, he's exactly what I need right now."

"I knew I should have gone with you," Celia lamented.

"Celia, Rhyder was there when I needed him," she countered.

There was a hesitation. "Obviously you saw the newspaper." Celia sighed. "I could have killed Rick for revealing everything that way. I can't believe how he's shown his true colors these past months."

"I'm better off without Rick, Celia," Evelyne said before her friend voiced the same thought. "I should hang up now, but could you please send the clothes to me right away?" She was glad to find Rhyder's address on a magazine label so she wouldn't have to wait for him to wake up to find out exactly where she was.

"I'll send them out on overnight delivery today," Celia promised, adding mischievously. "Think you'll be over your lust attack long enough to attend my wedding next month?"

"Brian proposed?" Evelyne squealed. "Or did you ask him to marry you?" She knew her friend well—

Celia would have thought nothing of proposing to the man she wanted.

"I didn't. He informed *me* we were getting married," Celia admitted, with a new note in her voice. "In fact, I'm sure this will be my last marriage. Brian also told me that he doesn't believe in divorce and that he intends to see how I look with white hair and wrinkles." Evelyne could imagine her friend's horrified shudders at the idea of allowing her flawless skin to wrinkle or her luxuriant hair to turn gray. "We're having a small ceremony in Beverly Hills. I'll give you more information in a week or so. You won't miss it, will you? I'm going to need all the moral support I can get," she pleaded, a strange characteristic for someone so self-assured.

"This is one wedding I don't intend to miss," Evelyne promised. Before she rang off, she gave Celia Rhyder's telephone number. She couldn't stop smiling at the thought of her strong-minded friend finally meeting her match. Though her own marriage had ended badly, she wished her friends well in their own endeavors.

"Do I smell coffee?" Rhyder asked hoarsely from the hallway.

"Yes, but I'm sure it's a bit stronger than it was two hours ago when I made it," she replied. "How did you sleep?" She looked him over in his jeans and lightweight V-necked sweater with his hair still sleep tousled and cheeks dark with his beard. He looked great.

"Fine." He stifled a yawn as he ambled into the kitchen to pour himself a cup of coffee. "Sorry I left you on your own so long. I didn't realize I was so tired."

"Don't worry about it. I called Celia and she's going to send my clothes out to me. I should receive them sometime tomorrow," she replied. "I'd offer to fix you something to eat, but I'm afraid your cupboard is bare."

Rhyder winced. "Give me time to shower and shave, and we can go out. I guess we'd better do some grocery shopping too."

Evelyne didn't like the idea of wearing the clothing she had worn on the plane but knew she didn't have much choice if she didn't want to freeze.

"I might have a sweater you could wear," he offered, guessing her thoughts. "I have a couple that shrank last year, and I never bothered getting rid of them." He sat back in a chair and sipped his coffee. "We'll just go out somewhere casual. That shouldn't be too difficult for us after the past few weeks."

Their dinner consisted of pizza at a nearby pizza parlor and a stop at a grocery store to stock up on the essentials. A few times Rhyder started to pick up a frozen dinner or canned chili only to watch Evelyne pluck it out of his hand and put it back where it belonged.

"As improbable as it may seem, I can cook," she told him, as she stood at the meat counter inspecting the available roasts. "And you won't have to worry about clinging domesticity. I only intend to repay you for your hospitality."

"I have a better way for you to do that." He then proceeded to whisper his suggestion in her ear.

Evelyne blushed, but later learned he meant to keep his promise. It was late when they finally went to sleep, although they had been in bed for hours.

Evelyne's clothes did arrive the next afternoon. She exclaimed with delight as she rummaged through the three suitcases for warm clothing.

"Do you realize how many suitcases you have here?" Rhyder asked, stunned at the amount of clothing scattered around the bedroom between clean clothing on the bed and clothes to be washed or dry-cleaned on the floor in neat piles.

"There's more at home," she replied absently, taking the hangers he had given her and hanging up blouses and dresses in the closet. Her lingerie was folded and placed in a drawer. She didn't tell him about a tissue-wrapped package she found at the bottom of one suitcase along with a note from Celia. The deep-coral silk-and-lace nightgown she found in the package was put at the bottom of one drawer for a special occasion, although every night was turning out to be a special occasion where Rhyder was concerned.

Rhyder stood in the doorway and watched Evelyne bustle about with her household duties. She seemed to belong there. While he had slept the day before, she thought nothing of making herself at home and hadn't complained that he'd left her on her own. Lora had always been determined to clean his house within an inch of itself and fix him proper meals and mainly make herself indispensable to him. Evelyne complained that he had left a mess in the bathroom and insisted he clean it up before she took her shower, and, no, she didn't need to have her back scrubbed or anything else washed. He found out that many times she braided her wet hair instead of taking time to dry it and later released the braid to allow shimmering waves to cascade down her back. He wanted her here, but he wasn't sure if he could handle it when she left.

"I think I'd better make some phone calls," he said gruffly, turning away.

Rhyder grimaced at Ken's crow of delight at the news of his return.

"I knew you wouldn't be able to stay away," he said happily. "When are you coming into the office?"

"Tomorrow, if you want me."

"Want you? Rhyder, we need you. Work is piling up around here like you wouldn't believe."

"Rhyder, where can I put these suitcases?" Evelyne called out from the bedroom.

"Is that what I think it is?" Ken demanded.

"I don't know. What do you think it is?" Rhyder countered, wondering what could be suffocating him.

"You brought back a woman." He laughed. "And she certainly doesn't sound like some old biddy who's leaving you her millions in her will. So, buddy, are you going to tell me what she's like?"

"No." Rhyder hung up and went back into the bedroom to gather up Evelyne's suitcases and put them in the storage area in the laundry room.

That evening they prepared their dinner spiced with laughter and kisses. Afterward, they sat on the couch watching television and celebrating commercials with more kisses.

"You don't want to watch the news, do you?" he asked huskily, moving his lips along the sharp lines of her cheekbone.

"The news won't be on for another two hours," she murmured, teasing his navel with her fingertip.

"Does that mean you don't want to watch it?"

"I don't think so." She stood up and held out her hands. Rhyder grasped them and also stood up, sliding his arm around her waist as they walked to the bedroom.

In the comfortable confines of the bedroom they slowly undressed and lay down on the bed facing each other.

"Do you know that every time I look at you I notice something different?" he asked in a loud whisper, caressing her cheek with the back of his hand. "Such as the way your eyes change color, especially when we make love. And the temperature of your skin changes

190

from cool to very warm. That happens when we make love too. And your voice changes from that melodic sound to a husky purr of satisfaction when you reach your climax. Isn't it amazing all the changes you go through during one particular time?"

"How do I know all of that truly happens the way you say it does?" she challenged.

"I could prove it to you," Rhyder recommended, moving closer until their hipbones nestled together in a very pleasurable way. He could feel the heat of her skin radiating outward to envelope him like a down quilt.

Evelyne felt his arousal pressed against her belly, and she couldn't help moving seductively against it. "I notice some very significant changes in you also," she said throatily.

"Now, I'd say your skin temperature has risen at least five degrees if not more," he murmured against the side of her neck. "Your pulse has speeded up and your eyes have deepened in color."

She pressed butterfly kisses along his jaw and up to his ear. She nipped the lobe and soothed it with her tongue. "Your pulse isn't lagging behind, I see." Her fingers tangled in his hair as she brought his face closer to hers for more kisses, with their tongues tangling in sweet delight. The hunger in her spread from deep within in wave after wave of need, racing through her until every nerve ending in her body cried out for fulfillment.

He cupped her breast reverently before dipping his head to take the pouting nipple in his mouth. Evelyne cried out at the desire raging through her veins as his tongue circled the dusky rose-colored nub that deepened in color from his loving. Even the aureole and the underside of her breast received his rapt attention before he turned to the other breast to give it the same treatment.

Rhyder rolled Evelyne onto her back while remaining on his side so he could view her body better. His hand smoothed her abdomen and down to her thighs before dipping finally to reach the fiery cove of her femininity, his skillful fingers igniting a need so urgent her breath came in short, urgent pants. Her hips arched up in silent invitation to deepen the loving invasion. He continued the light probes to taunt her further trailing his lips over her face and down to her mouth. His lips were hot and familiar as his tongue possessed her mouth with ease and she willingly surrendered to him.

"Rhyder, I need you." She gasped, surrounding him with her fingertips. He felt hot and urgent and she doubted he would be able to hold out much longer.

He groaned and moved over her, plunging into her core with one swift stroke. Evelyne wrapped her legs around his waist and rode the tidal wave right along with him. It could have been minutes or hours before they cried out together. Rhyder immediately rolled to one side to relieve her of his weight, but kept her close to him.

"Is this what Eskimos do to keep warm?" Evelyne asked, her voice a mere breathy sigh.

He picked up a lock of her hair and sniffed the exotic fragrance he would forever associate with her. "I don't know about that, but I sure wouldn't mind giving up an electric blanket for it."

She wrinkled her nose, recognizing his teasing mood. "The electric blanket might be safer at times." She propped herself up on one elbow and watched him reach for his alarm clock and set the hands for six-thirty.

"You're going into your office tomorrow, aren't you?" she asked.

Rhyder nodded. "I may as well see how much of a mess they've left the practice in. You don't know these guys, they could turn it into a disaster zone in a matter of days."

"You didn't seem to worry about that in Hawaii." She lay back in the warm security of his arms.

"No, but I wasn't worried about keeping up this place then." He stretched out and snapped off the lamp. "Not to mention feeding you. Now that you're finally putting some weight on, I don't intend to watch you return to skin and bones. Very lovely skin and bones," he added hastily, feeling her rise up and sensing her glare.

"That's better." She was mollified, but just barely. She snuggled back into the safe harbor of his arms and closed her eyes. As usual, with his arms around her she fell asleep immediately, and Rhyder succumbed soon after.

The alarm was a sharp intrusion into their slumber. Evelyne stirred and rolled over, mumbling incoherently as Rhyder stumbled out of bed into the bathroom for a wake-up shower.

He gazed bleary eyed at his reflection in the mirror while shaving and loudly decided he was too old for these early hours when he could have been sleeping comfortably in a warm bed with an equally warm woman. When he emerged from the bathroom, feeling a bit more human, he found the bed empty and enticing smells floating into the bedroom from the kitchen. He dug into his closet for a shirt, suit, and tie and dressed quickly. He took a quick look in the mirror, saw the man he remembered from six months ago, and left the room.

Evelyne was pouring coffee when Rhyder appeared in the kitchen.

"Your breakfast is on the table," she told him, handing him the coffee cup while she carried two glasses of orange juice.

"I didn't expect this," he said, viewing the plate filled with sausage and eggs along with lightly buttered toast. He didn't have the heart to tell her he usually made do with just coffee, since he didn't have the time or inclination to make himself a full breakfast before he left for the office.

She smiled. "I know. That's why I cooked it." She sat at his right and nibbled on a slice of toast.

"If you had been smart, you would have stayed in bed and tried to go back to sleep." He tried the eggs and found them just the way he liked them.

"It wouldn't have been fair to you if I did something you weren't able to do," she retorted, sipping her juice, looking beautiful in a sapphire velour robe and her hair brushed to a shiny curtain.

Rhyder wondered if there was a time she didn't look lovely, and said so aloud.

"I'm sure I didn't look very fetching when I had the mumps at the age of eight," she replied.

"You are so unique." He was as amazed as he had been the first time he'd talked to her.

"Unique? Why?" Evelyne shook her head, unable to understand his choice of words.

"Because of your accent and some of the words you use in conversation."

"I do not have an accent!" she argued.

"Sure you do. You just don't notice it."

"You're the one with an accent," she pointed out. "Sometimes you almost bite off your words, and I've heard other people around here talk the same way."

"And you talk like someone who's been educated in

Europe. You've had the American accent polished with a bit of the Continental thrown in." He glanced down at his watch and threw down his napkin. "I didn't realize it was so late. I should be home around six or six-thirty. If I'm late, I'll call you." He kissed her lightly on the lips, grabbed his briefcase from the couch, and walked out the front door.

Evelyne stared at the door closing behind him. "Have a nice day," she said with a wry smile as she got up to clear the table and wash the dishes, which she knew would take her all of ten minutes. After that she would have to find a way to keep herself occupied for the next eleven hours.

Rhyder was having an equally difficult time wondering if he could spend the next eleven hours away from Evelyne after having spent the past few weeks with her. He thought ironically about newly married men who return from their honeymoon complaining about having to leave their wives and go to work. He had always scoffed at their rapt expressions when they thought about their wives and how they would call home and indulge in some love talk. If he wasn't careful, he might be guilty of doing the same thing without even having a marriage license to back it up!

"Rhyder, you did make it in today." Ken, a lean dark haired man, greeted him with a hearty handshake.

"I told you I'd be here." He was disgruntled at his partner's assumption that he wouldn't appear.

"Sure you did, but the owner of that sexy voice I heard might have had something to say about that," he joked, walking behind Rhyder into his office. "You look great, old buddy. In fact, you look the best I've seen you in years, and I bet you haven't had much

195

sleep either." His knowing grin vanished under Rhyder's fierce glare.

"We'll just watch what we say, won't we?" he warned. Hearing his threatening words echo in the high ceilinged room, he sank down in the smooth leather chair behind the oak desk. "I'm sorry, Ken. There was no reason for me to snap at you."

Ken whistled under his breath as he took the chair across from Rhyder. "You just broke two of your own commandments. You didn't make a comeback about your love life, and you apologized to me. You're either sick or that broad means a lot to you." He held his hands up in self-defense under Rhyder's scowl. "Sorry, the lady."

"Exactly," Rhyder grated, sifting through the papers on his desk pad. He glanced up. "I see you were sure I'd be back. All of this is up to date."

"You could lie under the palm trees for only so long before you got sick of luaus and watching all those gorgeous women dancing the hula," Ken replied. "We've been overloaded the past month and need your sharp brain to get us out from under it. Be prepared to work late a lot of nights, Rhyder. Good thing you're all rested up and should be able to handle all the extra hours you're going to be putting in. After all, it's nothing you haven't done before."

"I'll see what I can do," Rhyder murmured, picking up a manila folder and scanning the contents.

Ken frowned. This wasn't the hardworking, slave-driving Rhyder he had worked with for so many years. Usually Rhyder would come back from his infrequent and extremely short vacations ready to pitch back in. His work had always come first with him, but he didn't seem to feel that way now. He was curious to find out more about Rhyder's new girlfriend, but wasn't sure how to go about learning anything without drawing Rhyder's ire on himself.

"Ah, did you meet the lady in Hawaii?" he asked casually, bracing a trousered leg across a knee.

Rhyder nodded, still reading the brief before him.

"Is she from around here?"

Rhyder shook his head.

"Then she's here for a visit?"

Another nod.

"Is she staying with you?"

Another nod.

Ken sighed. He could question a witness with the greatest of ease, but getting information out of Rhyder was next to impossible. He snapped his fingers. "Don't tell me, she looks like a gorilla and you're afraid I'll find out."

Rhyder shook his head.

"I know, she's cross eyed."

Another negative silent reply.

"She's old enough to be your grandmother."

Rhyder shot him an exasperated look that said enough.

"Then she must be young enough to be your grand-daughter," Ken said facetiously.

Rhyder shook his head. He slapped the folder down and stared at his friend. "You still enjoy following the gossip about the music industry?"

"Of course I do. I'm waiting for the day Dolly Parton comes to town and learns what a great guy I really am," he kidded.

Rhyder turned his chair around so he could look out the window, but only saw a cold gray day and a neighboring building. "The lady is Rick Winters's ex-wife," he announced.

Ken's eyes bugged out. "No joke?"

"No joke."

"Holy—" Ken's expletive was interrupted by the arrival of Rhyder's secretary.

Rhyder spun his chair back around and the two men stared at each other across the room. He didn't like seeing what looked like sympathy in his friend's eyes.

CHAPTER ELEVEN

"Just remember that old proverb about not saying anything if you can't say something nice about a person," Rhyder told Ken in an angry voice. He felt if another word was spoken against Evelyne he'd probably hit the man.

Ken showed surprise at Rhyder's temperamental reaction. How much did this woman mean to him? Ken had known Rhyder for over twenty years, and not once had he ever revealed a vulnerability where his current lover was concerned. This bothered him. As an avid follower of the rock music scene Ken remembered all the stories about Evelyne Winters when she had her stroke and later the news behind her divorce. How could someone as street smart as Rhyder get mixed up with bad news like that? It wasn't that Ken really had anything against the woman—after all, he hadn't met her—but a woman with a serious health problem and a loving husband who divorced her after ten years of wedded bliss meant there were problems not announced to the general public. He'd bet his last dollar those problems stemmed from the lovely Evelyne herself.

"I just don't want you ending up hurt, Rhyder," he said. "Six years ago, Lora left you with a bitter taste in your mouth that wasn't helped any by Debra's lawsuit. I don't want to see you hurt again."

Rhyder smiled. "Evelyne and Lora are as different as night and day, Ken. As for Debra, she isn't worth discussing. I know what people think of Evelyne, but I've learned about her over the past few weeks. What happened to me before was a picnic compared to what she went through. It took a lot of guts for her to endure what she did and remain sane."

"As opposed to her mother?" Ken interjected. "Didn't she have a nervous breakdown or something?"

Rhyder shot him a warning look. "Don't push your luck, friend." He picked up one of the typewritten sheets on his desk. "Why don't we talk about the Anderson will?"

Ken sighed. He recognized the need for changing the subject, but that didn't mean he liked it. He'd just have to meet the lady and find out for himself. He had watched Rhyder suffer through Lora's clinging-vine routine and the indignity of the lawsuit Debra had brought against him. It had just about ripped Rhyder apart and turned him into a bitter man who had to escape his life by leaving the state with the idea of never returning to his practice. Ken had been confident Rhyder would come back, but he admitted there were times he was afraid he could be wrong. He was glad to see Rhyder back, but he hoped he wasn't back for the wrong reasons.

"Old Man Anderson decided to cut his third son and fourth daughter out of his will," Ken told him. "The first son and fifth daughter are back in."

Rhyder chuckled. One of his favorite and most painful clients was a crotchety old man who periodically cut specified children out of his will when he grew angry at them. When he cooled off, he reinstated them and cut someone else out. "He'll be changing his will on his deathbed," he replied, glancing over the notes. "I'll have Helen set up an appointment for him a week from now. He may change his mind by then and hopefully save us some paperwork. I shouldn't complain, since he's never argued paying our fees, but there are times I feel as if I was taking advantage of him. I even suggested he send one of his grandchildren to law school and obtain his legal services that way. Of course, he wouldn't be able to cut that one out of his will." From there he went on to another client of theirs. Rhyder was back in his element.

Evelyne wasn't as lucky. After washing the breakfast dishes and making the bed she was left with the rest of the day to herself. She spent the next couple of hours doing the laundry, but there was time in between the wash cycle and the loading of the damp clothing into the dryer. She wasn't used to having so much free time on her hands.

In Los Angeles she always had her various committee meetings and luncheons to attend, and in Hawaii she and Rhyder were always doing something. She tried to watch television but soon became bored with soap operas she couldn't follow and game shows she couldn't become interested in. For the first time in years Evelyne didn't know what to do with herself.

The afternoon went a bit easier—she watched a movie her father's studio had produced years ago and viewed an afternoon talk show. Soon enough it was time to start the dinner preparations, and she happily occupied herself in the kitchen. She hadn't had a lot of opportunity to cook before, because Mrs. Lawson, their cook, didn't appreciate anyone "cluttering up her kitchen." How many times had Evelyne heard those words when all she'd gone in for was a glass of water? Well, now she had a kitchen all to herself and she was going to cook a meal never to be forgotten!

"I don't understand it," Evelyne wailed, looking down at the chicken that was underdone and potatoes that were decidedly overdone. "I was positive I had everything timed."

"Hey, don't worry about it," Rhyder soothed, getting up from the table and walking over to her. He slid his arms around her waist and kissed the top of her head. "It could happen to anyone."

"But not to me," she insisted tearfully, picking at the pink meat with her fork. "The last time I ruined a meal was my third cooking class in school, and we made omelettes."

"When was the last time you cooked a meal?"

Evelyne sighed. "Twelve years ago. The cook didn't like anyone fooling around in her kitchen, so I never dared bother her."

Rhyder nodded in understanding. "Is there a way we could salvage it?"

"I hope so." In the end they cooked the chicken in the microwave and tore it into strips for chicken sandwiches. The potatoes were better off thrown away. Evelyne silently vowed to purchase a few cookbooks tomorrow and work on updating her culinary skills.

After dinner Rhyder explained that he needed to look over some paper work, but he doubted it would take more than an hour.

Evelyne was watching a comedy show on television when the telephone rang.

"Evelyne, would you get that please?" Rhyder called out in a distracted voice.

She rose from the couch and headed for the kitchen to the wall phone. "Hello?"

There was a pause before she heard a woman's voice ask coolly, "Is Rhyder there?"

Evelyne's heart skipped a beat. "Who's calling,

please?" She intended to show the caller she could be just as intimidating.

"Debra Parker."

Her fingers turned icy. The woman who had sued Rhyder and turned him against women; and she had the nerve to call him? She set the receiver down and walked along the hallway to the second bedroom that doubled as Rhyder's study. He looked up with an irritated frown when she entered the room.

"A Debra Parker for you," she said quietly, and turned away.

Rhyder swore under his breath. She was the last person he would have expected—or wanted—to hear from. He reached for the phone on his desk. "Hello, Debra." There was a definite chill in his tone.

"Hello, darling, I just learned you were back in town." She sounded as if they had parted amicably those many months ago. "I had hoped you'd call me, but I guess the woman who answered your phone is keeping you busy. Is she your new bed partner?"

"What do you want?" He ignored her not-too-subtle question about Evelyne.

"I hoped we could see each other."

"Why?"

"Because of what we've shared."

"Past tense, Debra," Rhyder said bluntly, tapping his pencil against the edge of his desk. "I'm surprised you have the gall to call me after what happened." He was determined to get it out in the open.

"I merely did what I had to, Rhyder." He wondered why her purring voice had never bothered him before. Now it reminded him of fingernails on a chalk board.

"No, you didn't have to," he argued. "Debra, your suit against Palmer was for ten thousand dollars. You certainly got a great deal more than that out of me."

"Yes, I did, didn't I?" Her throaty voice was meant to remind him of the nights they had spent together.

Rhyder clenched his teeth. "You'd better get something straight, Debra. I told you my feelings in explicit detail the last time we saw each other. I would appreciate you not calling me at home again." He carefully replaced the phone in the cradle. Looking down at his paper work he knew he would not be able to return to it. He stacked the papers together and put them in his briefcase, then switched off the desk lamp and left the study in search of Evelyne. He found her curled up on the couch watching television. He knew better than to make any overtures to her after receiving a phone call from another woman and prudently took the nearby chair.

"Your paper work didn't take as long as you thought." Was her voice cooler than usual or was it just his imagination? He feared it was the former.

"I'm discovering it's harder to get back to the old grind than I thought it would be."

Evelyne nodded. She wondered whether to be bold and come right out and ask why Debra had called or wait and hope Rhyder would tell her without any prompting on her part.

"Would you like any coffee?" she asked.

"No, thanks." He rose to his feet. "I think I'd prefer some brandy. Would you like anything?"

"No, I'm fine, thank you."

Rhyder found a snifter and filled it with an inch of the fragrant amber alcohol. He walked back into the living room and took the same chair. It appeared that Evelyne wasn't going to ask him any questions, so it looked like he would have to take the initiative.

"Debra thought we would have no problem taking up where we left off." He might as well jump in all the way and see what reaction he would get out of her.

Evelyne looked up, the picture of indifference, while her stomach still churned from the wild thoughts that had been running through her mind while he was talking with Debra. "Oh, really?" She congratulated herself on the calmness of her voice, while in truth she wanted nothing more than to jump up and hit him.

Rhyder's fuse was much shorter than hers. "Yes!" he shouted, doing the jumping up. He slammed the glass down, the brandy sloshing up to the rim. "She thought she could calmly walk back into my life and back into my bed after what had happened. I told her no way. Does that make you happy?" he demanded, pacing the length of the room.

"Is it supposed to make me happy?" she countered, willing her face not to reveal the true nature of her feelings. So, he wanted her to reveal some jealousy, did he? Let him stay off balance for a while. It would do him a world of good!

"Yes, dammit!" He clenched his hands at his sides before he gave in to the urge to throw something. Why couldn't she shout or have a tantrum or something so he would know she cared?

Evelyne picked up the remote control and switched off the TV. "Rhyder, I have no control over your life, and I have no right to tell you how to run it. If it will make you feel better, I'll tell you that you would have been a fool to give in to her and that I'm very glad you didn't turn out to be a fool." She stood up and started to leave the room. "If you don't mind, I'm very tired and I'm going to turn in early. Don't worry about waking me when you decide to come to bed."

Rhyder breathed deeply to curtail the murderous images coming to mind. Half of him desired to follow her into the bedroom and show her just where his feelings were. The other half desired another shot of brandy. He settled for the latter.

Evelyne was positive she would still be awake when Rhyder came to bed, but she hadn't been in bed more than five minutes before she drifted off to sleep.

If Rhyder expected a repeat of the previous night's conversation during breakfast the next day, he was sadly mistaken. Evelyne served him French toast, sausage, and coffee with a smile and wished him a good day at the office.

The same pattern followed for the rest of the week and part of the following. Rhyder spent the greater part of each evening in his study going over the current cases and reviewing the work already done so he would be up to date. He would have preferred spending the time with Evelyne, but he knew his work was important and he had to prove to himself that she couldn't rule his life the way the other women had tired to do.

"Why don't you meet me for lunch today?" he suggested after finishing a second cup of coffee after breakfast one morning.

Evelyne's face brightened. "I'd like that," she enthused. "And I could do some shopping afterward. I've been curious to explore some of the stores."

"Why don't you come by at one o'clock?" Rhyder left the table and picked up his briefcase. "If you decide to do any shopping before meeting me, be careful and don't overdo it."

Hiding her smile she reminded him, "You're acting like a mother again, Rhyder."

"I just don't like nosy reporters," he mumbled, kissing her before leaving the apartment. "I also don't want to see you hurt." He buried his face against the curve of her neck, inhaling the exotic scent he always associated with her.

Evelyne's arms curved around his waist. She wanted to tell Rhyder that she couldn't be hurt by anyone as long as she had him beside her. "You're going to be late," she murmured, searching out his face with her lips.

His chest rose and fell with labored breaths. "A couple of minutes wouldn't hurt. It's not as if I punch a time clock," he whispered, lowering his face to hers. "Just this once." His kisses were devouring. In the end Rhyder was more than an hour late arriving at his office that morning.

With a warm smile on her lips Evelyne took care of a few telephone calls and attended to the business matters she had let slide too long. Before she knew it, it was time to meet Rhyder for lunch, and she was determined to show him she had more than shorts or jeans in her wardrobe. After perusing her limited wardrobe she decided on a conservative black wool crêpe dress and a royal-blue wool three-quarter-length coat with black velvet collar and trim edging diagonally across the front. A few twists of her hair tucked it up under a matching blue hat with only her diamond stud earrings showing. Sheer black hose and black leather pumps completed her outfit. She rummaged for a pair of her black gloves, transferred necessities into a black clutch bag, and prepared to leave.

Outside the apartment building Evelyne waited as the doorman secured a taxicab for her. She shivered in the cold wind and was grateful for the cab's heated interior as she gave the driver Rhyder's office address.

During the drive to the office building Evelyne withdrew a small notebook from her purse and jotted down a few notes regarding the errands she wanted to do that afternoon after her lunch with Rhyder.

Following his instructions she took the elevator to the twenty-fifth floor and stepped directly into the reception area for the Stewart and Marshall Law Firm.

"Yes, may I help you?" The receptionist, a composed blonde, asked Evelyne with a smile that bordered on boredom.

"I'm Mrs. Winters. Mr. Stewart is expecting me." Evelyne's smile was equally cool.

The receptionist sat up a bit straighter and immediately buzzed Rhyder's office.

"His secretary will be out in a moment," she informed Evelyne in a much warmer tone.

"Thank you."

Evelyne barely had time to take a seat before a tall woman in her early fifties entered the room.

"Mrs. Winters, I'm Helen, Mr. Stewart's secretary," she introduced herself with a warm smile. "Mr. Stewart is finishing up a conference call and asked if I would bring you back." She gestured with her hand.

During their short walk down the wood-paneled hallway, Evelyne was positive that Helen had mentally catalogued every stitch she wore and probably even estimated the cost of the designer outfit to the nearest dollar. She wondered how many other women the secretary had guided down this same hall to Rhyder's office. She found herself hating the idea of being one of many and knew she couldn't allow herself to dwell on the subject.

"Mr. Stewart will be with you in a few moments." Helen ushered her into a large corner office. "Would you care for some coffee or tea?"

Evelyne shook her head. "No, thank you." She glanced around the room as she unbuttoned her coat and allowed it to fall open, the deep blue a rich contrast against the stark black of her dress.

Helen returned her smile and left the office, closing the door behind her.

Evelyne looked around the office, seeing the personal touches she hadn't seen in Rhyder's apartment. She would have guessed that the two oil seascapes had been personally handpicked, along with the large oak desk and matching bookcases. The plush carpet beneath her feet had an Oriental pattern, one of the rich colors echoed in the deep-wine drapes accenting the window overlooking the neighboring office building. She looked down at his desk, seeing a pen lying across the desk pad, and papers neatly stacked to one side. She smiled, thinking how he left the bathroom in chaos every morning but seemed to hate the idea of one item out of place on his desk.

"Don't tell me, you're a spy for the opposition," Rhyder's loud whisper easily carried across the room.

Evelyne spun around, greeting him with a broad smile. "I certainly wouldn't find out very much here, would I? Perhaps I should seduce the man in charge to find out all his secrets."

Rhyder walked over to her quickly. "I certainly wouldn't fight you." His head swooped down, taking her lips with alarming ease. "I wish it could be more, but I don't want to disturb your lipstick more than necessary," he murmured, teasing her earlobe with his teeth. "My lady, you look ravishing. In fact, you look ready to be ravished."

"Rhyder, I never thought I would be attacked in a lawyer's office." Her chuckle held a hint of a husky croon related to arousal. "My, how kinky."

He sighed with regret and pulled away. "True, we could be interrupted at any moment, and as you know, I certainly don't believe in quickies. I hope you're hungry. I reserved a table for two at a very special place." He walked to the old-fashioned coatrack standing near the door and retrieved his topcoat.

"I'm starving." Her smile told him she was hungry for more than just food.

Rhyder took Evelyne's arm and led her out of his office. When they approached a man walking along

209

the hall, the man smiled at Rhyder and looked curiously at Evelyne. She could sense the sudden tension in Rhyder's body and gave his hand a reassuring squeeze.

"Ken." His voice sounded slightly strained. "I'd like you to meet Evelyne Winters. Evelyne, this is Ken Marshall, one of the partners."

"Mr. Marshall." She couldn't miss the curiosity in the man's face as he looked her over from head to foot. If he was looking for something wrong with me, he obviously couldn't find it, judging by his expression.

"I hope our cold weather isn't chilling you too much," Ken said politely, watching her with his keen eyes as if still searching for a major flaw. "After all, Chicago is a far cry from sunny California, isn't it?"

Evelyne stiffened. Even a casual mention of Los Angeles brought the old fears back to her. But she shouldn't be frightened of this man; after all, he was Rhyder's partner and friend. Wasn't he? She forced herself to relax. "I believe that the cold is good sometimes," she said politely. "It gives the blood a jolt and makes you more alert to your surroundings."

Ken nodded, understanding the hidden meaning within her words. Evelyne realized that while he was Rhyder's friend, he was reserving his opinion of her for the time being. She also knew the reason behind his mental pause and understood why. As long as he continued to think of Rhyder's welfare, she would try to like the man.

"Have a good lunch," Ken said before walking toward his office. "Pleased to meet you, Mrs. Winters."

"How did you get all your hair tucked up under that hat?" Rhyder asked while waiting for the elevator.

"Practice." She smiled knowingly, tucking her arm through his as the elevator door slid open. They stepped into the empty car and rode down in a matter of moments. Rhyder explained that the restaurant wasn't far and they could walk if Evelyne didn't mind. Since she didn't, they walked quickly down the sidewalk.

As they walked, Rhyder pulled her gloved hand into his pocket, cupping his protectively around it for added warmth.

"I'm glad you came," he said quietly, dipping his head so he could speak for her ears only.

"I'm glad I did too." She looked up at him with a bright smile. "While I'm shopping is there anything you would like me to pick up for you?"

Rhyder shook his head. "Just don't get too chilled," he advised, tipping his head back to feel the cold wind wash over his face.

"I don't get colds easily."

"But you might now."

Evelyne's face tightened at the mention of her health. "I told you, Rhyder, I'm perfectly healthy." She bit out the words.

"Don't get self-defensive with me," he chided. "You forget I know too much about you." He pulled her close to him to keep the chill away from her as much as possible. He cursed himself for not having grabbed a cab. He knew it would be all his fault if she fell ill. "It's just a warning, since I'm not very good around sickbeds and tend to cook the orange juice and refrigerate the soup. I'd also probably try to take your temperature in your ear."

"Some soups can be chilled," she replied. "And everyone knows where the temperature is supposed to be taken. I'm sure you'd make a very good nurse if the time arose."

Rhyder's expression turned perfectly serious.

"What I'm trying to say in my own clumsy way is that I hate the idea of you ever being in pain or ill."

She turned and placed her hand against his cheek. "Thank you," she whispered. "Thank you so very much for caring." She gave a smile of appreciation when they entered the restaurant set back from the street. "How lovely."

Rhyder nodded. "I knew you would appreciate it." They stood in the alcove waiting to be seated. He gave his name to the maître d' and guided Evelyne to the back of the dining room with its lush plants hanging overhead and greenhouse windows allowing the warmth to stay in and the cold to stay out.

"Mmm, everything looks so good." Evelyne pulled off her gloves as she scanned the menu, reading the various dishes written in an ornate calligraphy. "What do you usually have?"

"I try something different every time I come, and I haven't been disappointed yet. I'll probably have the steak soup this time. They serve warm sourdough rolls with it."

She continued to read the menu. "The spinach quiche sounds good," she finally decided.

Rhyder looked up and smiled at the waitress, giving her their orders along with the request for two coffees. "Do you have any definite plans for this afternoon?"

She shook her head. "I thought I'd just browse through the shops. Oh, I made a few long-distance telephone calls. I needed to talk to my business manager and my attorney."

Rhyder frowned, picking up his spoon and twirling the handle between his fingers. "Are there any problems?"

"No. I wanted to have some of my money transferred to a bank here," she explained.

"Tell me I'm being nosy, but why would you need a business manager?"

"I still own a good amount of stock in King Studios and my alimony payments are used for the household expenses. My business manager takes care of everything for me," Evelyne replied, giving the waitress a quiet thank-you when she placed a cup of coffee before her.

Rhyder digested this piece of information as their lunch arrived. "Meaning you're not as broke as you let on you were."

Evelyne smiled. "According to the standards everyone lived by in Bel-Air and Malibu, I'm practically destitute. If you talk about almost any other part of the country, no, I am not. I've learned that it's better not to discuss exactly how much money I have. The papers greatly exaggerated my settlement, and my attorney advised me not to go into the money matters with anyone."

"For fear a man might love you for your money," he said sarcastically, looking down at the bowl of thick rich soup set in front of him.

She stared down at her plate and picked at the melon next to her quiche. "It was for my protection, Rhyder. As a lawyer you should understand that."

"As a lawyer, yes. As your lover, no," he grated, tackling his soup with a vengeance that had nothing to do with hunger. "We've been honest with each other all along. Why did you feel you couldn't tell me about this until later on in our relationship?"

Evelyne shrugged. "It was a subject that never came up in our conversations."

Rhyder silently damned such logic. He also knew he was making an issue out of nothing and decided he would be better off dropping the subject.

213

"So, what kind of shopping are you going to do today?"

Evelyne's eyes turned a warm green. She understood what Rhyder was trying to do and felt sorry for him. She hadn't realized that the fact that she was wealthy would hurt him so. Since her divorce she knew some men would be only too happy to part her from her money, and by handing the monthly check over to a reputable business manager she was saved from everyday hassles.

"I thought I'd find a needlework shop and get some new patterns." She took a bite of her quiche. "And just do some browsing and see some of the city."

Though they continued to banter through lunch, the warmth had escaped for the time being. Rhyder acknowledged that Evelyne's settlement was none of his business, but he was surprised that she had been so open with other aspects of her life yet left that out with a deftness that said she could have easily left out something else from her past. When they parted in front of Rhyder's office building, he recommended several banks she could contact regarding a transfer of some of her money and told her where some of the best shops were.

"And don't be a worrywart that I'll get overtired or lost," she teased, kissing him lightly. "I'll see you at the apartment. Now go in there and do whatever you have to."

Even after Evelyne left, Rhyder swore he could smell her perfume and carried that thought for the rest of the afternoon.

"Buddy, you are in love," Ken announced, entering his office.

"Friend, you are right," Rhyder replied. "And it's one disease I don't mind having."

Ken shook his head. "You're heading for a fall." He

held up a hand in self-defense. "Wait a minute, let me finish. She's from California, the Golden State, and is used to parties and swinging times. How is she going to adjust to a stodgy lawyer from Chicago?"

Rhyder leaned back in his chair, his fingers forming a steeple in front of his mouth. "That's a good question. Lately I've been wondering if I'm all that stodgy after all. I think I was better off contemplating picking up rich old ladies on the beach."

Ken snorted as he pushed himself out of his chair. "Forget it. You would have been climbing the trees with the monkeys in no time. Just be glad you returned before you went off the deep end."

Rhyder spun the chair around and looked out the window at the gray, windy afternoon. It was a far cry from the warm, sunny days in Hawaii. How could he tell his friend that the more time he spent in Chicago with its rigid life-style, the more he wanted to return to an easier time? How could he tell him how tired he was and how much he needed to get away from the fast pace? The trouble was there were many things that needed to be taken care of before he gave any thought of leaving the firm permanently. He could only hope he would have the sense to walk away before it was too late for him.

Late that afternoon Evelyne returned to the apartment laden down with packages and vastly pleased with her purchases. Thanks to the doorman she was able to carry her boxes upstairs without any mishap. After tipping him she sorted the packages out and carried several into the bedroom. One large one was left on the living room couch while she put everything away.

"I smell something good," Rhyder announced, entering the apartment an hour later.

"Oh, ho, you get all excited over a roast?" Evelyne poked her head out of the kitchen.

He headed toward her, gathering her into his arms. "What I get excited over is your perfume," he said huskily. "It's got to have a sexy name."

"Obsession." Her own voice was breathless from his body angling itself against hers.

Rhyder gently nipped her bottom lip and drew it into his mouth to nibble on the tender skin. "How right they are. I am very obsessed with you," he whispered. "How long do we have until dinner?"

"About an hour."

"Sounds fine with me." He bent down and picked her up, carrying her into the bedroom. He laid her down on the bed and pulled her clothes off in record time, then went to work on discarding his own. "How about a kiss, Cinderella?" He wiggled his eyebrows suggestively.

Evelyne giggled. "It's Sleeping Beauty who gets the kiss. Cinderella got the glass slipper." She held her arms out for him.

Rhyder dropped onto the bed. "Right. I flunked fairy tales in kindergarten and I always get those two mixed up. All the same I still intend to kiss you and do a great deal more than that by the time I'm finished."

"Then do with me what you will," she crooned, running her hands over the now familiar planes of his body. "And then I can do the same with you."

"Sounds fine with me." Rhyder's mouth trailed over the slender curve of her shoulder and down her arm. Each finger received the same careful attention. By the time he'd reached her hips, Evelyne was breathing raggedly and whimpering his name. "You're on fire, baby," he rasped, looking up at her flushed features.

"Then help me put it out," she pleaded, reaching out for him.

When Rhyder finally moved up over her, Evelyne was more than ready for his possession. They melded together in a beauty only lovers of the soul knew, and when Rhyder shared his essence with Evelyne they knew their lives would never be the same again.

CHAPTER TWELVE

"I am not sick!" Rhyder argued, not very convincingly, since his voice sounded more like a weak frog's croak. "I just have a little sore throat, that's all."

Evelyne stared at him with an arched eyebrow as she shook down the thermometer. "And I say that your temperature is one hundred point one. That alone tells me you're sick, and you will stay in that bed until your temperature drops back to normal."

"Only if you stay in here with me."

She found it difficult to look stern when he resembled a small boy trying to get his way. "You will remain a complete invalid whether you like it or not."

Rhyder eyed Evelyne standing before him wearing black leather pants that hugged her lower curves and a lilac-and-black windowpane sweater tunic that hit her just below the hip. "If you want me to behave, you'd be better off wearing one of those starched uniforms nurses wear." He pushed away the blankets with an irritable twist of the hand.

Evelyne leaned down and pulled them back up to his chin. "You can't afford to get chilled," she admonished, placing the thermometer back in its box. "You stay in there while I fix you some soup."

"I don't want any soup."

"Then I'll only give you half a bowl." She walked

out of the bedroom with what Rhyder sullenly considered an exaggerated twitch of the hips.

Evelyne had never had the chance to wait on anyone, since Rick looked upon illness as a mortal sin, and taking care of Rhyder was pure joy for her. She waited upon him hand and foot and took care of his every whim. At night she slept beside his bed, on a rollaway bed that was usually kept in his study, so she could hear him if he had any trouble. At first she administered tender loving care in a way that would have made Florence Nightingale look like an orderly. But after the third day she was seriously considering sending for a private nurse to put up with Rhyder's irritability. As the hours passed his disposition grew much worse, until she thought she was taking care of a small child. In fact, she was positive a child would be much easier to care for than a cranky forty-two-year-old man! He refused to wear pajamas because they were constricting; he hated to drink orange juice or take aspirin; he hated sneezing and his sore throat. And he hated having to stay in bed without Evelyne to keep him company. He lay in bed hating his achy body and stuffed head. He especially hated Evelyne for acting so cheerful while he felt as if he would die at any moment.

"Evelyne, could you come in here and move the television around a bit?" He would call out. "I can barely see the screen."

"Evelyne, could I have some more ice water, please?"

"Evelyne, my covers are all knotted up. Could you help me, please?"

"Evelyne, it's too hot in here! Can't this electric blanket be turned down?"

"Evelyne, it's too cold in here and I can't reach the electric-blanket control!"

"Evelyne, I'm bored. Come in and talk to me."

She was convinced she wanted to change her name and that if Rhyder didn't ease his demands soon she was going to move back to Los Angeles.

"You're turning into a spoiled brat," she accused him, after serving him his lunch of a poached egg on toast, juice, and a small bowl of lime Jell-O. She stood back, her hands perched on her slim hips. "If you're not careful, your nurse is going to rebel."

Rhyder flashed her an endearing smile. "You wouldn't really leave me." He felt confident enough to make it a statement.

Evelyne shook her head, her arms now crossed in front of her. "If you could see the way you look now, you wouldn't even contemplate giving me any ideas."

A look of alarm passed over his face at her words. He pushed his covers aside and headed for the bathroom. Rhyder stared into the mirror at the bristle of four days' worth of beard, and at his blotchy features and sunken eyes. It was enough to give him nightmares.

"I guess I'd better behave myself and get down on my knees and beg you to stay with me," he muttered, returning to the bedroom and climbing back into bed, making sure to pull the covers up to his chin. "A dog would run off howling if he saw me right now."

Evelyne smiled. "Would you like an extra rug to protect your knees while you're begging?"

Rhyder had the grace to look sheepish. "I've been a real bastard, haven't I?" He pulled the tray back over his lap and cut his egg and toast into neat squares.

"That's a pretty good description for it, yes." She dropped into a nearby chair to watch him eat his lunch.

He chuckled at her pert reply. "That Swiss finishing-school education turned you into such a lady you're polite even when you're damning me. Where's that fiery temper I know you have?"

"It's there when necessary," she retorted. "It's just that I didn't care to upset you in your weakened condition."

Rhyder began laughing and ended in a coughing fit. "Damn, I hate being sick."

"You certainly sound better than you did three days ago," Evelyne assured him. "And your bloodshot eyes are gone. Colds just take time to go away. I think they're more of a nuisance than anything."

"It's probably better that I have it than you," he mumbled, tackling his Jell-O. "I hate food that wiggles."

She ran her fingers through her hair, smiling at his sullen-little-boy attitude. She doubted there was one thing he had liked in the past few days, but she still couldn't help loving him. Her smile slipped at that thought. She couldn't afford to fall in love with Rhyder. Before too long she would have to think about going back to Los Angeles and deciding what to do with the house and her life. Rhyder was settling back into his law practice, and she probably wouldn't be gone long before he wholeheartedly returned to his old way of life. And she would . . . she would what? She didn't like to think what her life was going to be like. Gathering her composure about her like a cloak, she flashed Rhyder an automatic smile, rose from her chair, and picked up his tray to carry it out to the kitchen.

While washing the few dishes and putting them away, Evelyne thought about her future. She wondered if she was essentially a weak person because she had relied on a man for so long. But did that honestly make her weak? She certainly had done many things without Rick . . . attended parties, luncheons, and

221

various social affairs when he was busy with his own work. She had never felt uneasy going somewhere without him, only sad that he couldn't be with her. So why did the thought of being without Rhyder bother her so much?

Evelyne knew she would have to come to terms with herself before she could truly get on with her life, and the best way to do that was to go back to Los Angeles and confront the ghosts of her past. Then she could become a whole person again. It was something she would have to think about after Rhyder became well.

Evelyne hadn't realized that Rhyder was wondering what was going through her mind when she left the room. His imagination conjured up his great fear: that she was leaving Chicago. He wanted to ask her to stay, but what could he give her? A life he wasn't all that happy with and a future that could be unstable if he decided to leave the practice. Was that what he should ask her to do? She did have a home to go to and another life where she might be better off. After all, he certainly wasn't the greatest catch in the country. He huddled under the covers and began feeling sorry for himself again. Picking up the portable TV's remote control he switched channels at random, finding nothing he cared to watch.

"I see we're playing roulette with the channel selector again," Evelyne commented, walking into the bedroom carrying her needlework bag in one hand. She settled back in the chair and sorted through yarns until she found the color she needed. She had begun working on a forest scene in velvet threads and could visualize the finished product hanging on Rhyder's bedroom wall.

"*We* are bored," Rhyder said sarcastically, silently wishing she weren't so cheerful all the time. She smiled even when she was angry at him!

"We are not bored, we are acting childish," Evelyne pointed out with maddening logic.

"You would, too, if you had to lie in this bed and do nothing," he grumbled. "I can't even look over my paperwork because it hurts my eyes." He had either decided watching TV wouldn't bother his eyes or preferred to ignore the fact.

"Perhaps you need reading glasses," she suggested sweetly, threading her needle.

Rhyder shot her a deadly glare. "Bite your tongue. I've been able to read just fine all my life without help."

"But you are getting to that age where glasses are needed." Her serene smile sent needles down his spine.

"I don't need glasses. My eyes hurt because I'm sick," he bit out each word with stunning clarity.

"Of course they do."

Rhyder narrowed his eyes. "You're too agreeable."

Evelyne finished a stitch before looking up. "As you said, you're still not feeling well, and I wouldn't want to upset you too much." Her voice was smothered in cotton candy.

Rhyder fell back against his pillow. "I can't wait until I'm well enough to get even with you."

Her eyes widened with innocence. "For what?"

"For treating me like a five-year-old child and feeding me Jell-O until it's coming out of my ears." He picked up the remote control and switched the channel again with manic glee until he reached a program guaranteed to make him truly ill.

It was more than a week before Rhyder felt more like his ornery self. When he felt well enough and swore he wouldn't collapse under the stress, they went out to breakfast, toured several museums, and had a late lunch. Rhyder suggested she eat heartily, because he wasn't going to allow her another meal for at least twenty-four hours.

Rhyder kept his promise. By the time they'd reached his apartment, they were in each others arms, kissing wildly, and groping through their clothes.

"How long has it been?" he rasped, covering her face with heated kisses.

"Nine days, ten hours, and fifteen minutes, but who's counting?" She slid her hands under his waistband and caressed his cotton covered buttocks.

Rhyder stepped backward, then sideways, in search of the hallway. "Evelyne, we've got a problem here."

"You're the one with the problem." Her wandering hands moved around to the front of his straining jeans and caressed the masculine bulge.

His mouth covered hers with undisguised hunger, his tongue thrusting into the moist interior. "Honey, right now I'd gladly make love to you here in the middle of the living room, but I'd prefer the comfort of my bed so neither of us breaks our back if we get too adventurous."

"Um, I'd go for that." Evelyne gurgled, digging her hands under the warmth of his sweater.

Rhyder groaned as her fingers ran through the curly hair on his chest. Forgetting his suggestion of moving to the other room, he gave in to the urges of his body and pulled her down to the carpet and quickly stripped her of her slacks and tiny panties. She wanted to laugh as she tried to slip off her jacket, but he was too busy trying to take off her sweater. Then the heat in her veins overtook any frivolous thoughts. It had been so long since she had felt the familiar weight of Rhyder's body over hers, and she needed his possession to make her whole.

His mouth fastened on her nipple, his teeth gently pulling on the deep-rose-colored aureole. Evelyne gasped at the spiraling sensations flowing all the way to the center of her femininity. When his hand smoothed over her stomach and down to the nest of dark hair, she arched up in silent invitation to his delving fingers.

"At least you can return the favor," he said hoarsely, dropping butterfly kisses across her eyes.

Evelyne complied happily. With sure fingers she found his strength and stroked him to velvety hardness. When she heard his groans, she guided him to where he belonged. She lifted her hips in welcome and easily kept up the rhythm he had begun even as she felt the pace increase and she flew outward until darkness engulfed her. She could hear Rhyder saying her name along with the ringing in her ears as she fell slowly back to earth.

"Damn you." He laughed roughly when he finally caught his breath. "Woman, you've wrung me out. I couldn't move if I had to." He shifted his weight off her and winced as a muscle protested. "I knew I was too old to roll around on the floor."

"It would have been worse if you didn't have plush carpeting." Evelyne felt a few tender spots herself. "I don't see why you have anything to complain about. I was the one on the bottom."

He grinned rakishly. "If you hadn't tempted me so much I would have given some thought to your more delicate areas." He covered her breast with his hand and kneaded the full flesh with a loving touch.

"*Me?* You were the one who attacked me before the door was closed," she accused, her eyes sparkling with laughter. "We probably gave your neighbors a great deal of gossip to take care of them for months."

Rhyder suggested something very unique for the neighbors to do, sending Evelyne bursting into laughter.

"I wonder if that's possible," she mused, before laughing again. She rolled over onto her side and snuggled up against him. "Think we could try it?" Her eyebrow arched in a way that delighted Rhyder.

He stood up and pulled her to her feet before sweeping her up into his arms. "Anything we try is going to be tested in bed," he announced, walking into the bedroom.

Rhyder kept his promise. They didn't leave the confines of the bedroom until the next afternoon.

What Evelyne remembered most was Rhyder slowing at the crucial point of their loving and looking down at her, his hair plastered back with perspiration and his features taut with desire as he said in a low voice, "You own my soul, Evelyne. Without you I'm nothing."

She could only look at him wide eyed and wish she could say the same words as easily as he had.

Evelyne found the apartment quiet after Rhyder had returned to work. Mrs. Cats kept the rooms neat and tidy, leaving Evelyne with little to do except for her stitchery. In a sudden fit of homesickness she tracked Celia down and talked to her for well over an hour. Celia commented how well she sounded and insisted she was going to have to meet the man who was doing so much good for Evelyne. Afterward Evelyne put in a call to the sanatarium where her mother was living. She suddenly needed to hear her mother's voice.

"Hello?" Evelyne's heart sank at the reedy sound that was a far cry from melodious tones she remembered from childhood.

"Mother." Evelyne was determined to be cheerful. "This is Evelyne. How are you doing?"

"Evelyne?" She could envision the perfectly arched

brow knit in confusion. "Dear, you're very late coming home from your friends, and you know how your father hates to wait for his dinner. Where are you?"

Her fingers pressed against her forehead to stave off the oncoming headache. Over the years she doubted that Amanda King had been in the present once. She seemed to prefer to regress back to a happier time in her life when her daughter was young and her husband was always there when she needed him.

"Mother, I'm in Chicago, remember? I've been calling you from here every week," she reminded her.

"Evelyne Louise King, I don't care to hear any excuses you have. You come home this instant," Amanda said impatiently. "I'm afraid you'll have to forgo any television tonight. After all, if you can't follow my instructions, there is no reason for me to give you any special privileges. You hurry home this minute."

"Mother!" Evelyne cried out, but she was too late. Amanda had already hung up and she could only hear the steady hum of the dial tone.

Evelyne set the receiver down and collapsed in a chair, allowing the tears to flow freely. She wondered if her mother would ever come out of her obsession with the past and remember that her daughter was grown and wouldn't mind having a mother who could love the woman she had become.

Rhyder rapidly discovered that his interest in his work was gone. The excitement of ferreting out little-known information and even the amusement of meeting with eccentric little old ladies or charming sexy young widows had disappeared. His accountant told him that his finances were now solidly in the black after barely a month of work. So why wasn't he happy? Why wasn't he pleased that he and Ken were taking on more clients than they could count and he was promised work until the end of the following year? The trouble was, this kind of fulfillment wasn't what Rhyder now wanted.

He picked up another file folder and scanned through the paper work detailing a case that promised months of work ahead of him. There was a time when the challenge had left him feeling exhilarated. Now he felt empty.

He closed the folder with a loud snap. "It's definitely time for a change," he murmured to himself, picking up another folder.

"A change of what?" Ken poked his head around the open door. "Women?"

Rhyder's stern expression said it all. "No, but it must be for you. You've seen Monica for what, two weeks? That's a record for you."

"Yeah." Ken sighed, walking in and dropping into a chair. "By the way, I'm having a get-together Friday night around eight and want you to come."

Rhyder groaned. "Your get-togethers are more like drunken bashes. I'll pass, thank you."

"You're turning into a real homebody, Rhyder," he jeered without malice. "From what I've read, the lady is used to a very heavy social schedule, and you've turned down four parties that I know of. Afraid she'll find someone else more to her liking?"

His look was fit to kill. "Not at all. It isn't a crime to enjoy a quiet evening at home, and the gossip rags you read don't necessarily tell the truth about people."

Ken straightened up in his chair, surprised by the vehemence in Rhyder's voice. "She's gotten to you more than I would have thought, Rhyder. Hey, I just don't want to see you hurt. She's all flash and glitter; you're herringbone tweed. Besides, did you ever consider that she could have another stroke at any time?"

228

That was a sore point with Rhyder because there had been many times he had lain awake with Evelyne sleeping in his arms wondering if a stressful situation would come up and Evelyne wouldn't be able to handle the pressure. Most important, what if he wasn't there to help her in her time of need?

"Her health is just fine," he said gruffly, silently indicating the subject was closed.

Ken shook his head. "Then there's no reason why you can't come," he said, rising from his chair. "It'll do you good to get out."

"We'll see." Rhyder wasn't going to commit himself.

But when he thought about it later, he decided it wouldn't be a bad idea to go to Ken's party. It was true he hadn't wanted to share Evelyne with anyone, while he should have wanted everyone to meet her and see the kind of beautiful woman she truly was. Better yet, he would tell her about the party and let her decide.

"A party?" Evelyne's face lit up so brightly Rhyder felt guilty that he hadn't taken her somewhere before. "Oh, Rhyder, that sounds wonderful. I would really like to meet your friends."

He winced at her open delight at the invitation. He had taken it upon himself to decide for her whether they should go out with friends or not, forgetting that she did enjoy going out. That didn't mean that she was bored with his company, just that she wanted to meet the people he worked and dealt with. He shouldn't have been so selfish all these weeks by keeping her to himself.

"It's more like a brawl than a party," he mumbled, concentrating on his stuffed pork chops and baked potato. "Most of Ken's friends aren't your run-of-the-mill stuffy lawyers."

229

"Like you?" she teased, leaning across the table. She shook her head, the silky strands floating around her like a dark halo. "Rhyder, in the past ten years I've attended parties that defy the imagination. Nothing could surprise me."

"I'm sure you won't be."

Evelyne frowned at the acidic note in his comment. "Rhyder, is something bothering you? Is it the party? Don't you want to go? Or is it that you don't want *me* to go?"

His face reddened at her perception, and she picked up on his uneasiness immediately. "So that's it." Her voice was so quiet he almost couldn't hear her. "I hope I'm wrong in thinking that the reason is because you're ashamed of me. Or do you think all I need is the beginning of a wild party to get me in the mood for an orgy?"

"That's bullshit and you know it!" he practically shouted. "I just didn't want to watch the men there drooling all over you and wondering what it would be like to be in bed with you."

Evelyne's anger evaporated at his confession. "And what about me watching the women cuddling up to you? If you don't want to go to the party, just say so, but I don't want you hiding in corners because of me. If it's because of my past, I can always stay home. I've never been one for socializing anyway," she lied, an admission Rhyder saw through easily, since he knew parties had been a good part of Rick's life.

"It starts Friday at eight," he replied in a low voice.

That night Rhyder made love to Evelyne with a tenderness he had never displayed before. It touched chords hidden deep within her soul and bound her even tighter to him. She knew she would have to leave soon or she would never be able to, until the time came when he would ask her to go. She couldn't bear the thought of forcing him to do so.

Friday night Rhyder ended up having to stay late at the office to finish up some paper work. He called Evelyne and suggested she eat without him, although he promised to be home in time to take her to the party.

Evelyne felt butterflies of apprehension as she bathed and dressed that evening. Social occasions had dwindled after her stroke, and she knew it wasn't because of people deciding she would need sufficient time to recover; it was because they were afraid to face her again.

During that time she learned that many people feared being around her, as if her illness were contagious. She had heard of that happening with cancer patients and the terminally ill, but she had never imagined it would happen with her. That was what hurt the most; people she'd thought to be her friends deserting her when she truly needed them the most.

Unsure what to wear she decided on a rainbow-striped sequined stretch tube-top and black satin pants with a cummerbund waist. With a man-tailored matching jacket, no one would have any idea how seductive her outfit really was unless she removed the jacket. By braiding her hair when wet and brushing it out later, she had shimmering waves flowing down her back. Her eye makeup was more dramatic than usual, with a brilliant cobalt-blue shadow highlighting her eyes and a deep-rose lipstick sculpting her mouth. A touch of perfume in all the right places, and she felt ready to take on the world. When she'd finished, she sat back and waited for Rhyder to come home.

"I'm sorry," he apologized, running into the apartment a little after eight-thirty. "I lost track of time."

231

"That's all right." She laughed. "It's fashionable to be late. I laid your clothes out for you."

Rhyder chuckled, pausing to press a warm kiss on her mouth. "By rights you should be yelling at me for working so hard I forgot about everything else. Instead you've managed to make sure I'll be properly put together without having to rummage through my closet. I promise I'll make it up to you."

She wiggled three fingers between two shirt buttons and tickled the skin beneath. "That's a vow I intend to see you keep," she crooned in the husky voice that always sent shivers up his spine.

Rhyder breathed deeply through his nose and only got a good whiff of her perfume. "I'd better take a quick shower, a cold one, or we'll never get out of here." He left her with a resigned expression on his face.

Not wanting to bother with a car, they took a taxi to Ken's apartment.

"We'll only have to follow the noise," Rhyder told Evelyne as they got off the twentieth floor of an exclusive apartment building.

She nodded when she heard the distinctive sounds of Wham. "He must invite his neighbors so he doesn't have to worry about any complaints," she commented as they followed several other people heading for an open door.

Rhyder nodded, ushering her inside.

"Glad to see you could make it!" Ken shouted, walking up to them with a drunken sway. "You know where the bar is." He smiled at Evelyne as Rhyder helped her off with her coat, but the smile soon turned into a leer when he saw her bare shoulders without even a thin chain to detract from the pale-gold skin. "Well, well, well. Is this the way you ladies dress in swinging L.A.? I think I'll have to see about opening a

232

branch office on the West Coast. In fact, I'll even volunteer to run it myself."

"Actually I bought this right here in freezing Chicago," she told him, unaware of Rhyder's stunned expression and his visible gulp.

Rhyder was positive the temperature in the room rose at least fifteen degrees. He had certainly seen Evelyne in less clothing and had even seen her dressed up a few times when they had dined out in Hawaii, but the top lovingly hugged her breasts as nothing else did. Not even the strapless dress she had once worn had accented her curves the way the top and satin pants did. He glared at several men who gave Evelyne more than a passing glance. He had an idea he would have a full-time job watching over her for the next few hours. Maybe he could invent a headache and they could leave early.

"What are you trying to do?" he demanded under his breath as he guided her between masses of bodies to the bar.

"What do you mean?" She smiled at a man who looked as if he wouldn't mind taking her home.

"You know exactly what I mean." Rhyder was certain the veins were popping out of his forehead. "That guy looks as if he's hoping to find you under his Christmas tree. And you wouldn't even have to be gift wrapped!" He draped an arm around her that literally screamed, *She's mine, hands off.* Since the bar was every man for himself, he fixed himself a double Scotch and found a bottle of Perrier for Evelyne.

"Stop glowering, Rhyder." She reached up and kissed him on the chin. "You look much better when those wrinkles on your forehead are gone."

"I would look much happier if you had worn more clothes," he gritted, swallowing his Scotch in one gulp and pouring himself another.

Evelyne took the glass out of his hand and set it on the bar. "I'm not going to demand we go home even if you begin acting like an ass. And you're well on your way."

Rhyder shook his head in denial and turned to retrieve his glass, only to find it gone. "Some things just aren't sacred around here," he muttered.

"Why don't you introduce me around?" she suggested.

"All right." He led her over to a group of two women and three men who turned out to be secretaries and law clerks. They recognized her face and name but had the grace not to comment on it. Some weren't as polite.

"Aren't you Rick Winters's ex-wife?" one woman who had obviously had too many asked, gazing nearsightedly at Evelyne.

"Yes." She was glad it didn't hurt as much to admit it as it used to be when the question came up.

"Girl, you were crazy to give up a hunk like him," she continued. She paused as if remembering something. "Oh, that's right. He dumped you, didn't he? Because you went crazy or something, wasn't it? Well, you can't win them all, can you? Don't worry, honey, someone else will come along. With your looks you won't have to worry. Just don't tell them who you really are or they'll run like hell."

Rhyder swore under his breath. How Evelyne could stand there and smile serenely was something he couldn't understand. But then he hadn't realized that she had come to terms about her marriage to Rick and comments about him couldn't hurt her anymore. He pulled Evelyne away.

"You don't look too happy, old buddy." Ken appeared, slapping Rhyder on the back. "Don't tell me you can't stay away from this beauty's body for more

234

than an hour. You should be more careful of her health."

"Watch it, Ken," he warned softly, beginning to see his friend and partner in a new light he didn't like. "You're getting way off base."

Evelyne froze, sensing something else behind the men's words. She groped for Rhyder's hand and squeezed it for comfort.

"I just don't want to see you hurt," Ken insisted, waving his glass about. "Look what that bitch Debra did to you. I can't afford to have you running off to some remote island when Evelyne dumps you for the L.A. orgies. Wake up, man, and smell the coffee!"

"Rhyder," Evelyne interjected softly, seeing they were attracting a small crowd of interested listeners, "let's go."

He shook off her hand, his gaze still boring into Ken. "Ken, you're treading on thin ice. I don't know what's making you talk like this unless it's the bourbon, but I don't want to hear it again. Just remember what we learned in law school: don't do any accusing until you have all the facts. Otherwise you're going to end up with egg or maybe even a man's fist in your face." He turned away and pulled Evelyne with him. It only took a few minutes for him to find her coat, and they walked out of the apartment.

Rhyder maintained his stony silence all the way back to his apartment. Evelyne could only sit there feeling miserable over the turn of events.

"People are always going to talk about me," she finally said, breaking the silence after they had entered the dark living room. "I'm still not all that used to malicious gossip, and I certainly don't appreciate hearing horrible things about me, but I can live with it. It appears that you can't handle it. Rhyder, I think it's time for me to leave and go back to Los Angeles. It's time for me to let you get on with your life."

The fierce look on his face told her an entirely different story. He grabbed hold of her arms and pulled her against him. "Don't you ever think that," he said fiercely. "I need you just as much as you need me. You can take care of any business you have just as easily from here. I need you, Evelyne. I can't let you leave me." His head swooped down to capture her mouth in a kiss that promised dark erotic pleasures never to be equalled. His tongue devoured the moist interior of her mouth and he whispered words of a shared loving no other mortal had ever known.

Tearing his mouth from hers Rhyder swept Evelyne up into his arms and carried her into the bedroom. If words wouldn't convince her how badly he needed her, action would.

CHAPTER THIRTEEN

Where had their clothes gone? Evelyne thought hazily, lying on top of the rumpled covers. She looked at Rhyder walking toward her, and suddenly she didn't care what happened to them. All that mattered now was that he was kissing her as if there was no tomorrow and his hands were warm and oh, so sure on her bare skin. She sighed, feeling his hands move up her legs, pause to caress the soft area behind her knees. He dropped a kiss on each knee before his hands trailed upward again, and she reached out, grasping his shoulders in an attempt to pull him toward her.

Rhyder looked up and smiled, his teeth gleaming white in the dim light. "Don't make me lose my concentration, witch," he said softly, dropping a kiss on her hipbone and smoothing a path across to the other hip. "I'm busy tasting every inch of your delicious body."

"I . . ." She gasped when he reached the other side. "I don't think you would be deterred no matter what I said." Her head arched backward as the fire shot through her body; his tongue, gentle but very insistent, flickered upon the part of her that ached so for his touch.

"Flow with it, love," he urged, blowing softly on her ultrasensitive skin. "Show me all the passion you have. Don't hold back with me."

Evelyne couldn't have held back if her life had depended on it. She loved Rhyder too much to keep any part of her from him. She held on to his head, urging him onward. As always it didn't take long for her to fly apart into tiny little pieces and soar among the eagles. That was when she discovered what she had known all along: she belonged with this man for the rest of her life. But there was something else she would have to do first. When she regained her breath, she pushed him onto his back and raised herself up.

"And now it is my turn." Her smile promised the same dark pleasures he had given her. Evelyne began with light, fluttery kisses along his chin, just missing his mouth. She explored the shell-like exterior of his ear with the tip of her tongue, and found the sensitive area just behind it. Her fingertips ran through the crisp hair on his chest that arrowed out into soft silk as it passed his waist before turning coarse again. Her lips curved into a knowing smile that transferred itself onto his mouth as she flicked her tongue across the male contours and delved inside.

"I bet you wore braces when you were young," she crooned.

"Nope. My family is known for its straight teeth." He was finding it very hard to breathe. "It's in our genes."

"And here I suffered with braces during my formative years." Her hand found his masculinity and caressed it lovingly. "What did you suffer with during your formative years?"

His laugh turned gutteral at the light teasing touch of her fingernail. "I had to deal with girls who were convinced they were wiser than their years when it came to dealing with the dark area of sex when I wasn't too sure what was going on."

"Oh?" She looked at him with a delicately arched

238

eyebrow. "I can't imagine you were the type to wrestle with girls in the back seat of an old Ford."

He covered her hand with his and showed her exactly what he liked. "It was an old Chevy and I sometimes did a bit more than wrestle with them." His other hand found and covered one breast, his thumb rubbing her nipple into a dark rosy peak. Evelyne's soft moan brought a broad smile to his face. "I think there will be a bit of wrestling done here before the night is over." He lifted his head to continue kissing her, but she shook her head.

With a slight smile on her lips she dipped her head and found a small brown nipple nestled among the light-brown hair. It only took a few strokes of her tongue to turn it into a tiny pebble of searing need that swooped down to the pulsating center of his body with the searing accuracy of a guided missile. By the time she transferred her attention to the other nipple Rhyder was positive he was just one step away from insanity. He ran his hand over the clean line of her back and down to the rounded shape of her buttocks, needing to feel the warmth of her skin, and smell the exotic scent of her perfume. When she lifted her head he grabbed hold of her waist to pull her over him.

But Evelyne wasn't finished. With a smile she gently pushed him back onto the covers. Her kisses again left a moist trail down his chest and along his waist. Soon Rhyder's groans weren't breathy, but gritty, as she encompassed him with burning lips. Her hair drifted about her face in a dark cloud and floated over his skin like waves of molten lava. His hips bucked as she caressed him with passion and love. Now Rhyder was positive he was riding the line of insanity. His entire body tensed and he gasped out her name, a plea for her to love him fully before he went crazy.

Evelyne moved up over him with the grace of a

dancer. When she sheathed him, he knew he was home at last. He gripped her hips, following her every movement as she began a rhythm calculated to drive them over the edge.

"Beautiful. So beautiful." His dry lips were moistened by her tongue. "Give in to me again, Evelyne. Let us see that other world again."

Her skin was damp with perspiration as she strove for that star in the galaxy only lovers knew. Nothing mattered to Rhyder but that he loved her and couldn't let her go. His face grew taut, every muscle in his body tightening as he prepared himself for that final fall. His mouth opened, but he wasn't aware of the shout that left his lips as he shared himself with her.

Evelyne only knew that she felt as if she had been shattered into millions of tiny pieces and the only person to make her whole was Rhyder. Breathing raggedly she collapsed on his chest.

It was a long while later before she drifted back to the present. Rhyder kept his arm curled around her body that fit so perfectly against his, her head pillowed on the damp skin of his chest. Skin made even damper by her tears.

There was nothing for her to be sad about. Their loving had been even more beautiful than before, and she doubted either of them had ever known such heights. The trouble was, he made it more difficult for her to leave him.

"We'll tear each other apart in the end, Rhyder," she spoke softly, feeling the ragged tenor of his breathing beneath her ear. "Is it really worth it for us to suffer so much? Haven't we done enough of that in the past? I need to come to terms with the person I've become, and I sense you need to come to a few terms with yourself. I also have to see my mother. She isn't doing well at all, and I'm hoping that if she sees me in person and I have the chance to sit down and talk to her the way I should have when she first had problems, she might begin to think about the present *and* the past."

Rhyder's arm tightened. "I won't beg you to stay with me, Evelyne," he said finally. "I've lost a lot of pride where you're involved, but I do know when to quit. I will ask, though, if you'll stay until the end of the month. That's only another ten days. Since you seem to have some paper work to handle when you go back, there's no reason why you can't go over most of it here, and you'll be better prepared when you leave. Of course, if you need some help I'll assist you in any way I can."

"All right." She didn't want to leave him, but she knew she had to go if they were to find out if they were truly meant for each other. She knew from her marriage that involvement with a man meant a fifty-fifty partnership; she was determined to remain a whole person physically and emotionally.

Rhyder's arm relaxed at her reply. For a long time they lay in the same position without a word spoken between them. They were taking another turn in their lives and it would take time to prove if life would be on their side this time.

Saturday morning Rhyder suggested they take a drive outside the city, and with Evelyne's enthusiastic agreement he made arrangements to have his car brought around front.

"A typical attorney's car," Evelyne commented as he assisted her into the front seat of the dark-blue BMW.

"A practical car," he corrected, sliding behind the wheel. "It's not overly large, and it isn't so small that I could be overturned during a bad storm. Besides, I don't really use it all that much. We're not like L.A., where you take a car just to go around the corner."

"It isn't that bad. It's just that our freeways are a way of life." Evelyne glanced out the window as they drove down the city streets. A thought came to her. One she didn't care to voice but hoped to learn the answer to. "Why doesn't Ken like me?"

Rhyder swore softly. "I wish I knew," he admitted with a sigh. "To be honest, he acts as if you're going to corrupt me with your easygoing California ways."

She smiled wryly. "And he wasn't worried that the 'hang loose' attitude in Hawaii wasn't going to change you? Obviously he worries more about the women you come up against than the call of the Islands."

"He honestly didn't think I'd stay there very long. From the beginning he said I'd be back because the slow pace would drive me crazy."

"Did it?"

Rhyder shrugged. He glanced in the side-view mirror before flipping the turn signal and changing lanes. "Hard to say. In many ways I enjoyed sleeping late and not worrying about sticking to a strict schedule. I haven't had what you'd call a real vacation in years, and at the time I was more than happy to get away from the practice and find out what I've been missing from life." He spared a quick glance at her, silently indicating that *she* was what he had been missing.

Evelyne looked down at her hands clenched in her lap. "From the time I was born, I depended on a man for my existence," she said softly, so softly the words barely reached Rhyder's ears. "At first there was my father; he was there to write out the checks for my school fees and dancing lessons. I barely graduated from school and Rick was there to take over. When I got my divorce, my first thoughts were that I wished my father were still alive because I didn't know what

242

to do. I was in a complete fog. After the divorce was finalized, Celia flew me back to New York to recuperate. And I ended up leaning on her."

"Then you go to Hawaii to get away from all your little watchdogs and you end up with me playing camp counselor," he said wryly. "You really haven't had a chance to be on your own, have you?"

Evelyne scooted over and rested her head on his shoulder. "I don't see you in that light." Her voice turned teasing. "Unless you count when you shanghaied from Kona to Honolulu to Chicago without letting me take a breath. That did take a bit of arrogance."

But Rhyder couldn't see it as a joke. "I did, didn't I? I didn't bother to find out your opinion. I just took over because I was so afraid some smart-ass reporter would show up and harass you until you broke."

"I'm tougher than I seem, Rhyder," she chided, unable to feel anger at his overly protective attitude because she finally realized he had only done it for her sake and not necessarily because he had to be in charge. "At least I'm pretty sure I am. I'm still trying to find out."

When they stopped at a red light, he leaned over and pressed a kiss against her forehead. "What did I ever do to deserve someone like you?"

"I'm not really sure. After all, you did practically insult me the first time we met."

"I didn't insult you. I just spoke my mind."

"Oh, was that what it was?" She feigned innocence.

"This is not a joking matter, Evelyne," Rhyder warned.

"No." Her voice softened. "But I don't want either of us to be sad now. Not after all we've shared."

"You're still going to leave." It was an accusation.

"I have to."

Evelyne's declaration didn't necessarily spoil the rest of their day, although it did give them both something to think about as they walked along the shoreline. Their arms were wrapped around each other as if in hopes of not losing each other too soon.

That night Rhyder didn't attempt to make love to Evelyne. Instead he held her in his arms and lay awake fearing the day she would leave and he would be alone again.

During the following week Evelyne and Rhyder tiptoed around each other as they went their separate ways. Much to Evelyne's despair Rhyder brought paper work home with him and stayed in his study until the early morning hours. He explained that he had a difficult case that required a great deal of his time, but she was afraid he was merely initiating the break a little early so it wouldn't hurt so much when it finally happened.

She decided that, if she was going to leave, she was going to leave a reminder behind. One afternoon Evelyne went shopping and came home with a painting to hang on one of the bare living room walls. During her search for the painting she discovered some throw pillows that would add a bit of color to the room along with a rose-colored vase that she knew would look perfect on a small table near the window. By the time she had finished with her shopping expedition, her arms were filled with packages. She was positive she was going to enjoy setting everything up when she got back to the apartment.

Rhyder came home dead tired. The day had been filled with conferences and a few heated disagreements with Ken. Rhyder couldn't understand what was going on with his friend, but he didn't have the patience to put up with the other man's cocky attitude where Evelyne was concerned.

When he entered the apartment he blinked, backed up, and glanced at the number on the door, convinced he had somehow blundered into the wrong room.

"You're home early," Evelyne greeted him, caught in the act of placing the vase filled with dried flowers on a table.

Rhyder slammed the door behind him and walked to the middle of the room. He turned around slowly, taking in the brilliant colors of an abstract painting on one wall, the bright-blue and paprika velvety throw-pillows on the couch.

"What's this?" he asked in a quiet voice that usually signified an oncoming storm.

"This place looked more like a hotel room than a home, so I decided to add some life to it," she explained, stepping back to view the vase, then moving forward to inch it over to one side. "What do you think?"

Rhyder's face was pinched with the tension that had been building up inside of him for the past week. Didn't she understand that the last thing he wanted was any reminders of her after she'd left? "I think you'd better find out if it's all returnable, or you'll be carrying a lot of extra items back with you to L.A," he gritted.

She looked incredulous at his announcement. "Rhyder, I bought all of this for you. The place looked too sterile."

"And now it will refuse to let me forget you," he practically shouted. "I can't let that happen, Evelyne, or I'll go crazy."

Now she understood the reason for his displeasure. "Rhyder, I'm not going away forever," she told him softly. "I just want to settle everything and make sure

245

I'm a whole person before I come back to you. I don't want any problems between us again."

"And if I don't want you when you've finally decided I'm all right to stay with?"

Evelyne gasped at his cruelty, but she understood that he was only lashing out in self-defense. "That's just a chance I'll have to take, won't I? Because I do plan to come back to you, Rhyder. I just wish you could believe me." She walked slowly into the kitchen. "Dinner is almost ready. You have enough time to wash up."

Rhyder dropped his briefcase on the couch and walked into the bathroom. He stared at his face in the mirror and rubbed the heels of his hands over his eyes. He was tired, very tired, but that was no excuse for taking it out on Evelyne. In adding some homey touches to his apartment she felt she was doing something wonderful for him, and he had thrown it all back in her face. After the crass way he acted he wouldn't blame her if she never came back. He certainly wouldn't want to live with an idiot like himself. He wondered how she could afford items that were obviously very expensive. She never mentioned much about her alimony payments, only that they did cover the household expenses and that she had a trust fund from her father's estate and stock in King Studios which she had never touched. The clothing she wore certainly wasn't cheap. He had once seen a pair of leather pants like hers, and they were priced at over three hundred dollars.

Rhyder took time to splash some cold water over his face and changed into a pair of jeans and a gold pullover sweater. It wasn't until he turned away from the closet that he realized the comforter on the bed was new and made of soft velvet squares. He passed his hand over the smooth fabric and couldn't help but think of Evelyne's skin. He recalled her words promising she would be back. The trouble was, did she mean it or would she find out that the fast-paced life in Los Angeles was for her after all? He had to leave the room before he went any crazier.

Evelyne was dishing out fettuccine in two pasta bowls when Rhyder arrived at the table.

"If I say I'm sorry and am willing to hang by my toes until the year two thousand, will you forgive me?" he asked.

She set the bowls down and put her arms around him. "No one can hurt me the way you can," she confessed. "Not even Rick had as much power over me."

"Don't go," Rhyder pleaded, burying his face against the fragrant cloud of her hair. "Can't you understand that I'm afraid you won't come back?"

"The same way you have to understand that I need to find out just who I am right now," she replied, rubbing her face against the soft wool of his sweater.

Rhyder gripped her chin and tipped it upward. "*I* know who you are, and that's all that matters," he said roughly, his eyes glittering.

Evelyne lifted her hand and placed her palm against his cheek. "I love you, Rhyder. I love you so very much, but I have to give you a whole woman. Anything else would be unfair. I called the airlines and made my reservation for the first of the month."

Rhyder stepped away. "Then that's that." His tone was flat. "I guess we'd better eat." He sat down and gazed, without any appetite, at the food set before him.

Neither ate very much that evening. Rhyder stayed long enough to help Evelyne with the dishes, then escaped to his study mumbling something about work to look over. He knew he couldn't stay in the same room

247

with her without rehashing a subject that only brought pain to both of them. Evelyne spent the evening watching television and working on her needlepoint. The trouble was, her needlework needed little concentration and all she could do was think about Rhyder and wonder whether she was right in leaving him. She had to believe it was, because that would be the only way she would be able to step on that plane when the moment came.

The break had already begun. Rhyder decided he had to separate himself from Evelyne early so he wouldn't hurt too much later. Evelyne was just plain hurt. In an attempt to keep her courage up to take that flight, she called her mother. This time she was in for a shock.

"Dear, I am so happy to hear from you." Amanda King's voice was clear and coherent, without any of the misty vagueness Evelyne had been used to in the past. "How is Chicago? Is it very cold there?"

"You . . . you remember where I am?" She was stunned.

"Well, of course, dear. You told me you were staying in Chicago with a friend for a little while." Amanda's voice betrayed amusement at her daughter's surprise. "Truthfully, I never liked it there. It was always so cold, and you know how I hate the cold. I did enjoy that time the three of us went to the Bahamas, remember? And you had a crush on the tennis pro?"

Evelyne held the phone so tightly, her knuckles turned white from the effort. She had just reached her sixteenth birthday when that trip had occurred. It appeared her mother hadn't recovered as much as she thought she had. For a moment she had dreamed . . . but dreams didn't always come true.

"Yes." She cleared her throat. "Yes, I do remember.

And Daddy complained that you spent too much money at the boutiques."

"My dear, are you happy?" Amanda asked suddenly. "You mean so very much to me, and I'd hate the idea that you aren't happy. I know you loved Rick, but it appears he never loved you enough. If you recall, he didn't like to visit me either. Oh, you always made excuses that he had to work and such, but I knew the real reason he didn't come. He can't abide anyone who is ill. There were times when your father was that way. Some men just are. I want you to find someone who isn't as selfish and who will love you no matter what. Don't let your bad experience with Rick embitter you against all men."

"I haven't, Mother. In fact, I have found someone," Evelyne said in a choked voice. What had brought about the miraculous change in her mother's behavior? Whatever it was, she was grateful, because Amanda now sounded the way she used to. "He's wonderful and he knows about my stroke and the extremely slight chance there could be another, but it doesn't matter to him. He loves me for myself."

"Don't lose him, dear," her mother advised. "I can tell by your voice that he's special. Keep hold of him and never let him go."

Evelyne edged toward a chair and sank down into it before her knees gave out. It was so difficult to believe she was talking to her mother the way she once had. It was so wonderful.

"His name is Rhyder Stewart." She kept having to clear her throat of the tears threatening to overtake her. "He's an attorney, and while he can be a bit of a bear at times, he doesn't frighten me because he's also very gentle and sweet. He—ah—he means a lot to me."

"When do I get to meet this wonderful man? I

should put my seal of approval on him, although I have an idea he's already passed the test with flying colors."

Evelyne smiled through her tears. "I'm planning on coming back to L.A. in a week or so. Perhaps he can fly out later when the case he's working on is settled." If he was still talking to her then, she thought silently.

"We've been having sunny days for the past two weeks, as if it were June instead of the end of February," Amanda told her. "You can leave the fur coat and wool behind. It will be so good to see you again, Evelyne. It's been a long time since we could sit down and talk."

"Yes, it has." She gave up and allowed the tears to fall. "I'll call you as soon as I arrive."

"Evelyne, I love you very much." The declaration was sudden and very fervent. "Please don't ever forget that. No matter what has happened in the past, I've always loved you."

Evelyne sniffed. "I love you too." She slowly replaced the receiver and burrowed down in the chair for a good cry, where Rhyder found her an hour later.

"Honey, what's wrong?" He rushed over to her and crouched down beside her. He framed her face with his hands and studied her tearstained features. "What happened? Are you sick? Did something go wrong? What is it?"

She shook her head to each question. "It's my mother," she wailed, gripping his wrists.

Rhyder stiffened. "Is she—Did she—" He was afraid to voice the words.

"No," Evelyne said irritably, her words muffled by her tears. "She was just fine."

"And that was the problem?" he asked gently.

"She's always lived in the time before Daddy died. She seemed to think I was still a small girl and would scold me for staying too long at my friends' or remind me I had to clean my room. But she wasn't that way at all today," she replied, holding her head still as Rhyder took out his handkerchief and carefully dried her damp cheeks. "She talked about Rick and told me not to be upset over my divorce. She also wants to meet you."

Rhyder smiled. "And what did you say?"

"That I wanted her to meet you too." She offered a shy smile.

"I'd like that too." Rhyder straightened up and held his hands out to pull her from the chair. "Come on, let's clean up that blotchy face of yours."

"My face is not blotchy!"

"I'm sorry to disappoint you, but you are not one of those women who can cry beautifully. Your eyes look as if they had been part of a week-long drunk and your face looks as if it has big red freckles on it."

Evelyne groaned, picturing Rhyder's description all too vividly.

"Why don't you lie down for a while?" he suggested, steering her toward the bedroom.

She ventured a faint smile. "Are you going to lie down with me?"

"I had planned on it, yes. Any objections?"

"Only if you hadn't planned on it."

Late that night they lay in bed after a time of rich, tender lovemaking, Rhyder's body curved spoonlike around Evelyne's back and his arms linked around her waist.

"Evelyne, I do want to meet your mother," he said quietly, nuzzling the tender spot behind her ear and blowing gently into the tiny shell. "I want to know what you were like as a small child and as you were growing up. I want to find out everything I can about you."

"Does that mean I'll get to meet your mother too?"

He chuckled. "She'll probably tell you you're getting a great deal and talk about grandchildren." Evelyne's heart skipped a beat at the thought of carrying his child. Would her health allow it? That might be something she would have to consider if the time ever came. "As for my brother, he would tell you I was a holy terror and someone as beautiful and sweet as you would be better off without me and I didn't deserve you." His voice turned hoarse with longing. "Do I deserve you, Evelyne?"

She turned in his arms and covered his face with kisses. "Oh, yes, you certainly do deserve me," she murmured, rotating her hips against his. "And right now, I'm going to prove just how much you deserve me."

One thing Evelyne's mother had taught her was to always keep her promises.

Over the next few days Rhyder began to relax. Maybe it was because the early hostility between Ken and himself was gone or maybe it was because he had begun to hope Evelyne wouldn't fly to Los Angeles just yet. Or at least that she would wait until he could travel with her and protect her from any cold-blooded reporters that might lay in wait for her. He didn't believe that old news was no news.

But she didn't want any more protection, his conscience reminded him. She wanted to face the world herself without any help. Of course, that didn't mean he couldn't try, did it?

"This case is going to take longer than we'd expected," Ken announced, walking into Rhyder's office.

Rhyder groaned. "Now what?"

Ken threw a sheaf of papers on the desk. "It appears Calvin Walters has a niece in Florida and we're

252

going to have to check out her claim to the estate. The funny thing is, I don't remember the old man saying anything about his having any brothers or sisters."

"If you had listened to Walters, you would have thought he was hatched out of an egg," Rhyder grumbled, looking over the report. "Damn, she is going to have to be checked out. Did you get hold of an investigation firm out that way?"

"Yeah, but one of us will have to fly out there if the claim looks legitimate," Ken suggested.

Rhyder looked up. "Meaning me?"

"Old Man Walters was your client," the other man pointed out with maddening logic.

Rhyder turned back to the report and read it through. Ken was right, he would have to be the one to go out there if the investigator came up with strong evidence. And Ken didn't look all that unhappy that Rhyder would be out of the office.

"What is it about Evelyne you don't like?" he asked abruptly, lacing his fingers together and placing his hands on top of the desk.

Ken feigned ignorance. "What are you talking about?"

"You know very well what I'm talking about," he said harshly. "You've been against her from the beginning. Why?"

"Look, I have nothing against her personally. But I've read a lot about her and her ex-husband. She's lived a way of life you and I have no conception of. She's used to fast men, fast parties, and who knows what else? Do we really know that she had a stroke or was it covering up something else more sinister or illegal?"

Rhyder half rose in his chair. "I don't know what's happened to you over the past few months, but you're not the man I went to law school with. You're pushing, Ken, and I don't appreciate it."

Ken held up his hands. "I'm only going by what I read in the papers, and not all of it can be hype."

Rhyder shook his head in disbelief. He could probably talk to Ken from now until doomsday and he still wouldn't understand the kind of woman Evelyne really was. He was so sure of the media rags he read that he wouldn't believe the truth if it was in front of him. This glimpse of a new side of his partner and friend was a revelation Rhyder didn't like; he was rapidly losing his respect for the man.

Rhyder stared down at the report. Maybe it was for the best that he might have to fly to Florida. After all, Evelyne would probably be gone then and he'd need to keep himself as busy as possible so he wouldn't go crazy. He slipped the papers into his briefcase. He'd look it over more that night.

Evelyne made one of Rhyder's favorites for dinner that evening, chicken and dumplings. He exhibited pleasure at her thoughtfulness and ate two large helpings, then complained that he was getting fat as he helped her with the dishes.

They had just dried the last dish when the telephone rang. Rhyder grabbed the receiver.

"Hello? Who's calling, please? Just a moment." He covered the mouthpiece with his hand. "It's a Dr. Simpson." He looked at Evelyne inquiringly.

"He's my mother's doctor." She took the receiver from him. "Hello, Dr. Simpson, is there anything wrong?" As the man spoke, her face turned ashen. "No," she whispered, gripping the receiver tightly. "No, you're wrong, I spoke to her a few days ago and she was fine. She was the way she used to be. There has to be a mistake." Her voice grew shrill. A moment later she hung the phone up and gazed at Rhyder with large dark eyes filled with pain. "My mother is dead." With that announcement she fell to the floor unconscious.

When Evelyne came to, she found herself in a sterile-looking examination room that could only belong to a hospital. She gazed fearfully at the doctor standing over her and immediately thought that everything that had happened had only been a dream.

"Please lie back down, Mrs. Winters," the doctor requested, placing his hand on her shoulder. "You've had a bad shock, and when you fainted, Mr. Stewart brought you here."

"Rhyder?" she croaked between dry lips. It wasn't a dream after all! "Is he here?"

The man smiled. "He's pacing the hallway outside. You gave him a pretty good scare." He instructed the nurse to place the blood-pressure cuff on her arm. "How are you feeling?" He checked the dilation of her pupils.

"I have a headache," Evelyne admitted, wincing at the bright light in her eyes. "Nothing else."

The nurse jotted down her blood pressure on a chart and handed it to the doctor.

"Am I all right?"

"Mr. Stewart explained your medical history to me," the doctor told her. "But I believe this was nothing more than a fainting spell due to the shock you received." His expression was grave. "You do remember why you fainted, don't you?"

Her eyes filled with tears. "Yes," she whispered. "I'd like to see Rhyder, please."

He nodded to the nurse, who walked over to the door and gestured to someone. Rhyder was in the room in seconds, looking at Evelyne as if she were a miracle. He scooped her up in his arms and held on to her tightly.

"I was afraid I would lose you," he muttered. "And I couldn't live if anything happened to you."

"It was an ordinary fainting spell," she assured him, holding on to him just as tightly. She tipped her head back and found his eyes moist. "I told you I was too tough to go easily." But her efforts at a joke fell through. "I didn't get to see her again, Rhyder. And she sounded so well in our last phone call. Why is everything going against me now? What will I have to do to make everything better?"

Rhyder shook his head. He only wished he could give her an answer or make her hurt go away. Since he could do neither, he settled on giving her his love and comfort. When he glimpsed the controlled expression on her face, an icy chill ran down his back.

"There's no choice about it now, Rhyder," she said in a voice that was much too calm. "I'll have to return to Los Angeles on the first available flight."

CHAPTER FOURTEEN

Rhyder had no choice but to let Evelyne go. How could he keep her with him when her mother had just died and she would have to make the funeral arrangements? And due to the damned case in Florida he couldn't go with her with a clear conscience. He did insist that she wait until the next day in order to rest up for the ordeal ahead of her.

The morning of her flight he sat on the bed and watched her pack her suitcase. It should have helped to see that most of her clothing was left in the closet. But she had called her friend to have her things sent to her. Who said she wouldn't contact him with the same request? Who said she wouldn't go back there and decide she wanted more from life than a boring lawyer?

"That's all I'll need," Evelyne murmured, carrying her cosmetics bag out of the bathroom. She looked at Rhyder with terribly sad eyes. "I wish you weren't driving me to the airport."

He felt a stab in the direction of his heart. "You're not going to stop me."

"I know. It's just that I hate good-byes." She zipped her suitcase closed. "And this is hard enough on us as it is."

"No kidding," Rhyder muttered, picking up her suitcase.

Their ride to the airport was silent, as was their walk to the ticket counter where Evelyne received her seat assignment. Rhyder was tempted to suggest they adjourn to the bar, but Evelyne still couldn't drink and he didn't feel right drowning his sorrows in front of her. They walked down the long hallway to the gate and sat down, not looking at each other and saying little.

It wasn't until Evelyne's flight was announced over the loudspeaker that her composure broke. She picked up her purse with stiff fingers and stood facing Rhyder, who looked just as miserable as she felt.

"I have to go, Rhyder," she whispered. "But I'll be back, I promise. Just let me find the true me. I don't want you to be cheated. Please understand."

"How can I understand when all I know is that I love you and am afraid you won't come back to me?" he asked hoarsely.

Evelyne's lips trembled. She threw her arms around Rhyder's neck and kissed him with all her heart. His arms wrapped around her and held her tightly against him. Their tears mingled as their kiss escalated to tongues dueling and harsh whispers of love. When the loudspeaker announced final boarding, they parted reluctantly.

"I will be back, Rhyder," she assured him, tears streaming down her cheeks. "Please don't hate me." With that she turned away and ran down the tunnel to the waiting jet.

Rhyder stayed long enough to see the jet take off before leaving the airport.

He couldn't believe how quiet the apartment was. He walked into the bedroom and could smell Evelyne's perfume permeating the air. No wonder— she had left a bottle on the chest of drawers. Was she trying to drive him crazy? He dropped onto the bed, his head cradled by his hands. If he didn't convince himself he was an adult and above strong emotions, he would certainly begin crying. Instead he shucked his clothes and crawled into bed, cradling Evelyne's pillow and inhaling her soft womanly scent. It may have been the middle of the day, but he had no desire to do anything but sleep and forget she was gone.

Evelyne remained in a fog throughout her flight to Los Angeles and as she arranged a rental car at the airport. The agent gazed at her quizzically with that Don't-I-know-you? look but didn't pursue her thoughts, thank God.

She had forgotten how bad the L.A. freeways were, even when it wasn't rush hour. She battled the traffic, which didn't improve as she traveled along the highway to Malibu. When she pulled up to the garage of a three-story redwood-and-glass house, she felt drained and more tired than she had felt in a long time. Evelyne didn't bother putting the car in the garage. She unlocked the gate facing the road and walked down the flagstone path to the front door. Before opening the door she took a deep breath and let it out slowly. Feeling calmer she entered the house that held so many memories.

Evelyne stood in the entryway and looked up at the stairs leading to Rick's office and a small sound studio he used when entertaining some of the bands his company represented. Downstairs was the master bedroom and her private sitting room. She walked slowly into the living room, over the narrow bridge that spanned a small pond filled with koi. Nothing had changed. The modernistic furniture with its comfortable cushions in white with cherry-red pillows for accent was the same, as was the fireplace. The hot tub near the balcony had been maintained and looked ready for immediate use. She walked into the adjoining den. The movie screen had been rolled up into the ceiling, the pieces of video cassette tapes had been swept up. Nothing was left to show of her tantrum so long ago. After that evening she had closed the den door and hadn't opened it again. She should have known that Mrs. Miranda, her overly efficient housekeeper, would have taken care of anything. There wasn't a speck of dust anywhere, and nothing was out of place. She had called the woman the night before and asked that the kitchen be stocked. She checked that room next, poured herself a glass of iced tea, and sliced off a chunk of Swiss cheese to help ease her hunger pangs.

In the next hour Evelyne carried her suitcase inside the house, although she knew she wouldn't need any of the heavy clothing. She sorted out what would need to be dry-cleaned and put away the rest. She changed into something cooler and wandered out onto the balcony.

From her vantage point she could see a famous television star jogging along the waterline, an actress walking her dog, and another popular television actress walking along the sand with her new baby. Evelyne turned around and stared at the telephone. She should call Rhyder and tell him she had arrived safely. She was afraid to call him. She was afraid she would take the next plane back to Chicago—back to him. But she had to call him and hear his voice.

Rhyder answered on the first ring.

"Hi," Evelyne said softly, twisting the cord between her fingers.

"Was your flight all right?" His voice sounded hoarse. *I wish you hadn't gone.*

She nodded, then realized he couldn't see her. "Yes,

it was fine." *I wanted you to go with me.* "It's much warmer here."

"Are you feeling all right?" He hoped she wouldn't grow defensive about her health. *I want to be with you and make love with you.*

"Yes." She sat on the bed and lay back. "I'm going to call my doctor and make an appointment to see him." *I miss you.*

Rhyder sat up in bed. There was no way he could have slept that night until he heard from her. "Evelyn, if you need anything, anything at all, you will call me, won't you?"

"Yes." Her voice sounded oddly husky. "I should go." *Please, keep on loving me.*

"I'll call you tomorrow night," he promised, his own voice having that same husky note. "I love you, Evelyne. I always will."

Her eyes filled with tears. "Don't make it sound so final. I'll be back before you know it." She gently replaced the receiver in the cradle.

After two weeks had passed, Evelyne thought back on her words to Rhyder and wondered if they had been spoken too soon.

She was grateful for the family attorney's assistance in her mother's funeral arrangements and sat through the reading of the will that left everything to her. She also had a very interesting talk with her mother's doctor the day she drove out to the sanitarium to pick up Amanda's personal belongings.

"I don't understand how she could have gone so quickly," she had told him. "I talked to her only a few days before, and she sounded more like her old self. She was perfectly coherent and even knew where I was staying. I felt convinced that she was finally getting well."

261

The silver-haired man smiled and shook his head. "Mrs. Winters, your mother lived entirely in the past, when you were twelve years old and had a tendency to be late to dinner."

"No," she insisted. "She was herself again. She discussed my divorce, everything."

The man looked at her with pity in his eyes. "I'm sorry, Mrs. Winters, but if that was so, then you were very lucky, because her coming out of her regression would have been tantamount to a miracle."

Evelyne sat back in her chair, not entirely convinced the doctor was right except in one area: it was certainly a miracle. One she wouldn't have missed for the world.

She only wished for another miracle, and that was to talk to Rhyder. She had called his home only to hear an answering machine explaining that he was away and for the caller to please leave a return number; she never did. She called his office and was told he was out of town, and if she would leave her number, Mr. Stewart would return her call when he came back, or could Mr. Stewart's partner help her? No, Mr. Stewart's regular secretary was on vacation and his number could not be given out for any reason. She didn't bother asking for Ken after that taste of his hostility at his party. She left her name and wearily went about the task of sorting out the many household effects filling her home.

Many times Evelyne felt the need to call Rhyder and tell him she loved and missed him and wished he could be with her, but all she could do was grit her teeth and get on with her work.

True to her word she contacted the newspaper reporter, Elliot Hayes, and granted him an interview, talking candidly about her illness and her subsequent recovery. She was grateful he didn't ask her any pointed questions about Rhyder. She did admit to Elliot that she'd learned many men were afraid of women who had suffered a major illness—while expecting their wives or girlfriends to cope with them after they had been struck down with a stroke or heart attack. In talking Evelyne felt the last of her anger toward Rick leave her heart. All she mentioned about Rhyder, preferring to keep his identity a secret so he wouldn't be bothered, was that she had met a wonderful man who wanted her no matter what.

"No one is perfect in this world," she said to the enthralled reporter, who kept the tape recorder running so he wouldn't miss a word. "We all have to learn to live with one another, whether the man has lost the use of a limb or the woman has undergone a mastectomy. If there is true love in the relationship none of that will matter, because it isn't the heart and the soul that will have been damaged." She laughed, conscious of the dampness on her cheeks. "That's enough of me on my soapbox."

"I think this is going to turn out to be one hell of an article," Elliot announced, shutting off his tape recorder. "And the guy in your life is pretty lucky. He's the one who was with you in Hawaii, wasn't he?" He grinned. "Strictly off the record, Mrs. Winters."

She grinned back. "No comment, Mr. Hayes."

In the end the article about Evelyne Winters ran in newspapers in all the major cities.

Rhyder read the article and accompanying photographs in a Florida paper. He had been trying to call Evelyne for the past week but had been unable to reach her. He cursed the fact that she didn't have an answering machine. He had checked his, but there were no messages, and Ken said she hadn't called the office. If he was smart, he would write her a letter, but while he could write the most concise brief he couldn't handle a simple two-line note and he didn't want to dictate even the shortest note to a secretary. He would just have to try more often to get her on the phone. His insecure half questioned if the man she'd talked about in the article was someone else, and that was why she wasn't home. The secure half said there was no problem and perhaps it was best that he not talk to her while she took care of her life and he slaved away to iron out the problems in the current case. Why couldn't Calvin Walters's niece just move to a foreign country and forget about any kind of inheritance? After all, it was only twenty million dollars.

He picked up the telephone and tried Evelyne's number again. He let it ring thirty times and decided no one was there. Didn't she ever stay at home? He turned back to the papers on the table and forced his mind to turn off the part about Evelyne and concentrate on the case. The sooner he got it unsnarled, the sooner he could take off for California and kidnap Evelyne.

Evelyne spent her days walking on the beach or going to visit old haunts. She ran into a few of her old friends, some of whom looked embarrassed, muttered something about meeting for lunch, and went about their own business. Evelyne didn't mind. She was too busy thinking about her life in general and what she wanted for her future. One part of it was very easy; she knew she wanted Rhyder, and as soon as her affairs here were settled she would fly back to Chicago. Some nights she would dig into her purse for her key to his apartment and hold the metal object as if it would send her back to Chicago without benefit of transportation. She talked to a realtor about listing the house and learned there would be no problem selling it. Her days were long and filled with work and, sometimes, stress, but she learned she could handle it. She felt stronger each day.

One morning Evelyne was in the midst of going through old photographs when the doorbell rang. Since most of her neighbors knew she was back, she thought nothing of going to the door. When she opened it, she stepped back in surprise at the sight of a woman with bright-orange hair, wearing torn jeans, high-heeled boots, and an army fatigue shirt.

"Hello, Evelyne," she said shyly.

"Kayla." Drawing upon her training she stepped back another pace. "Come in, please."

The woman stepped in hesitantly. "I wasn't sure if you wouldn't just slam the door in my face," she confessed.

Evelyne looked at Kayla's thin figure. "I'm afraid that isn't my style. Would you like to come in and sit down?" She led the way into the living room.

Kayla studied the small pond, the carefully arranged furniture, and the terrace—all part of an extremely expensive piece of real estate that Rick loudly cursed Evelyne for having received as part of her divorce settlement. Some questions that had run through her mind the past year and a half were now being answered.

"Would you care for something to drink?" Evelyne was the perfect hostess even as she burned to know Kayla's real reason for coming to see her.

Kayla shook her head. "I don't have very much time." She blushed, something odd for someone who looked so hard boiled. "I'm supposed to meet Rick for lunch in an hour."

"Oh." Evelyne sat back and waited.

Luckily she didn't have to wait long for her answer.

"I—ah—I'm sorry it all ended up the way it did," Kayla said slowly. "I know Rick played some dirty tricks concerning you, and I wish it hadn't ended up that way."

"What happened to your upcoming blessed event?" So much for good manners.

"I miscarried a little over a month ago." Kayla looked toward the open drapes leading to the terrace.

"But you still have your other child." Oh, how it hurt to talk about a child that should rightfully have been hers!

Kayla nodded. "I want you to know, Evelyne, that my son isn't Rick's. I just let him think he was. Rick doesn't know about any of this."

"Then why are you giving me such a deadly weapon? For all you know, I might use it against you for revenge." Evelyne asked. "I hate to think what Rick would do to you if he knew the truth. He'd begin by destroying your career, and you know it. And he certainly wouldn't stop there."

"I read the article about you." Kayla looked uncomfortable. "And I read the part about you wanting children. I also read between the lines. I think you hated Rick for not giving you children that he supposedly gave me. I just wanted you to know that it isn't true. I understand you met someone, and I'm sure you got the better deal." She smiled faintly. "I understand Rick much better than you can. I can flow with his moods because we both started up the hard way, but you always had money to pave the way for you. He envied you your background and hoped that by marrying you it would rub off. Unfortunately he learned it doesn't work that way."

Evelyne nodded. "Rick isn't ever going to grow up, Kayla. Are you sure that's what you want?"

"Yes," she said without hesitation. "I loved him the first time I saw him, but I wasn't about to poach on someone else's property." She shrugged under

266

Evelyne's wry expression. "Okay, so I let up my scruples after a while, but I didn't give in too easy either."

Evelyne laughed, shaking her head. "It's difficult to imagine we're sitting here talking about my ex-husband—your present husband."

"Hey, if we can't complain about him, who can?" Kayla giggled. "I just wish I had known he likes to watch the late show in bed with the sound all the way up."

Evelyne groaned. "Oh, yes, one of his nicer habits. Along with eating pretzels in bed."

Before they knew it, the two women were comparing notes—and little did Rick Winters know that he was definitely not coming out on top.

When Kayla left a little over an hour later, the two women felt more comfortable with each other, and Evelyne sincerely wished Kayla luck with her marriage. She privately thought the younger woman would need it if Rick ever decided to show his true colors to her.

With the house empty again, Evelyne wandered through the rooms feeling the quiet steal around her. Rick's old office was cleared of furniture and the sound studio also emptied of equipment. She walked the length of the room, the heels of her shoes clicking against the wood floor. From there she explored the second-floor rooms and went down to the bedroom and bathroom with its octagonal sunken tub in beige marble and matching double sinks. Her sitting room was furnished in French provincial, the soft colors and fabrics very feminine.

She sat at the delicate writing desk near the floor-to-ceiling window overlooking the beach and composed a letter to Rhyder, read it over, and tore it up. It took seven drafts before she wrote what she truly felt. As

she read it over she was afraid she sounded too melo-
dramatic—even if it was the truth. She stared down at
the cream-colored stationery with the blue monogram
at the top of the page before looking over the words
that came from her heart.

My darling Rhyder,

I've tried to reach you by telephone but have
been unable to find you. I don't know if it's inten-
tional or whether I've just been unable to connect
with you at the proper time, so I am writing to
you.

I know you didn't want me to come to L.A.
and I understand why, but it was the best thing I
could do for myself.

I entered a house I had spent a good part of my
married life in, but there are no longer any ghosts
to haunt me here. You should be very proud of
me, because I've learned to bury the past and go
on with the future. I only hope that you will be a
part of my new life.

I love you so much that I hurt with it. I find it
difficult to sleep because you're not beside me.
Many times I walk along the beach or visit a favorite place of mine and I wish you were there
with me to share the experience.

I have truly learned that the mistakes of the
past were not all of my own making; that it took
two to inflict the pain. I'm not a broken woman
anymore, and so much of that is due to you and
your love. You allowed me to work at being myself and not just an extension of you. But I'm
selfish, my love, because I now want it all. I want
you along with the new me. I want to marry you,
have your children, and grow old with you. I
want us to argue over my spending too much

money, over you indulging our children too much, and whatever else may come up. Because even then we'll be certain of our love.

The past few months have taught me so much about what love truly is, and you're the one who showed me the way. A tiny part of me is frightened that you'll now reject me, but my saner half knows better because a love such as ours can stand anything. I want to come home, Rhyder. Yes, I said home. This is no longer my home, because you are not here.

I love you.

Evelyne

Before she should lose her courage, she slipped the letter into an envelope and addressed and stamped it. She ran outside to her car and drove to the post office so the letter would go out with the next pickup. Then she stopped by the grocery store, bought enough fattening food to last her a year, and returned home to wait for her telephone call from Rhyder.

Three days later it hadn't come, and Evelyne was convinced it never would. She cooked herself a batch of fudge which she promptly consumed, suffering shortly afterward a tremendous stomachache. The next day she kept her stomach calm with soup and was convinced the pimple on her chin and another on her forehead came from the rich fudge.

She stayed up to watch a late movie, then another film, and fell asleep during the late late late show. Evelyne wasn't sure how long she had been asleep when the doorbell rang. She only knew her eyes refused to open any farther than a slit.

"Whoever it is has a lot to answer for," she muttered, groping her way upstairs. "Couldn't you wait until later in the day, say noon?" she asked loudly, trying to find the light switch. When she failed to find anything remotely resembling one, she continued to stumble blindly in the dark toward the unrelenting doorbell. "I hope this is good." If she could have, she would have snarled on pulling open the door. She suddenly woke up at the sight of her early morning visitor.

"Do you realize how much trouble I had to go to to get here?" Rhyder demanded, marching inside and slamming the door behind him. He dropped a small suitcase on the floor and looked at Evelyne. "Did you forget to pay the light bill or do you always receive your guests in the dark?" He didn't bother waiting for a reply; he merely searched around until he found the light switch.

Evelyne blinked at the sudden intrusion of light. She stared at Rhyder, unable to believe her eyes.

"I couldn't get on a direct flight here, so I took one to Atlanta," Rhyder continued. "The trouble was, I missed the direct flight out of there, so I flew to Chicago. And from there to San Francisco. I feel like I've been on a plane for half my life. Luckily I missed out on traveling to Seattle, Dallas, Houston, and Kansas City. Well, aren't you going to kiss me or something?" He braced his hands on his hips.

Evelyne could only look up at him. "Don't look very closely. I—I have a pimple," she faltered, pointing to her chin, unable to think of anything else to say.

Rhyder's gaze softened; he'd recognized her surprise at seeing him so unexpectedly. He should have called her instead of being in such a hurry to see her. "Is it contagious?"

She shook her head, her lips trembling. She was so happy to see him, but her arms refused to throw themselves around his neck.

"Then I wouldn't worry about it if I were you. It

certainly doesn't bother me." He pulled her into his arms. "I think you'd better kiss me before I turn into a frog."

"Oh, Rhyder," she cried, throwing her arms around him and covering every inch of his face with kisses. "I've missed you so much, and your receptionist wouldn't give me your phone number in Florida, and I tried to write you but I couldn't put it into words. I didn't say all I wanted in my letter, but I tried to!"

"Wait a minute." He grasped her arms and pushed her gently a few inches away from him. "What letter?"

"The letter I wrote you. The one that brought you here," she insisted.

"I didn't get any letter. Honey, I flew here straight from Florida. I shipped all the paper work back to Ken, told him to finish everything up, and I began flying every damn airline in this country to get here."

Evelyne frowned. "I mailed the letter to your Chicago office three days ago. I was afraid you had given up on me."

Rhyder pulled her back into his arms and hugged her tightly. "There was no way I would give up on you." He stood back wearing a stern expression on his face. "First of all, no more Mr. Nice Guy. We are getting married as soon as the law in this state allows, and I'm not letting you out of my sight for anything. If you don't have everything settled yet, I'll be around to help. But I'm not letting you go off to find yourself, because as far as I'm concerned you're good and found!"

"All right," she agreed softly.

"And I don't want to hear any arguments, Evelyne," Rhyder went on, not hearing her reply. "We're getting married."

"Anything you say, Rhyder."

271

"There certainly can't be anything more you need to know about yourself."

"You're absolutely right."

"If there is, I want to be around when you're finally ready to settle down."

"I'm ready now."

"I mean it, Evelyne, I don't want any protests on your part." By now Rhyder was getting up a full head of steam and was pacing the length of the entryway. "We are getting married."

"Yes."

Rhyder's mouth closed with an abrupt snap as her words finally sank in. He spun around. "Did I hear a yes?"

She smiled broadly. "I said yes five minutes ago."

He shook his head to clear the cobwebs that were clouding his brain. "You did?"

Evelyne nodded. "Several times, in fact. If you'd like it in writing, I can do that for you. I know how lawyers like everything in writing."

His unrestrained laughter bounced off the walls. "Honey, with you a verbal agreement is just as binding." He rushed over and took her in his arms. "You realize there's no backing out."

"I don't intend to."

Rhyder closed his eyes, just enjoying the sensation of having her close to him. "I do believe that this kind of contract deserves more than a handshake."

"I certainly agree on that." Still smiling she took his hand and led him downstairs. The drapes were wide open, allowing the moonlight to flow into the room, and the sounds of the sea filtered through the open door. Evelyne slipped his coat off and draped it over a chair, then went to work on his shirt. In no time she had him undressed and pushed him onto the bed.

"Just give me a few minutes." She gave him a seductive smile before heading for the bathroom.

Rhyder felt relaxed for the first time in weeks. After having spent hours in various jets, he enjoyed the idea of lying in a bed, even if there wouldn't be any sleeping done for a while! It was an excellent way of celebrating their engagement. He flopped back on the firm mattress. He couldn't imagine anything feeling so good, unless it was having Evelyne beneath him. He closed his eyes. It certainly wouldn't hurt to doze a little before she came back. What was taking her so long anyway? He settled into the mattress a bit more and pulled a pillow under his head. There, and he could hear Evelyne when she returned and they could get down to some serious loving. Yes, this was much better than sitting upright. So much better. A soft sigh escaped his lips.

Meanwhile, Evelyne was busy powdering every inch of her skin and adding perfume to some erotic spots. She moaned her displeasure over the not-too-new cotton gown she had worn to bed hours before, but she couldn't do anything about that. She began to pull it over her head. Then, with a broad smile, she tossed it into the hamper. She had no need for the gown. Rhyder would only take it off again. After running a brush through her hair, she pinched her cheeks to give them added color and quickly gargled with mouthwash. Now she was ready to go back into the bedroom and allow Rhyder to seduce her. She opened the bathroom door and leaned against the jamb in a sensuous pose.

"Here I am," she murmured seductively. Silence. "Rhyder?" More silence. Evelyne straightened up and walked toward the bed and the supine figure sprawled across it. Sounds of soft snoring floated through the air. She looked incredulously at the sleeping man.

"I don't believe this," she said to herself. "He fell asleep." Then Evelyne remembered Rhyder's telling her about the many planes he'd taken to get here, and she could only guess at the hours he'd spent traveling. No wonder he was tired. She leaned over and carefully pulled the covers over him and climbed into bed beside him. She laid her head on the pillow and pleased herself by just watching him. Rhyder was with her, and right now that was all that counted. With a contented sigh she soon fell asleep.

Rhyder was slow to wake up. He rolled over and opened one eye. This wasn't his bed. Where he came from, he didn't have warm sunshine streaming into his room, and he certainly didn't hear the sounds of the ocean and voices from below. He opened the other eye. He certainly didn't have a wall-to-wall bed and furniture he thought was called Danish Modern. If he had found himself on silk or satin sheets he would have been positive he had somehow stumbled into a bordello.

"I see you decided to wake up."

Rhyder whipped his head around. He breathed a sigh of relief. "I was scared for a moment I had stumbled into the wrong house. What time is it?" He glanced down at his watch, held it up to his ear, and shook it.

"Two in the afternoon."

"I thought my watch had stopped." He sat up in bed and eyed her wearing a brief sunsuit. "I like the outfit. Is that part of California's decadent way of life?"

"Of course." Evelyne entered the room carrying a large tray. "I'm surprising you with lunch in bed, since you slept through breakfast. I'm sure you're dying for a cup of coffee."

Before she could set the tray down he had wrapped one hand around the back of her head and brought her lips down to his. "I need this more," he murmured, flicking his tongue over her lips.

Evelyne felt the light touch all the way down to her toes. "Rhyder, I spent a long time fixing your breakfast," she halfheartedly protested as his hand found its way down the v-neck of her sunsuit.

"I'm sure it will be as good cold." He took the tray from her and set it on the floor before tumbling her onto the bed. His fingers wandered over her face and down to her shoulders. "You did say yes to my crazy proposal last night, didn't you?"

"I wasn't allowed to say no." She snuggled up against him, feeling like a cat sleeping before a warm fire.

"And I wasn't going to take any chances." He gazed over the pale-blue cotton. "How does this thing come off?" He fingered the narrow straps.

Evelyne lifted herself up on her knees and reached behind her to unfasten one very large button. Dropping back down she pushed it off onto the floor and dispensed with her bikini panties the same way.

"Too bad you missed the floor show last night," she said with a provocative tilt of the head.

Rhyder grimaced. "I was more tired than I thought. I think it was the flight from San Francisco that finally did me in."

"I shouldn't have teased you." Evelyne kicked the covers back. "Hmm, it appears you're wide awake now." She traced a pattern over his hipbone.

Not caring to bother with too many preliminaries Rhyder rolled over her, grabbing her wrists and pulling them up over her head. "Should I wait for you to take care of anything?" he asked huskily.

275

She smiled and shook her head. "I believe in planning ahead . . . just in case."

"Good girl." He slanted his mouth over hers and slipped his tongue inside. "I almost forgot how good you tasted," he murmured, moving his body in slow, blood-warming movements. "And how good you felt."

"It's always nice to revive memories, isn't it?" she asked softly, doing some tasting of her own. The musky, warm scent of his skin brought back a few recollections of her own that were much more than nice.

Rhyder rested his palm over her breast and teased the nipple with his thumb. "So many nights I would lie awake and remember our times together and how I'd feel inside of you and the way you'd cry out when you climaxed. But I'd also think about the evenings when I'd be reading and you'd be doing your needlepoint. Those times were just as good as the times we made love, because we were together. That's all that mattered. While I missed making love with you, I also missed just talking to you. This is just to tell you that it isn't your body I want."

Evelyne stretched, her hips rising just enough. "Are you trying to tell me that it's only my mind you want?"

He pretended to consider her question. "I'll get to that when we're both ninety and unable to do much more than talk. Until then we've got to make up for all those years we didn't know each other."

Her tongue appeared, sliding over her lower lip. "You'd better hurry up, then."

Rhyder groaned, and returned to the treasures of Evelyne's mouth. For a long while the only sounds were soft sighs and moans as their mouths melded and their tongues performed a loving duel. His hands warmed the swelling mounds of her breasts and ca-

276

ressed the tips to aching nubs. Evelyne was content to rediscover every plane of Rhyder's body and thrill to the sounds of his whispers of desire and happiness they were together again. When Rhyder slipped inside of her, she gasped with delight, wrapping her legs around his lean hips. The pace was gentle, because they had all the time in the world and no one to worry about except themselves. But it couldn't remain slow and gentle for long. They hadn't been together for a long time, and the fire refused to be banked for much longer. Evelyne felt the core of her body tighten as she felt Rhyder begin to thrust faster and deeper until they were truly one. When they fell into the stars, they fell together.

"This isn't a weekend, is it?" Rhyder asked once he'd finally got his breath back.

Evelyne shook her head. She felt content and happy and wasn't about to move one muscle for anything. "Why?" she murmured.

"Because we're going out to get a marriage license today. I told you, I don't intend to let you get away from me again," he said sternly.

She smiled and ran her hands over the warm, damp skin of his back. "It could wait a little while, couldn't it?"

Rhyder threw his head back and laughed. "I have an idea I won't have any say in it."

"You are so right."

CHAPTER FIFTEEN

After their trip to the license bureau, Rhyder insisted on taking Evelyne out to dinner. During after-dinner drinks he presented her with a small dark-blue velvet box. She looked at the diamond flanked by emeralds and felt like crying with happiness.

"It's beautiful, Rhyder," she whispered, watching him slip the ring on the appropriate finger.

"Just wait until you see the band that goes with it." He grinned. "Evelyne, I'd felt pretty raw about women in general when I met you, and given your past I admit I didn't think too much of you in the beginning. I'm very glad you proved me wrong."

"And I'm glad you talked me out of playing musical beds," she replied softly. "You're all I want and need."

He reached across the table and grasped her hand. "Shall we go somewhere else for a quieter celebration?"

She nodded and prepared to grab her purse.

"Well, look who we have here."

Evelyne froze, but not for long. She looked up with a composed smile on her lips. "Hello, Rick. Kayla. How are you?"

The other woman looked uncomfortable as she stood next to the tall blond man Evelyne had once been married to.

Rick didn't look the least bit uneasy about interrupting a private conversation. He stood before them dressed in faded jeans and a chambray shirt, his blond good looks a beacon for every woman in the room. Except for Evelyne. He looked down at Evelyne's left hand and grabbed it.

"Didn't waste any time, did you?" he sneered.

Evelyne recoiled, not just from his touch, but also his tone of voice. She saw Rhyder begin to rise and shook her head. The last thing she wanted was any kind of adverse publicity for Rhyder and her.

"I at least waited until the body was cold before seeing about replacing it," she said coolly, inclining her head toward Kayla, who blushed. She regretted embarrassing the other woman, but she wanted Rick to get her meaning loud and clear. "This is my fiancé Rhyder Stewart. He's an attorney in Chicago."

Rick's smile was false. "It's going to be awfully cold out there. But you do have a bit of cold blood in you, so maybe it won't be too bad. Send me a wedding announcement so I'll know when to stop the alimony checks." He nodded and went on with Kayla following him.

Evelyne looked down at her drink and smiled. "All that makes him happy is not losing any more money," she told Rhyder.

"How much alimony does he pay you?" he asked, then promptly choked on his drink when she told him. "That much?" He hesitated. "Maybe we should live together instead of marrying. I sure wouldn't want you to lose out on all that money." He chuckled at her glare. "You know very well I was kidding. It just seems like a large amount of money."

She nodded. "There's a great deal of upkeep on the house. It also meant I wouldn't attempt to take away from his company profits, which my lawyer thought I had a good chance of doing. The house is up for sale

279

now, and that shouldn't take long. If it won't bother you, we could think about using the money as a down payment on a house."

"After we decide where we're going to live," he replied mysteriously.

"Are there that many places to live in Chicago?"

"That isn't where I'm planning on us living." Rhyder sipped his drink. "But that's part of your wedding present, and you're just going to have to wait until after the man pronounces us man and wife."

"What if I don't want to wait that long?" she asked archly, leaning over to nuzzle his ear with her lips. She smiled when she heard his breathing deepen. "Ve haf vays to make you talk," she murmured in a passable European accent.

Rhyder chuckled. "Honey, you can interrogate me all you want, but I intend this to be the surprise of all surprises."

Evelyne inched her fingers under his shirt and over his warm skin. Her nails scratched lightly, then rubbed seductively, and with her mouth doing unspeakable things to his ear and throat, she knew Rhyder wouldn't have a chance. What she didn't realize was that he was enjoying her torture all too much and wasn't about to give in to her too easily. Finally Evelyne stood up, held her hand out to Rhyder, and led him out of the restaurant.

Once they were home and he was in her loving arms, he finally gave her a very strong hint regarding his surprise. The hint was more than enough. She squealed with joy.

"I do hope you're going to finish your seduction?" he requested.

A broad smile graced her lips. "My love, you can expect your seduction to last for the next fifty years and beyond." She moved over him to begin the first installment.

EPILOGUE

"You can't be home yet!" Evelyne wailed when she watched her husband of six months walk in the front door.

He seemed surprised by her attack. "Sorry I'm ruining your day, but I thought I'd leave early. If you have a boyfriend in the bedroom, he's going to be in a lot of trouble," he teased.

She rolled her eyes. "Ha! As if I had any time between running the boutique and keeping up with you." She tossed her braid back. Dressed in denim cutoffs and a flimsy cotton camisole top, she looked much younger than her thirty-three years. She approached him and gave him a kiss calculated to raise his blood pressure. "And how was your day?"

"I saw a very sweet old man who wants to leave his worldly goods to his parrot," Rhyder announced, sliding his arms around her waist and pulling her toward him. "Larry said he once had a guy who wanted to leave everything to his goldfish." Keeping his arm around her he walked her into the sunny kitchen, where the interesting smells of baked fish were permeating the air. Rhyder rummaged in the refrigerator for a beer and popped the can's top before speaking again. "Did you find an assistant for the shop?"

Evelyne nodded. "The first woman I interviewed. She's perfect for the shop. Lani's children have all left home, and she wants to get out and do something for herself now." She stared out the window at the stunning view of the beach and ocean before her.

What a surprise it had been when Rhyder told her he wanted to move to Hawaii after they married. He had been in contact with a few law firms on the Islands, and several were optimistic about taking him on as a partner, not to mention making use of his admirable skills. He had to take courses familiarizing him with state laws, but there would be no problem in his practicing there. What mattered to him was that he would be out of the fast lane in Chicago and Evelyne would be away from her past in California. He strongly felt it was what they both needed.

Another thing Rhyder guessed Evelyne needed was a sense of worth. He had suggested that she invest some of her money in a boutique, since she could certainly pick out beautiful clothing and sell to the tourists. She fell in love with the idea and had now found a way to keep herself busy, but there was none of the stress she had endured before with Rick's life-style. Any parties she and Rhyder had in their new home were casual barbecues and took little planning.

Rhyder had gone to work with a law firm in Hilo on the island of Hawaii and they had bought a home that had everything they could imagine, including a huge sunken tub with Jacuzzi jets, and a swimming pool and spa in the patio area. The couple had everything they needed and couldn't imagine a more satisfying life.

"I missed you today," he murmured, nibbling along the side of her neck.

She chuckled. "You say that every day. You're turning into a sex fiend, Rhyder. For a man who's pushing forty-three, you're doing an admirable job of playing the satyr."

Rhyder groaned. "That's what happens when you marry younger women. They inspire old men like me."

"Hey, I see nothing wrong with your age." She rotated her hips against his. "I'm the one who's dead tired all the time. And not the kind of tired you're thinking about either," she interjected, reading the concern in his eyes. "I am just fine and you know it. The doctor said I'm so healthy it's disgusting, and there's no reason for us to worry if we decide to have a family."

"Only if you want kids and there are no problems," he said, raising an old argument between them, although their arguments never lasted long because they had vowed they wouldn't go to bed until their arguments were settled. Usually that's exactly where they were settled.

Rhyder still looked skeptical. "You know what the best thing I ever did was?"

"Hm?" Evelyne was busy nibbling his ear. "What?"

"Letting you pick me up."

She tipped her head back. "Wait a minute. You did not let me pick you up. I practically told you to get lost."

"Then why wouldn't you let me alone? After all, you were the one who sneaked into my room, remember?"

"I sneaked across a stranger's balcony. I had no idea it was your room, and if I'd had any brains, I would have forgotten about watching that ship leave," she shot back.

"But look at what you would have missed out on." He picked her up by the waist and set her on the counter.

Evelyne curved her lips in a knowing smile, aware

284

of the deep love they shared. "You are so right. You would have missed out on the perfect woman for you." She leaned forward, covering his mouth with hers to make sure she would have the last word.

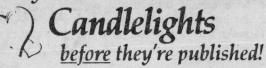

Now you can reserve October's
Candlelights
before they're published!

♥ You'll have copies set aside for *you*
   the instant they come off press.
♥ You'll save yourself precious shopping
   time by arranging for *home delivery*.
♥ You'll feel proud and efficient about
   organizing a system that *guarantees* delivery.
♥ You'll avoid the disappointment of not
   finding *every* title you want and need.

ECSTASY SUPREMES $2.75 each

☐ **141 WINDS OF A SECRET DESIRE,**
   Deborah Sherwood 19548-9-18
☐ **142 MYSTERY IN THE MOONLIGHT,**
   Lynn Patrick 15991-1-18
☐ **143 ENDLESS OBSESSION,** Hayton Monteith   12310-0-19
☐ **144 MY DARLING PRETENDER,** Linda Vail 15279-8-11

ECSTASY ROMANCES $2.25 each

☐ **462 OUT OF THIS WORLD,** Lori Copeland 16764-7-29
☐ **463 DANGEROUS ENCOUNTER,** Alice Bowen . . . 11741-0-10
☐ **464 HEAD OVER HEELS,** Terri Herrington 13489-7-38
☐ **465 NOT FOR ANY PRICE,** Suzannah Davis 16454-0-32
☐ **466 MAGNIFICENT LOVER,**
   Karen Whittenburg 15430-8-25
☐ **467 BURNING NIGHTS,** Edith Delatush 10885-3-18

☐ **7 *THE GAME IS PLAYED,* Amii Lorin** 12835-8-49
☐ **19 *TENDER YEARNINGS,* Elaine Raco Chase** 18552-1-47

Dell DELL READERS SERVICE—DEPT. B1229A
P.O. BOX 1000. PINE BROOK. N.J. 07058

Please send me the above title(s). I am enclosing $_____ (please add 75¢ per copy to cover
postage and handling). Send check or money order—no cash or CODs. Please allow 3-4 weeks for shipment.
CANADIAN ORDERS: please submit in U.S. dollars.

Ms /Mrs Mr_____

Address_____

City/State_____Zip_____